Published by Piscataqua Press
An imprint of RiverRun Bookstore
142 Fleet St., Portsmouth, NH 03801
www.piscataquapress.com

ISBN: 9798-1-939739-81-0

Printed in the United States of America

Visit the author at:
asiaislandic@yahoo.com
http://asiaislandic.wix.com/greg-may-author

Cover art: *Nude Lying on the Rocks* ©Horacio Cardozo
Used by permission. Thanks!

A WICKED TIDE

Greg May

In Appreciation

-Freytag-Loringhoven, Elsa von, *Body Sweats:The Uncensored Writings...*

-Irene Gammel & Suzanne Zelaco, *The First American Dada: Introduction*

-Dr. Deborah J Haynes Ph. D, Religion & Fine Arts, Harvard University

-Gammel, Irene, *Baroness Elsa: A Cultural Biography*, & *Baroness Elsa: Gender, Dada, and Everyday Modernity*

-Dr. Irene Gammel Ph. D, English, McMaster University

-Barnes, Djuna, *Nightwood* & *Book of Repulsive Women*

- John D. Bardwell, *Ogunquit-By-The-Sea*

-Chris Ritter, *Ogunquit Maine: A Photographic Essay*

-Vernon Fimple, Artist: 'Corona' 1961, 'Masquerade' 1962

Countless hours were spent harassing the kind and patient staffs of the Ogunquit Library, Historical Society of Wells & Ogunquit, Ogunquit Museum of Modern Art, Portland Museum of Art

Interminable pestering for information from Richard & Mary Littlefield, Richard Knight & family, Mike A deVallier, Bob York, Sharon Cummings of SoMe Old News and other local folk is much appreciated.

…for Maria Julia…
of course…and always…

Author's Notes

The story you are about to read resulted from countless hours of research involving libraries, historical societies and interviews with local people, many of whose family histories reach back to the 1600's, when they arrived in the Ogunquit, Maine area. Most of the characters in this story were real people, and in some cases I have changed the names in a manner that might, should the reader wish to play detective, allow them to solve the identity riddle of each. In some instances I have taken local people 'out of their generation' and placed them into the village of Ogunquit in 1920. Such is the privilege of a wandering imagination.

In recent years many museum displays, historical sites and history books have experienced revisions in an effort to discard politically correct interpretations of times past, in favor of a more accurate portrayal of historic events, however uncomfortable those might be. The foundation for *A Wicked Tide* is somewhat akin to these types of revisions though no one can truly be sure of the real facts. In 1898 an artist named Charles Woodbury opened a school of art on the Ogunquit rocks in what is now called Perkins Cove. He often and wisely advised his students to *'not draw what you see of a wave, but rather draw what it does.'*

In a feeble attempt to honor his sentiment, I have chosen not to describe what was depicted in history books about the people living in 1920 Ogunquit, but rather imagine what they might have been thinking, given the events of the day. The results of this imagination, based on research, photographs, personal letters, interviews with generational descendants, and accounts about that time, is what lies on the following pages.

Snuggle into a quilt in front of the hearth on a gray, stormy winter Maine morning as the wave's crash on the jagged rocks, and let your imagination churn in the angry, frigid waters...

The Setting

The village of Ogunquit, Maine in 1920 was a microcosm of an America in transition. This quaint, 'Beautiful Place by the Sea'; a geographical transition in itself since time eternal, is where sandy Atlantic beaches are first overwhelmed by the rocky coast that Maine is so noted for. Bald Head Cliff and its craggy edges rise out of the sea less than a mile from the last vestiges of sandy beach expanse that reinvigorates itself along a four mile stretch from Ogunquit north to Kennebunk, where the inevitable Maine rocky coast explodes forever with fervor.

In addition to terrain transition, the 900 souls of Ogunquit had found themselves witness to boundary pushing mores of the day thanks to two art colonies gaining anchorage in its quaint little cove, known now as Perkins Cove. In 1920 these two art schools existed within eyesight of one another atop the rocky coastline in this small inlet. The older school was devoted to conventional and accepted painting styles, while the newest devoted itself primarily to *Dadaism*, (a relatively new approach to the arts), and creating, among other forms, depictions of the naked female human form. The new crop of artists also brought shocking, avant-garde, bohemian lifestyles from the big city with them and nestled their enclave in between the bawdy, hard working, hard drinking fishermen on one side, and the matronly artists of the established school on the other. These new age *Dadaists* pressed the boundaries of the standards of decency in this small village, just as they did in the entirety of modern European and American society. Decades later television like *Saturday Night Live* and MTV, as well as musical acts like Madonna and Lady Gaga, would press societal boundaries in a similar manner.

1920 America was in transition on a number of fronts, as

women had just won voting rights, alcohol was banned, and small wealthy women's colleges in New England were being challenged from within, struggling with women's burgeoning and new found freedoms, sexual and otherwise. At the fore was women's health and reproductive issues, thrust into the consciousness of the male dominated religious mindset. The medical community was forced to consider such outlandish concepts as birth control and abortion. While it would be forty years before women would be burning their bras in public, the foundations for equal rights among the sexes across the spectrum of American society were being laid in 1920 New England. Representative of this condition was the gathering of a small gaggle of young women from these colleges, as well as some prostitutes from the Manhattan bowery, converging into this new age artist enclave to openly pose nude in full view of the tourists and fishermen on the rocks of Ogunquit, as well as in view of the wealthy middle aged matrons of the more staid art school located a stone's throw across the cove. This happenstance most assuredly elicited colorful conversation from all quarters.

This cove was also a favorite haunt for those smuggling alcohol to the region as Prohibition had just became the law of the land, making the sale and distribution of alcohol a crime. The continuous cat and mouse game, between the smugglers and the revenue agents, had residents constantly on edge anywhere near the coastline, and particularly in this oft-used hidden cove. A certain element of danger and risk for enjoying a simple sailing excursion was fraught with the worry of being approached by the government authorities or worse yet, by hardened criminals shanghaiing a pleasure craft to make a quick "rum run". This seemingly ambivalent, newly formed art enclave with naked women lounging on the rocks attracted much more attention than the smugglers wanted, and a degree of friction formed between all of the competing interests.

1920 Ogunquit was also being discovered as a premier

tourist locale for wealthy folk from Philadelphia, New York and Boston. These folk, "from away", brought their spending power, privileged mindsets and their tastes for the finer goods and services along with them for the entirety of the summer months, further jeopardizing smuggling activities and livelihoods. Many of the 900 locals soon found that they could be builders, gardeners or housekeepers for the summer and make enough money to last them through the harsh Maine winters and then some. Teenage daughters would no longer have to be packed up and shipped to the textile mills down in Massachusetts to work dastardly hours so they could contribute to the family coffers. Loyalties and lifestyles were purchased or altered, and many of the heretofore "hardscrabble farmers and hard luck fishermen", found that they were no longer "hardscrabble or unlucky", as long as they kept the rich folk afloat during their summer visits.

In the small mixing bowl in Ogunquit called Perkins Cove, the ingredients of this unpredictable recipe were:

Hard working, thrifty and tight-lipped fishermen and farmers;

A conservative group of serious artists from wealth;

Women emboldened by an evolving society;

Wealthy tourists injecting handfuls of money;

The stresses associated with smuggling;

and a new collage of artists that bordered on the obscene.

As if this mix wasn't volatile enough, the last ingredient added to this recipe was a singular sinister mastermind. And as this mixture was about ready for the oven heat, a final ingredient came upon Ogunquit like a storm brewing out to sea on a chilled-gray autumn New England morning.

An evil was approaching Ogunquit, sailing in on *a wicked tide…*

Prelude

"I'm really starting to dislike those sons of cast aside mothers, Din," whispered Eben as they watched the oars of the federal boat dip into early morning slack tide waters. The revenuers were on their tail again.

"Maybe those bastards will get hung up aground and not know it as the slack sucks away. It'd be a real giggle if'n those bastards have to muck onto the trolley for all to see! We'll just set by and let this little Josias Creek cover our hidey-hole for us a little while longer. Heck, they can't hear squat amidst all the gurgling and cain't smell us neither," Eben spewed on.

"Hell's bells Eben, we got close to thirty tins of hooch sittin' up here in the weeds, our biggest haul yet! If we get caught on this round Gunnyquit will be dry for a month and the hotels will be screamin', and then they won't buy from us no more."

"Keep it down Dinny!" Eben whispered. "There looks to be six of 'em in that dory roundin' the point and comin' on, but they're still a hunnert yards away. If'n they come past those dories settin' by they're gonna get beached for sure if'n they get out and hunt for us a spell. Maybe ole Valentine Meadows will roust them up to his dingbat mansion and paint the bastards! Heck, that spooky bastard is probably poppin' a nut settin' up his easel contraption now!"

"That sucker still spooks me Eben, you ever get a look in his eyes? I'm still sayin that he's an evil sonofabitch even if he throws his money at us locals. I ain't the brightest bloke, but that sucker is buyin' our loyalties and laughin' about it up in his lair."

I know you got the hots for that Holly gal, and she is a looker fer sure, but how did you let yourself get all het up for that gal anyway? Here tell that once them models get in that

i

house they shed their duds before the door hits em' in the ass, just sayin'." Dinny declared.

"Now that's a tender subject Din, and I can't deny it neither. I'm sweet on her fer' sure, and I get so angry every time I think about what she's doin' in that eerie house. But when she comes over to the house and closes in on me personal-like I just can't help but love her all the same, regardless of what she's doin' in that place, or who is doin' whatever to her. She won't tell me how much Meadows pays her, or the other gals, but I do know that she goes in there 'cuz she wants to and she says it's fun. She says that mostly all they do is pose nekkid for the artist dudes, but it's the "mostly" that gets me het up. She tells me not to worry, that all she thinks about when she leaves is bein' with me, but dangit, it ain't like I can take her to church with Ma and Pa, now is it?"

Both young men let Eben's short heartfelt dissertation sink in for a few moments before Eben finally whispered, "Hey Dinny, I think they're leavin' us be. Maybe they've figured out that by the time they might find us, they'll be left high n' dry by the tide, and the chance of findin' us ain't worth the embarrassment of gettin' hung up on the sand bar? They just don't seem to have grown a pair this mornin', and methinks we're in the clear… this time!"

The Story

"Oh deah, I haven't thought of them days in forevah", responded the weathered old man dressed in a worn, checkered button-down shirt that had seen more sea salt than the shaker he was fumbling with. "That was back in the twenties fer chrissakes."

He tugged at his shirtsleeves while trying to keep the mist in his eyes hidden from the young girl who had asked him the question. It had seemed harmless enough, the question that is, but somewhere back in the early morning frost in the lobsterman's memory, a long forgotten tide had churned up the waters.

Jessie was a recent arrival to the local high school and was doing her final term paper about the history of small commercial fishermen in her new community of Ogunquit, Maine. A Wisconsin farmer's daughter, she had large blue eyes, a curvy figure and an innocent manner that along with her short blond hair gave her birthright away amidst the stockier, dark haired daughters of rural Maine. True Maine daughters were given to brooding, plain features and downcast outlooks on life in general. Jessie, on the other hand was always bright eyed and smiling and her giggles always included an unintended snort or two. It was mostly impossible not to like her, match her smile nor decline to answer such an innocent question. Such was the fix that ol' Richard Day found himself in on this afternoon, settling in for his daily end-of-day cup of coffee at the local café.

Every afternoon the lobstermen would convene after

returning from hauling, baiting and setting their traps on yet another cold and gray early spring day.

Settling in to his chair that no other lobsterman dared to occupy, as he had been doing for nigh onto fifty years, Richard lorded over the table of lobstermen without ever having to say a word. He was just as stunned as his brethren when Jessie bounced into the café, bells hanging off the door clanging in irreverence to the somber mood that the lobstermen always brought into the café with them, and proceeded to march directly over to Richard without a care in the world.

"Good afternoon, Mr. Day! My name is Jessie and I was told that I could always find you here around this time," she bubbled. Almost too stunned to speak, he began to open his mouth to do so but she continued before he could catch his breath.

"Mr. Day, for my senior project I am doing a paper on Perkins Cove and the lobstermen who lived there during the time when the artist colonies were there also. I was told that you were the only person who might help me learn about that time. May I ask you a few questions, Sir?"

A small, wry grin appeared on his face as a devilish twinkle in his misty blue eyes returned, his partly opened mouth still shocked out of whatever already forgotten response he intended to give. It was that spark in his eyes that always belied his rough appearance, favoring his generous soul that all those close to him knew about. He looked at his table-mates, all still similarly stunned in silence and awaiting the bawdy quip that was sure to come, but were yet again surprised by this man's good nature. When he finally found his voice, and breath, he turned his eyes away from the girl and spoke to no one in particular and began, "Lads, I been lobsterin' nigh onto fifty years, and I've often tried to imagine what it must be like when a lobster takes his first bite of my bait, only to then realize that he's been trapped. Now I know."

Before any of his tablemates could muster a syllable, ol' Richard latched his eyes on the still wide-eyed girl, who met his stare without a blink, and sighed, "Oh lordy, I'm happy to help you Jessie, though I'm not sure I'm gonna like it much. Let's set over there in the corner and get your pen to workin!"

Jessie had already bounded over to the corner table and slid a chair out for the older man, even before he had completely left his seat. Richard Day was still so befuddled by the events of the past five minutes that by the time he turned around to grab his cup of coffee that he had forgotten, Jessie had already latched onto it to bring it over to their table. Day stopped in mid-stream only long enough to mumble, 'Jeezus', and then completed his slog over to the table that Jessie had chosen. As he began to take his seat, he shuddered and attempted to take a degree of control of the situation but before he uttered a word, Jessie caught him in mid-sitting position by stating, "Oh Mr. Day, I am so excited you have agreed to talk to me. Everyone in town told me that I would be wasting my time, but I knew the first moment I saw you that you were not as ornery as they all say you are."

They held eyes for an extended moment again while Richard fathomed the innocent words from this beautiful little bundle of exuberance, and once again his brain felt like a trapped lobster. All he again could muster was a muffled, 'Jeezus', under his breath. Not only had this cute little gal, "from away", confused him, but he also felt like he had just been neutered by her pearly whites like a sheep up in the Montana highlands. If Richard had been a volunteer fireman in the village, he would have been hoping for the emergency siren right then, calling all to arms so as to rescue him from this little gal's clutches, but since he wasn't a volunteer fireman, nor was the siren blaring, he peered over to the lobstermen table for rescue, but only found gazing eyes of comedic mirth awaiting his glance.

Richard was a caught shedder-shell lobster, snared into revisiting his earliest remembrances of what he had witnessed so many years before down in Perkins Cove. This wide-eyed little girl was only asking about what life was like when the two art schools were operating in the Cove, but he was deathly afraid that she would ask a question about one of the teachers, Valentine Meadows, and if she did, he wasn't sure he could not only keep his composure, but also keep long since hidden emotion and shame from exposing and revealing those marrow-numbing encounters.

Richard had spent the entirety of his adult life attempting to rationalize and purge such unpleasantries inflicted into his soul by that obviously evil spirit, and his true regret was that the bastard responsible for his torment died of pneumonia, or so it was said, before Richard was old enough to exact revenge on the asshole himself.

Now came this bright eyed, effervescent, virginal girl child asking questions about times he had long since forced into dormancy. Day was known as the hardest and toughest lobsterman along the coast. He now found himself deathly afraid of being reduced to an emotional wisp by this spit of a girl in full view of his mates in the café that worshipped his every utterance.

If she asked the wrong question, and she probably would, the entire town and his family would likely soon learn of his pain, which he had so successfully hidden from view for his entire adult life.

"Sonofabitch," he muttered under his breath.

"Excuse me?" she questioned, not quite sure that she heard him correctly, but instinctively asking because that is how decent girls were supposed to respond to cussing.

He hung his chin a bit, wiped a tear from his eye and smiled, realizing that he was finally about to free himself of that emotional anchor that had been dragging his vessel for decades.

"Jeezuz, may as well start with your questions young lady, I couldn't make it to the door with my dignity intact even if I wanted to now."

Before she could speak, he started in, and the café went silent...

I was just a bundle back then, hadn't even discovered what my pecker was truly for, but I was a tick on a dog for my uncle, Eben. He musta' been in his early twenties back then and he and his pals tolerated me some. Now I gotta say, some of what I'm 'bout to tell you is stuff I learned later in life about them days, but I don't rightly remember how much I really saw or how much I learned, if'n you get my drift.

It was quiet times I guess, and everyone in the cove got along. When the first batch of artist folks showed up and settled on the shore, us locals, or them locals I should say, for I was still a smidge, kinda enjoyed somthin' different, and though we didn't understand them, they were harmless. Better yet, that crowd started throwin' money around like it was litter while they were here, and pretty soon some of them middle-aged gals, *virginal wayfarers* we called em', began to hire us all to build them houses an' such, 'cuz they kept comin' back with their brood each summa. Those who didn't build new houses hired us all to make their rental places more fancy, and paid a lot of us to be their drivers at their beck n' call. Heck, some of us went over to Berwick with cash money to buy a wagon and team to bring back so them rich folk would always have a ride to York or Wells for their groceries. They'd pay us to jus' set around with the stock all harnessed up jus' in case they wanted to go somewhere.

By and by more people started to come to Ogunquit for the summa' months and hotels started to spring up and people started to rent out rooms. Us locals started to hike our prices, and damned it all, those folks would pay it without comment, so we raised prices some more. Little shops sprung up in the village and the town and the cove was quite lively. Us fisherfolk couldn't catch enough to keep up with the demand. By the time I was hatched Gunnyquit was a thriving little summa' community and artists come from all over the world.

Then that otha' artist fella showed up and started his school jus' about the time that Prohibition set in, and everything changed. There was gals out loungin' on the rocks in their birthday suits for all the world to see and not a care in the world. My uncle Eben almost got hitched to one if'n I recollect. I'll never forget her. Her name was Holly and by god she was a looker, just beautiful. She had a friend, a gypsy from royalty of some such, that used to dance out on the beach and she was somethin' to see also. Then there was this other older lady who everyone called the Baroness, but she was loony as a duck. They were all really nice to me though. The honcho of the place, well, let's just say I'd a liked to feed him to the fishes. Oh, but the parties they'd have… You could see them all dressed up in costumes actin' out plays and rehearsin' their lines all day in these getups! They all had to be drinkin' or smokin' somethin'. All day and all night, sometimes for days this went on. Some of the locals, as well as the rich folk over to the art school on the other side of the cove would just sit on the rocks and watch the goin's on! Quite entertainin' really! Sometimes you'd see some of em' gettin' on, if'n you catch my drift. The fishermen sittin' down at their shacks repairin' nets n' such, were havin' a fine ol' time hollerin' up to the house when all this was goin' on, cat callin' the girls to flash 'em some skin n' gen'rally bein'... well, fishermen. I remember my uncle Eben's best friend, Dinny, would be laughin' so hard that sometimes he'd be cryin'. I always remember that Eben would never watch though. He'd always turn away or go away, never thought about it much though, but Uncle Eben never drank or cussed, nor missed a Sunday in church that I can recall. He was different than the rest of the fishermen, but everyone really liked him and boy was he a worker. The summa' I remember most there was a French boy at the mansion named "Ro-bare", not Robert like its spelled, but "Ro-bare". He and I became pals for a while til I got, er... sick, I guess from somethin' I ate while visitin' him up at the house. Never saw him after that, but I didn't go down to the cove neither, after I started feelin' better. I disremember much. Anyway, it was a sorrowful thing about Eben, he just passed on a few years back. Fished his whole life out of his dory, never went to power. I guess he was rich enough that he didn't feel the need for it. But he never got married neither, nor had any girlfriends that I remember. I guess he never got over that Holly gal...

"Can Eben come out and play?" Holly chuckled outside the Ewert home.

"Dang Holly, shush up will ya! Ma and Pa are in the kitchen and they'll hear ya, and all hell will break loose. I'll meet ya over at the woodpile in a couple minutes if'n I can get past the folks and shed that little Day fella," Eben quietly pleaded.

"Naw, I think I'll just knock on the door and say Hi to your Ma, and maybe wink at your Pa, whatya think?" teased the girl. Eben just shook his head with a smirk and ducked back inside the window and closed it. She could see through the glass as Eben was hiking up his britches and reaching for his shirt, while wondering how long it would take her to reverse the process as soon as they made it to one of the shacks or barns or wherever he was going to take her this time. She was going to be eighteen in a few days and wondered what her boyfriend, for that's what she considered Eben to be, was going to get her for her birthday. What she hoped for was that they could take the train down to Portsmouth and spend a day or two walking around arm in arm like a regular couple, and not be ashamed to do so at that. Once Eben had closed the door inside, the window she was peering into lost its glare and became a mirror, and Holly caught sight of herself and measured the reflection. Her icy green eyes were her best feature she thought, but her thin supple lips ran a close second. She had to agree that she was indeed, a beautiful creature, as the artists who sketched her often commented. Even the artists that liked boys rather than girls, or the ones who weren't intending on enjoying her charms remarked favorably. She had as long a set of legs as a young woman could have for being just a bit over five feet tall, and she thought that Eben's lanky six foot frame fit perfectly with hers when he was lying on top of her. She liked her straight sandy colored hair and often enjoyed frizzing it up a bit. Even if all the people in Ogunquit didn't know she was one of the models down to the cove, they'd stare anyway if she simply walked down the street, for she knew herself to be a head-turner for sure.

An honest appraisal of her beauty, she thought as she gazed at her reflection, turning her head slightly from side to side. As she swiped a knot of hair away from her eyes the sun caught the glass just a bit and made half her reflection disappear for a moment, just long enough for her to seemingly glance into her soul, and she shuddered. She whispered to her reflection, "I'm not sure I like you much, but I do sometimes, and I really want to all the time, why won't you let me?" She turned away and took a few pensive steps toward the road that led past the woodpile where she would rendezvous with her only true lover. She was wearing a plain blue patterned cotton dress and underneath a set of underwear she had just taken off the clothesline. She had bathed in one of the tubs in the house and lathered herself all the way to her toenails. She caressed herself with a more diluted solution of lemon juice on her hair and skin than she always used to kill the man juice up inside her after sex. As she strolled down the path she wondered if Eben would truly appreciate how fresh and wholesome she felt all over.

Holly had completed her freshman year at Vassar College, one of the finest women's colleges in the country, if not the world. The school was noted for its strong liberal arts curricula and she had breezed through the first year of classes with flying colors. She boldly concentrated her studies in mathematics and art history, the former still unsuitable for women according to most male academics. One of Vassar's stated visions for its students was to empower a 'willingness to experiment', and Holly used that honored statement to qualify her promiscuity, and to attempt to come to acceptable terms with the sexual abuse she endured from her father and his pals beginning when she was fourteen years old. Her recounting of her college dalliances intrigued her dormitory pals to no end, and she was a most popular counselor and confidant among her virginal peers. On Sundays and at campus events her pals always seemed to find a way to avoid her company however, lest their reputations be sullied by association. Holly was initially hurt by these slights but eventually disregarded the emotions such conduct would have normally brought forth.

She was only now beginning to stress about her future beyond her summer employment in Ogunquit. Her father, a lawyer who had recently passed away, left enough to keep her mother in her societal station but not by much. Appearances for her mother would have to be maintained, but with a strict frugal eye. In a few months time perhaps a job could be discreetly sought, if only to, 'ward off the burdensome boredom of widowhood', which ladies of her station would certainly understand. In the meantime, Holly's mother had written a short note stating that she would be unable to provide tuition for the coming school year. The letter was short, friendly, but somewhat terse, ending with a 'Your Loving Mother' signature.

Holly was instinctively positive that her mother knew about Holly's promiscuity with her father and his friends, and likely blamed her for instigating such dastardly conduct, though most assuredly knowing that her late husband was a true scumbag. If Holly had conducted herself as a true lady, her father would never have been enticed to share her charms, mother convinced herself.

Holly was sure that this is what her mother thought, completely disregarding any sentiment that all Holly had done that first time was to help her father off the bathroom floor after he had passed out drunk. All she remembered was being forced to kneel in front of him and stick out her tongue. Holly had closed her eyes and seemed in a daze when he had finished splashing her face with his seed. She didn't have any idea what her father had sprayed her with but felt its warmth and creamy stickiness. After washing her face off for what seemed like hours she had finally fallen asleep in her bed, only to be awakened at first light to the same episode while clutching her pillow. After he was finished, her father had ordered her to wash and get to breakfast in short order, where at the table all was normal again. Over a plate of eggs young Holly had started to whimper and was immediately scolded by her mother to never disrespect her father's table ever again. From that point forward she was a dutiful daughter, and consort for her father, and any other man she was ordered to 'kibitz' with; 'kibitz' being their new private term for compliancy.

The situation only got worse when her father began to freely instruct her in the presence of her mother to kibitz with him in his study after her chores, and her mother scolding her if she was late for a kibitz with her 'very respected and busy father'. At some point Holly decided that her mother assumed that these kibitz sessions were private education lessons bestowed on the girl by a great and learned man, and she should feel entirely privileged to be so fortunate to receive them. Holly's mother had constantly nagged at the girl to express profound appreciation to her father for taking time out of his busy life to share his wisdom with his daughter. Holly's mother or any of the maids were never permitted entrance into her father's office, which was another motivation for her mother to hound Holly about expressing appreciation for the secular opportunity to enter. Shortly after Holly had fulfilled her worldly education from her father, he began to include other esteemed gentleman in these kibitz sessions. The gentlemen always handed her father envelopes with cash after her education sessions were concluded. Mother expressed much admiration and appreciation to her wonderful husband for permitting their daughter's educational horizons to be expanded by the tutorship of such learned and esteemed gentlemen. Mother was particularly appreciative when priests agreed to bestow their wisdom on her young daughter. Her mother began to refer to Holly as the most fortunate girl in the world, and after countless educational sessions with a variety of teachers, Holly began to comically agree.

Holly had arrived on campus with an exuberance to excel in her coursework and lay her foundation with every male in a decision making position. At the time, she figured she had four years to establish the necessary groundwork to blackmail her way into a lucrative career or marriage, or whatever else her expertly applied charms could procure. Her father and his pals had educated her exceedingly well. Unfortunately, her tuition was no longer assured, and she would have to expedite her chosen path with Valentine Meadows and his associates that she had met during his numerous visits to campus as a visiting professor, as well as the many social events he had invited her to.

She was quite unsettled about Meadows because he simply wasn't as eager to clamor for her potent charms. He had more sinister desires with children rather than a yearning all other men had for her wares, and this left her vulnerable to his whims. Still, she more than adequately served as his arm candy and he always complimented her on the profound affect she had on others at social gatherings. She truly was an asset to not only his lofty station in the art community, but also by allaying casual references and rumors about his true desires for kids. As long as such an engaging and striking young woman as Holly was on his arm, no one could ever lend credence to the whispers about Meadows' ultimate decadence.

As she approached the woodpile she was still deep in her own world and a bit out of sorts with her immediate future. If Meadows cast her aside at the end of the summer, she would be homeless and with only a few hundred dollars to her name. By the end of summer she might have close to a thousand just with wages and part-time waitress work over at the Sparhawk Hall & Hotel, but waitressing held little appeal. As she sat on a stump in the sunshine awaiting Eben, she suddenly came to the conclusion that if Eben had no intentions for her beyond slap n' tickle, she simply couldn't afford to disrupt her potential relationship with Meadows, even though he outwardly encouraged her fling with the local boy. She figured that even though Meadows kiddingly chided her about 'taking advantage of that good looking local chap', she figured it had to scratch his craw somewhere in his fiber. He may be a deceitful child molester, but he still had the pieces and parts of a man, and that man did enjoy taking occasional turns at her being, simply to enforce his rule over her. He would simply command her to satisfy his wishes, usually to demonstrate to others that she was his property, and he would finish in whatever fashion and continue his conversations with others as he withdrew or toweled himself off. He might pat her on the head or on her bottom when he was done, usually quickly and sometimes not even to climax, and might even offer a 'thank you' before wandering off to other business. Sometimes if students or friends were watching, he would offer others the opportunity to 'step-in' as if they were dancing in a ballroom. She needed more ammunition with Meadows than just her willingness to satisfy his whims. She needed some kind of hold that would force him to keep her around on his payroll and then some. That gypsy whore named Byzar he brought from the streets of Manhattan was very beautiful, accomplished in social settings and every bit the sexual specialist that Holly was, and maybe even more accommodating than she. This was worrisome.

Sitting on that stump she made her decision. Eben needed to treat her right for her birthday by taking her to Portsmouth, or she just couldn't afford dilly-dallying around with this very handsome young man. She would have to discard him, even though she knew she loved him with all her heart.

She was still deep in thought when she heard the snapping sticks in the woods behind the woodpile. Expecting Eben sooner than this, and given her current mood, she was a little annoyed that he hadn't arrived at the woodpile sooner, knowing what delicious delights awaited him. Heck, guys would cross fire for her charms, who was he to think he could assume their availability? He better demonstrate suitable appreciation and ask forgiveness for making her wait, she concluded. His tardiness was fortifying her resolve to demand his attention, and intentions for her birthday.

As Eben strode out of the clearing she stood and drew her finger across her forehead to brush a few strands of hair away. Trailing Eben was that little Day boy, as per usual. That kid was a real mood breaker and it further annoyed Holly that Eben let that little boy tag along with him just now, knowing that he was heading for some skin time with Holly, his girlfriend, or so she had hoped up until the last hour or so.

Holly, being Holly, stepped forward to give little Richard Day a big hug and smooch on the forehead, which flabbergasted the little boy to no end. He really liked the attention, even though he feigned that he was too old for such nonsense. To Richard and the other boys his age, Holly was as close to a goddess as one could ever hope to find or see, especially when viewed amongst all the local Maine girls. Being the conniving sort, Holly bent down and teased, "So Richard, what did you get me for my birthday, it's this week you know?"

The boy was a little embarrassed and tucked his thumbs in his overalls before sputtering, "I don't know Miss Holly."

She playfully tousled his head and said, "That's alright Richard, I know you love me don't you?"

"Yes ma'am," was all the boy could muster.

"Maybe you can tell me what my fiancé Eben got for me then, could you?"

To this Eben rolled his eyes and wished he had sent the boy on an errand or something before going to the woodpile. Now the entire town would learn of his impending nuptials to that slutty girl from the art school on the rocks. Eben could only imagine the horror on his mother's face when she heard the rumor. Holly could be a real frustrating critter he decided.

Holly still hadn't acknowledged Eben even a bit as she

held the little boys rapt attention, and then he wondered, "Miss Holly, what is a feency?"

Holly let the weight of the question linger for a moment thereby creating further anxiety in Eben before finally letting him off the hook with, "Aw Richard, it's just a saying when a boy and a girl like each other, pay it no mind. Now Richard, I have to talk to Eben alone for a while, is that okay with you?"

"Sure Miss Holly, I'm heading down to the cove to do some crabbin' anyway with my new pal Bobby, he's from France you know. He says he knows you too, and you're real nice."

"I know who you mean Richard, Mr. Meadows brought him with him all the way from France, he's a very nice boy. You two should get along just fine. Have you met Mr. Meadows? He likes your new friend very much."

"Yup. He gave us some gumballs yesterday. I used to be scair't of him but he was real nice when I was with Bobby. He said that if I'm good that he might hire me to do some chores for cash money around his place while Bobby is in his school, so I'm gonna go crabbin' down to the cove and hope that Mr. Meadows hollers for me."

"That's just fine Richard, I'll bet Mr. Meadows will put you to work and I'll be sure to put in a good word for you. You run along and if you see Mr. Meadows, promise me that you'll tell him that I sent you, won't you? It would be our little secret and a big favor for me."

"I'll tell him Miss Holly, I surely will, ma'am."

"Our little secret, Richard?"

"Our little secret, ma'am."

The mesmerized little boy took off after Holly released him from her spell, and he was so bedazzled by being so close to Holly and so seemingly important to her that he completely forgot about Eben who was still standing quietly next to the woodpile. "What was that all about, Holly?" Eben finally sputtered as the boy disappeared onto a trail in the woods that led onto a well used footpath.

"It's a private matter between me and my new boyfriend, little Richard," Holly chided. She moved into Eben and demurely stroked her right index finger lightly along the length of Eben's zipper and purred, "Why Eben, are you a bit jealous of my new little friend?"

She was close enough so Eben could not escape her fresh female scent even if he wanted to, and his firmness was beginning to press against the inside of his zipper under her delicate touch, but just as he reached for her, Holly spun away feigning complete disinterest. "So Eben, what *shall* we do this weekend for my birthday?" she asked innocently, even though her question was anything but. Eben stepped after her and attempted an embrace but Holly stepped along and turned her shoulder abruptly away from his first touch and continued her slow stroll toward the same path little Richard had taken. She knew full well what immediately jumped into Eben's mind by doing so, that being there was no loving to be had if she continued on. She also knew that Eben realized that he had to choose his next words carefully for stopping her stroll with a grasp would surely not halt her. If he wanted to enjoy Holly's charms this day, and the pressure against the inside of his zipper said that he most assuredly did, then he needed to conjure up an answer, and the right answer, to her question real quick.

"Holly, I was thinkin' we could go out to Isreal's Head above Lobster Point with a blanket and watch the moon?" he offered hopefully. She stopped her stroll and stared at him hard.

"Why not have a picnic there at lunch, Eben?" she demanded. She knew the answer but she wanted to force Eben to say the words aloud. By now Eben's pants were hanging completely free from his solid frame without any hint of encumbrance near his zipper and he blurted, "Aw Holly, we both know the answer to that, this town would kill me and my folks would do worse if we were to be seen carryin' on like a couple." Even before the words left his lips he knew he was proverbially screwed, and that 'proverbially' was the only screwing he was bound to get on this day. He stepped toward Holly outstretching his arms, "I'm sorry Holly, I didn't mean it to sound like that, I love you so much dammit. You're my…"

"I'm your what…Eben, exactly?" Holly calmly interrupted. "I'm your girlfriend, I'm your lover, I'm the woman you want to marry? What is it exactly that I am Eben?" Holly was flushed and dead serious now, but in full control of her emotions as she stood before the only man she knew that she might ever truly find love with. The kind of love that permeates the marrow, that physically aches when apart. The kind of love that stutters a step, or jumbles an attempt at forming a sentence. She was so close to crying and falling into his arms, but she found a long dormant sense of self worth and pride somewhere in her soul. She would stand her ground and somehow not display a single tear. With a purposeful calm she softly whispered directly to the beautiful, innocent young man standing before her, "Eben, the saddest part of what is happening now is that I know with all my heart that you will regret this day until your last breath. You and I are like waves and the ocean; we simply belong together for eternity. Just because other men have had me, and I have been physically forced to submit on occasion, does not now, or ever mean that what I have shared with you isn't the most sacred thing on earth to me. And either you're too fucking dumb to realize this, or you're too much of a god damned faggot to be a man about it and marry me while you have the chance. The woman you make such passionate love to, and she to you, is worth a good poke but not loved enough to take to your church, or to dinner at a nice restaurant, or home to your family. What does this say about you, Eben, and your manhood?"

They stood there in the small meadow staring into each other's soul and Holly drew a measure of satisfaction as the first tear fell not from her eyes, but from Eben's. They just stood. After an interminable minute, Holly gently turned and strolled away. It was done.

Byzar Bedrosian was a petite, extremely flexible and accomplished ballet dancer. She was too short and not quite graceful enough to be accepted as a serious study, though she practiced her craft daily. She adored being in Maine and away from the dinginess of the Manhattan bowery. She was just eighteen, and had been servicing men since she was twelve years old, as was directed by her gypsy clan. Byzar never knew her mother, or if her mother was in the clan of twenty or so, she never identified herself. Her aunties always told her that they were all her mother, and that's just the way it was and to think no more about it. Brown, slightly wavy shoulder length hair, deep set dark eyes, supple thin lips and a nose with a bit of a hook—these were her alluring facial attributes. Not a stunning beauty like her new friend Holly, but very exotic when she applied a touch of mascara with deft skill. She was a hairy creature, with an almost single eyebrow, fondules of hair springing from her nipples and a light spread on the backs of her thighs. She refused to shave her armpits, but relented when trimming her privates. Her one imperfection she surmised was a small growth of excess skin just above her anus, which by the time her lover's peered at such, they were usually too engrossed with the task at hand to care much, beyond a inquiry as to whether it was uncomfortable, which it was not to Byzar. Shame at being used by men had long since been cast out of her soul, and Byzar was simply matter-of-fact about the concept. Something akin to the necessity of having to poop after meals, she concluded. Her 'aunties' had instilled this concept in her bones early and often. If a man expressed satisfaction after a session with Byzar to her aunties, she was duly rewarded and congratulated. She had been taught to squirt a small amount of red dye up inside her to make her customers think that they had popped a virgin, for that was how she was offered to the market by her clan. It had been a successful ploy for her first four years in the trade, and it made the clan a great deal of extra money per session. By the time Byzar turned seventeen, she could no longer hide her experienced needs to pull off the ruse any longer. Her entire goal at this point in her life was the acquisition of an old, wealthy husband. Escaping the clutches of her clan to accompany one of her regular and most demanding customers was her best shot at her goal. This customer, a wealthy, young art patron from Brooklyn named Valentine Meadows, spent most of their sessions watching her be violently abused by one, or more, men in his studio. He paid handsomely for the pleasure. He would create the most outlandish and sometimes horrific scenarios for Byzar to be the focus of: drunken sailors, innocent schoolboys, men of all races and sizes and sometimes women. When the play-acting was concluded and the actors paid and dismissed, Meadows would simply stroll over to Byzar and bend her over and quickly finish himself in her butt. After bathing individually, they always set down for a cup of tea while watching the ships in Brooklyn harbor.

One afternoon, after a particularly brutal session with two priests Meadows had found, he handed her an envelope with five hundred dollars and instructed her to pack a single suitcase for the summer, as she was going to Maine with him to his art school. Their train was scheduled to depart on the following day and she was instructed not to be late and to dress as fashionable as possible. She stood up, pecked him on the forehead as per usual, and left his flat without a word. When she arrived at the station the following day, he placed her arm in his and they strolled along as a fine couple before boarding the train, where they shared a cabin, as well as a splendid lunch in the elegant dining car. Byzar played her role exquisitely and Valentine Meadows was extremely pleased with her flair and conduct.

Once in Maine and settled into Meadows' lavish home on the rocks above Perkins Cove, Byzar was free to explore the little village of Ogunquit as well as the expansive beach a mile up the trail. At low tide, Byzar found herself a veritable playground where she danced and performed pirouettes much to the delight of those visiting during the late spring days. The Sparhawk Hall was still in the process of opening for the summer tourist season and many early season guests were taken by Byzar's hour long displays of ballet and modern dance. Meadows had settled her into a second floor bedroom overlooking the cove, which she was to share with another model that had yet to arrive. He had told Byzar about her new roommate to be, and stated that her name was Holly, and that she would arrive as soon as her college term had concluded. He stated that Holly was very bright and as vivacious as Byzar, and they both shared the same *duties* for the summer. Both would get on just fine he had said. When the art school would be in session, in another three weeks or so, she, Holly and other *models* would be requested to 'sit' before his students in various positions and dress, and he expected his two *finest* girls to represent his esteemed name in fine form and to the level of their compensation, which was one thousand dollars for the summer. The clear understanding was that should the artists request sexual favors of any type, she and Holly were expected to comply in good humor. Their room was to be kept tidy and no visitors were to be invited without Meadows' permission. Their meals and laundry were provided by the French woman who, with her husband and young son, stayed in the room next to the kitchen on the first floor.

It was arranged that both Byzar and Holly would work in the elegant dining room at the nearby Sparhawk on Friday, Saturdays and Sundays only, and only then for breakfast meals. Meadows stated that once the tourist season was in full swing, that he would be taking many of his meals there and both girls could expect to be introduced to many and varied guests as he might choose to do so. The girls would be introduced as his 'fine art' protégés and during slack time would have free reign of the student studio section of the house, so as to explore their artistic talents and observe excellence at work among his students. Meadows concluded his remarks to Byzar by stating that some of the Sparhawk guests would be personally invited to observe the art school inner workings when in session and that certain accommodations for these guests would be required.

All of this was glorious news to Byzar and she looked forward to meeting her new roommate. Until that time she had a couple weeks to explore the rocky coast, the sandy expanse of Ogunquit beach, and visit the village shops of Ogunquit and the more expansive little town of Wells, a short trolley ride to the north. Foremost on Byzar's mind however, was where to hide the five hundred dollars she carried in her purse; more money than she had ever thought possible to possess.

"Eben, you look like the sun ain't shinin', and your pockets is empty even though we jus' parlayed that last batch of hooch for a brand spankin' new dory, complete with a false bottom. What's got you so glum all the sudden?" Dinny wondered. Dinny was half a foot shorter than Eben and nowhere near as handsome. He already had the beginnings of a Boston Ale paunch and a rummy's nose to go along with premature thinning brown hair. An unremarkable intellect was offset by as dry a humor one could ever hope to find, which surprised most he knew. Most folks with satirical insights were generally quite bright, but Dinny's brain certainly didn't qualify on that score, so folks just considered that Dinny's humor was drawn from a simpleton's mindset, nothing more.

"It ain't nothing Din, I'm just tired. Between lobsterin', my chores at home and our midnight runs out to the rum line I'm jus' played out I guess."

"Whyn't you find your gal, she'd relax you some I expect,"

Dinny smirked.

"Holly ain't in the frame no more Din, and I trust you know that I'm hurtin' some about it. The truth of it is Din, that she dumped me for certain, and on one side I'm relieved that I don't have to hide it from my folks and others, but on the other side I surely miss her somethin' awful. She was stickin' to me worse than that little Day kid and I figured I could shuck either of em' any time I wanted, but now I feel like my guts is empty missin' her so bad. I messed up. I most surely did I'm thinkin'," Eben lamented.

"Every time I catch a glimpse of her she's smilin' and gettin' fawned over by some old geezer or rich guy over at the Spar, or she's posin' nekkid on the rocks at the cove. How can a guy marry that and live with himself, Din? It really hurts cuz I still love her somethin' awful. What a jackass I am," Eben moaned.

"Eben, we got some jangle and Doctor Dinny will see you now. Meet me back here in an hour cleaned up and with an overnight bag, we're goin' whorin' in Portsmouth. That's your prescription and that's final," Dinny ordered.

"Nah Din. I don't feel much for it and with my luck I'd surely get the clap and feel worse than I do now, dangit."

"It ain't up for discussion partner, cuz' I'm goin', and if I'm goin' you are too, cuz you bein' my friend and all, I'll know you got my back and I won't get shanghaied to China or some such place. I hear tell of a gal with a crib on the second floor near the waterfront that has'em linin' up ten deep on weekends, but since it's Tuesday, it might be slow, and we could stick our peckers in her own juices rather than that of the thirty fellas before us, savvy?" Dinny chuckled as he turned to go to his shack to clean up and fetch his possibles.

"That don't sound too appealin' Din, but like you say, I

prob'ly need some strange and if'n you got shanghaied I'd have to haul all our hooch myself, so yup, I'll meet you at the train directly. Hello Portsmouth!" Eben was perking up already.

The train ride to Portsmouth took less than an hour and it was still daylight when Dinny and Eben set to their wanderings.

"Well our first big decision I suppose is where shall we grab our first brew, Eben? We'll consider sleepin' arrangements when the situation allows, eh? Right now let's get some suds n' see if we can find a couple gals who are just startin' business for the day; less chance of the clap methinks?" Dinny chattered as he was already heading for the docks and associated dives along same.

"Oh and by the way, Eben, you ARE drinkin' tonight. No ifs or buts about it. Nobody here to see you fall off your high ridin' wagon and come to think of it, why don't you cuss a little just so's I'm sure you're a regular human? Doctor Dinny's prescription ya' know. By the way, have you seen that little gypsy gal Eben? Friends with Holly I'm told. I've seen her dancin' out on the sand over at Gunnyquit beach a bunch of times. She wears only a bathing suit that shows all her arms and legs right up to her little ass, and it's tight enough that it ain't difficult to imagine what the suit is coverin' at that. She causes quite a stir at the Spar but the owners always say that she is only wearin' what ballerinas in New York City wear, so it's acceptable. Still pisses off the wives and older women though from what I hear. When she's waitressin' she faces them women head on and she comes off as sweet as poison when she speaks. Jeez I'd like to fuck her," Dinny announced as they turned into the nearest pub.

It only took 30 minutes before Eben was coming down the

stairs from the second floor cribs where one of the forty-something harbor whores had taken him. Din had paid the gal and directed her to Eben as he headed out back to take a leak. Eben hadn't even finished his beer when the gal swung to his side and ordered him to come with her and said she was already paid for by his pal. By the time he warily shut the door behind him she had grabbed his crotch with a couple squeezes and lifted her dress over her head all in one motion. She had said, "I always like to start with you young guys, your quick to stiffen and even quicker to squirt, what you waiting for sailor? If it's a kiss, forget it. Shuck'em and get with it. How do you want me anyway, front or back?"

Eben managed to choke out a garbled "From behind" as he dropped his pants to his shins, and she replied, "If you try the wrong hole, I'll slice it off and that's a fact, savvy? I've got half a dozen shriveled up wankers in my top drawer if ya' don't believe me. Try for my bung and I'll surely shit my seventh! Need another tug or are you ready to pump, you handsome sailor?"

Eben was understandably dazed by the woman's speech but was completely over the edge of reason, as well as being stiff as a yardarm, so he shut his brain off to the whore's further meanderings and proceeded.

It did feel good to have his pecker in a pussy again, but it wasn't Holly's scent he was smelling, or her cute little firm butt he was staring at as he pumped as fast as he could. He had a momentary spasm of concern for the next guy so he decided to squirt over her back rather than inside her—just to be polite. He snatched a towel from her dresser, which was in reach, and dried himself off before drawing up his pants. She still hadn't straightened up but had her right hand behind her head as she griped, "Hey asshole, you got that shit in my hair, and on my sheets. It's a wonder you didn't hit the wall, shithead. Hand me a towel would ya'? Eben gently tossed the towel that he had just used, on her back as she was beginning to straighten up. He was out the door just as he zippered up and made a half-hearted attempt to swing the door shut but knew when he let the doorknob go that he didn't give the door enough pace to get to the frame. She was still yelling at him as he got to the top of the stairs and quickly descended, "Hey you rat-fuck, at least you can close the fuckin' door... asshole."

He could still hear her faint yelling as he elbowed Dinny on his way out the door, well ahead of the bouncers who had just started their shift. Both young men were stepping lively on the red brick sidewalks as they turned the corner into an alley and on to the next pub.

"Listen Eben," Dinny announced, "try not to get us knifed before dark will ya' for chrissakes! What the hell did you do to that gruesome tramp anyway?"

"Jus' pumped her and left, that's all," Eben chirped with a grin. "I guess I ruined her expensive hairdo with my stuff. Pissed her off I expect. Weren't intentional. I'm feelin' better already Doctor Din, and your prescription was spot on, though I'm hopin' for no side effects."

As they hurried away from the waterfront up toward Market St., where there were pubs aplenty, Dinny started speaking in an almost confessional tone, "Well that tickles me to no end Eben, and while you're in such a good mood I ought to tell you what I saw up at the Meadows place the other day deliverin' hooch to that spooky bastard. Usually I just drop the tins on the kitchen table for that French lady and she goes and gets the money from Meadows somewhere upstairs. She always has a piece of cake or some pie for me while I'm waiting."

Dinny went on, "So she disappears and a few minutes later I hear footsteps comin' down and it's Meadows and the little French kid that your little pal Richard is always playin' with. Anyway Meadows is only wearin' tight shorts big enough to barely cover his jewels, and the little kid is in the same getup. Meadows sets down at the table across from me as if it's as natural as can be, and the boy hops up right on his knee, and adjusts his seat by using the table and Meadows crotch with either hand to brace himself. Meadows greets me as if we're old pals, pats the kid on the ass, and asks me how much he owes. I tell him it's the same price per three gallon tin, and that its 180 proof from Belgium, and that it is the finest stuff available. He says that he knows all that, and that he considers me 'most trustworthy', but would like to give me a bonus for my good service. He introduces the kid as 'Robare', or some such French thing and the kid sticks out his right hand as if I'm supposed to smooch the back of it, like those frenchies do. I shook the kids hand and it felt limp and shit. I tell ya' Eben I was almost about to puke seein' all this. But it gets more fucked up, I'm tellin' ya. You sure you want me to keep goin' Eben? I really should tell ya' jus' so I can sleep some, ok?"

"May as well Din, you're on a roll and I can see it's somethin' you gotta tell. But let's grab a shot n' a beer first. If I'm gonna drink I may as well get an early start don't ya' think?"

They had walked clear to the other side of the docks below Market St. just to clear themselves of any possible meeting with those ruffians from the first pub. They found a pub that wasn't too crowded and grabbed a table, ordered some beer, rum and stew and Dinny started in again.

"Like I was sayin', this little kid and Meadows is obviously queer and I think that the French lady is the boy's momma, but apparently doesn't care that the guy is probably diddlin' with her boy. Eben, it gets worse. The bastard reaches into the boy's underwear and fetches an envelope and hands it to me. He says that inside is payment for the hooch as well as a bonus. He says that as long as he and I have an 'understanding', winking towards the boy, and that deliveries are timely, bonuses for such conduct may be expected. He says that our arrangement is valid as long as our 'trust' is. I was athinkin' that as long as I delivered booze and kept my mouth shut as to the goins' on in that spooky place, I, rather we'd, get paid more than the usual. I felt sick. Then the guy pats the boy on the rump and shooshes him up the stairs and says for me to follow him into the studio. I do, and what do you suppose I see? Holly is settin' there with six artists painting behind their easels. She has a flimsy dress over her shoulders and is posing with her legs parted and her head tilted back sucking a strawberry. She smiles over to me and says, "Howdy Din, like the view that Eben will never sniff again?"

Dinny continued, "She never even flinched and the artists at their easels didn't neither. She kept on posin' and the artists kept on paintin'. Then Meadows asks me if I like art. I didn't say anything 'cuz I was still looking at Holly... sorry but I was. Then a lady about your Mom's age prances forward and introduces herself as Baroness Von 'something such what the fuck', and squeezes my chest in both hands. She says with a heavy accent, 'Ah you must be the handsome lad that brings the liquid joy to our clan, is that so?'... I said that I do, in fact, supply the hooch that Mr. Meadows orders, and that my name is Dinny.

"She laughed and then said, 'I know all about you and your friend Eben. What would he think if he knew you were gazing at Holly's charms right now, as you are? Of course it would strain your relationship, ya?'

"I nodded a bit I guess and then she said, 'Dinny, who ever named you that, eh? Nonetheless, while you stare at Holly, I will give you a miraculous blowjob, ya?' The lady was Russian I guess and when she opened her robe, she had postage stamps stuck all over and a couple tomato cans coverin' her nipples. Weird as hell!" Dinny went on.

"I'm tellin' you Eben, that by the time I got my senses back the Baroness was on her knees workin' my pecker somethin' awful and Holly was smiling at me like a Cheshire cat. Holly looked over at me and said, 'Hey Din, if that marvelous nutcase doesn't suit your fancy, I'll be done here in a few minutes. The woman that is suckin' you off is quite famous ya' know. We call her Mama Dada 'cuz she is the lady that started the Dadaist movement in Europe and New York City. She says she didn't but she probably did.'

"Holly then says that a Dadaist is someone who makes themselves into a canvas, like a live artist, and tries to shock the rich folk into trying to hide their own curiosities and fantasies.

"Then Holly says, 'We're all Dadaists here, you might try it Din, er, when she gets done with you! By the way, it wouldn't break my heart to fuck you to death just to spite your pissant of a friend, Eben.'

"She was speaking mean, Eben, she surely was. I'll have you know that I never got there, Eben, for the Baroness sucked me dry without much say-so on my part. That lady pulled up my pants, tucked me in and buckled me up, and before I had a notion to say anything to Holly, I was led out the door and the old gal slapped me on the butt. Whilst this was going on old Meadows was sittin' in the corner playin' with himself and the artists were still paintin' away like nothin' was goin' on. To tell the truth Eben, I felt like I had been cast in a play that had been pre-arranged as I stumbled down the rocks toward my, er our, dory. I jus' had to tell you Eben, mostly cuz' of that little Day kid that hangs around you so much. I seen him playin' with that fairy little French kid and I wonder if that bastard Meadows has designs on his little ass also. The little French fag seemed to be on drugs by the way, and I wonder if that sinister bastard Meadows spikes the lemonade, as it were?" Dinny finished while staring at his beer and steaming stew.

Eben just sat there as if struck by a codfish until after a minute or so piped up, "You ain't shittin' me, are ya?"

"I kinda wish I was, Eben. The whole place was freekin' looney, but the artists at their easels seemed real serious about their work. Everybody else, including Holly seemed as if they were suckin' on laudanum or something. The just weren't right in the head," Dinny wondered.

"To tell you the truth Eben, I'm a little spooked to deliver there again, blowjob notwithstandin' an all. Eben, here's your half of what Meadows gave me in the envelope, one hundred smackers. If George Weare, Bish Young and his pals ever caught wind that Meadows was payin' us so much for booze they'd likely steer the Dixie III right up on the rocks personal like to Meadows door! I'm supposed to deliver another four tins next week, you sure you don't wanna switch with me, and I'll deliver the homegrown stuff to Adams, Maxwell, Perkins and the rest of them shipbuilders at the Gunnyquit wharf?"

Eben changed the subject like everything that Dinny had

confessed was of little consequence, "I'm glad you mentioned the Dixie III Din, we got to start thinkin' about whether to get us one of them speedboats. And by the way, how many tins we still got left in the hold under the hay in the barn? Last time I counted we had forty left. That's better than money in the bank, and I'm pretty sure my folks still don't know about our cellar. Anyway let's not worry about who's gonna deliver where, if'n you don't want to mess with Meadows anymore I'll deliver to the bastard. Knowing that Holly is all het' up to make me jealous just convinced me that I got no use for her anymore. I don't give a crap what she does, and I'm glad to be rid of her, thanks to your prescription and tellin' me what she said. Their all weirdos in there, and I'm gonna have me a talk with little Richard and keep him out of that bastard's evil mitts. If I find out that Meadows has touched little Richard I'll gut him. Then them squirrely artists will really have somethin' to paint," Eben fumed.

Relieved that Eben had received the story that Dinny was so worried to tell his friend, he got back to business and said, "Let's eat a'fore this stew gets chillsome and ponder whether we ought to get us a speedboat like the Dixie III."

Eben continued, "Near as I can tell, if we invest in a speedboat, we can make it out to the rum line three miles out in about thirty minutes dependin' on the seas. Even if'n we aren't as fast as the Coast Guard's boats we could still beat em', but we ain't so fast as to outrun their guns! I'm not sure I wanna get tangled up with that kind of life, Din. We got a good thing goin' now, it's steady and we're too small an operation to bother them Dixie III boys anyway. I'm sure they know that we run a little hooch on the side of our fishin' biz, but those guys are supplyin' half the State as it is. We're just supplyin' some of the hotels, shipbuilders, and a few select folk like Meadows, Juddy Dunaway, and some of Cap'n Tunkers pals. Throw in a preacher or three and we've got us a nice little thing goin' Din. Them big boys ain't gonna mess with us, 'cuz it's mostly family and friends we're supplyin', and hell, they live in this town too. I also don't think they really know how many folks we do supply and with your connections at the Sparhawk as the Chief Bellhop, you get first crack at the new guests as they come in, right? You also get to chat in private with potential customers while you're doin' your gardening, right?" Eben calculated.

"So the way I got it figured is that it makes more sense for you to become pals with that squeaky voiced, stutterin' bastard Meadows than it does for me, you follow? Maybe he's likin' your pretty little butt also, Dinny?" Eben chuckled.

"Go chase yourself, Eben", Dinny laughed, and piped up for another round of brew, only this time with whiskey instead of rum.

"I'm with ya' Eben, whilst I'd like a Dixie III tied to my mooring, let's not spoil the good thing we got goin'. We're getting' rich quiet-like, and now that we got our false-bottomed fishing dory, Ogunquit style, we can carry our midnight hauls in from the schooners anchored out at the rum line with no one the wiser. If any of the revenuers boats or the Coast Guard boats show up on the horizon, we just start settin' out our nets like we always done and be friendly-like," Dinny stated matter-of-fact-like before continuing, "I don't like the thought of getting' shot at neither, Eben. Say did you know that the Dixie III has her wheelhouse walls filled with sand to catch the bullets? Ain't that somethin'? Ole' Cap'n Tunker told me that, as well as the false bottom it has. He said that she was built in New Jersey somewheres and that once the Coast Guard saw what she could do for speed, they went to the same builder and paid to have a faster version built! I guess the builder can't be blamed for what his boats get used for now can he?"

"Ladies and gentlemen," Valentine Meadows announced in his signature high pitched whimper, thankful that his first three words rang over the elegant dinner table without his typical stuttering. "It i-i-i-s m-m-m-my distinct honor to-to-to welcome my dear fr-fr-fr-friend and pa-pa-patron of the f-f-f-fine arts, the lovely a-a-a-and world renowned B-B-Baroness Elsa Von Freytag Loringhoven."

Holly was seated next to Byzar, both beautifully attired in sleek, lacy, high necked, cream colored full length gowns. Both quietly clapped along with the other twelve guests at the table. There were seven art students, (of which four were male), two artists-in-residence (sculptors both), one new female model who hadn't been introduced to Holly and Byzar yet, and two male guests from the Sparhawk, who were likely expecting to share in the girls' charms at some point in the evening. The Baroness bowed to all at the table and proceeded to reveal her breasts she had painted with black with bright white circles around her nipples. In a deep, Russian voice she grandly announced, "It is wonderful for me to join such a group of most talented people, ya? I look forward to exploring all of our collective talents and journeys. Vee shall commence dahling Valentine, ya," to which Meadows smiled, nodded and signaled the two borrowed waitresses from the Sparhawk Inn to begin service. Robare's mother supervised the serving but her son and husband were nowhere in sight.

Both Holly and Byzar were fascinated with the Baroness, who was seated directly across from them. After a few moments of serving, the dinner table chatter commenced and the Baroness at one point held both the girls eyes in mutual satisfaction and wonder. Byzar in particular was almost trembling in the presence of such an illustrious woman from 'the old country'.

"You two lovely creatures are going to be my protégés, ya?" the forty-something Baroness announced to the table. Both girls blushed, nodded but neither could find their voice.

"We have all summer to share our talents and expand our boundries, shall we not? Vee shall meet out on the rocks at sunrise my lovely young morsels, yes?" to which both girls immediately nodded and meekly replied in concert, "Thank you very much, Madame," and softly giggled at doing so.

The Baroness found this delightful and questioned Holly, "You are?"

"Holly, Madame"

"And you, dear?"

"My name is Byzar, Madame," to which the Baroness queried, "Romanian?"

"Yes Ma'am, though I have never been there," replied Byzar.

"I adore your people young lady, und you must be a very talented young vomen, as you must be also, Holly dear!" the Baroness stated confidently.

"You may address me as Dada or Elsa, dahlings, ya, und I look forward to a new day dawning tomorrow vith my new friends. Now let us enjoy our dinner und make new friends." The Baroness held out her two hands to be clasped by each girl, after which all three nodded with glee and polite laughter.

Holly and Byzar were craftily seated between the two gentlemen guests from the Sparhawk, and as per their implied directives both gals demurely introduced themselves to each gent, which delighted the men immensely. The girls knew to prime their conversations with the gentlemen and to divulge as little about themselves while seeming to be enraptured with their dinner partners' conversation. As the dinner went on, the Baroness closed her robe at some point and Holly and Byzar stole a few moments of stealthy conversation away from their suitors.

Holly whispered without looking at Byzar, "How's yours?"

"He's farted twice that I know of!" Byzar demurely replied. This brought forth an uncontrolled spasm from Holly who had to quickly cover her mouth from spitting water at the Baroness, which she successfully accomplished, as well as making the table believe that her short gag was a result of water going down the wrong chute in her throat, rather than that of bursting out laughing. Byzar, complete with welled up eyes as a result of her own stunted laughter, quickly patted Holly's back while feigning great concern over her roommate. It was a grand 'gotcha' moment for Byzar, which both girls, and likely the Baroness would all derive boundless joy about at sunrise on the rocks in the morning.

As soon as the still blushing Holly recovered and offered her apologies all around, which were acknowledged and dismissed with amusement, even Meadows was delighted, Holly dabbed her eyes with her cloth napkin and began to fan her face with her hand for a few moments. This little event afforded her tablemate from the Sparhawk a fortunate opportunity to put his arm around the girl as well as his hand on her naked forearm, much to his delight. Holly recovered and thanked him while slightly turning away from his touch in the most ladylike fashion while not causing any outward embarrassment for the gent. She, and the table recovered and resumed the chatter and as soon as conversations were re-engaged Holly whispered to Byzar a quick, "I'm going to get you for that you little punk!" as Byzar innocently replied with a face full of mirth, "I'm sure you will, my dear." Both girls looked at each other and giggled and when they turned their attention back to the table they found the Baroness staring at them both with her hard set dark eyes, which immediately terminated their smiles, and when seeing this, the Baroness leaned forward in a very serious manner and whispered, "You two vomen are vicked! I can see this is going to be a very fun summer!" The Baroness then leaned back in her chair and winked at both of the girls and smiled with delight, to both Holly's and Byzar's great relief and joy.

The Baroness, and both girls instinctively turned toward the head of the table to find that Meadows was immersed in this interchange, when the Baroness leaned in the direction of Meadows and said, "Valentine my dearest, you have impeccable taste, as per usual." To which Meadows chuckled and nodded his approval to the girls and then back to the Baroness, "Ya Elsa, ya!" and all laughed accordingly.

Prior to the serving of dessert, Meadows suggested that all might stretch and stroll about while the table was being prepared, and one of the borrowed waitresses politely announced that a bell would be rung when dessert was ready. As the guests rose to explore the house and breathe the cool coastal aroma on the veranda, Holly, Byzar and the Baroness excused themselves to the ladies toilet, where when all three entered, they all broke down in knee bending laughter as if they were all pals from way back. All were in tears when the Baroness finally managed to speak without any hint of old country accent, "You two devious sluts are hilarious!"

The lack of accent and the bold words absolutely shocked Byzar and Holly, until the realization that the royal Baroness act was just that, and all three broke down laughing yet again in each other's arms.

"Elsa, what is 'Dada'?" Holly asked.

"Holly dear, we'll talk about that tomorrow morning, but you two have to reappear in the dining room and take care of your guests, correct?"

Byzar giggled, "I'm going to get my guy drunk if I can 'cuz I don't want to attend to the smelly old fart."

Elsa wagged her finger at Byzar and said, "The trick, my dear, is to find out how long he is staying at the hotel, and if he is travelling with his wife. If so, be sure to 'acquire' a piece of jewelry or notice a birthmark if you can. Also carry a small purse with you and make sure he sees you fondle with it when you are finished; it makes them feel obligated to fill it!"

"Always willing to learn new tricks of the trade Elsa, I look forward to learning more," Byzar sweetly commented. "Are you in our line of work?" motioning to Holly, who had not yet accepted that she was actually now a full-fledged prostitute.

"I chose the marriage path my girls, all four of them so far, but in between husbands I have supported myself in a manner befitting a Baroness station." Elsa mused as she ushered the girls out the door. "Valentine invited me here for the summer, and one of the reasons was to provide some guidance for his two favorite young women. Now scoot your little fannies out there and make those gentlemen yearn to come back and tell all their wealthy pals to do likewise!"

Sunrise on the chilly Perkins Cove rocks was cloaked in an early morning hoarfrost fog as well as on the sparse stunted evergreens on the barrier island protecting the Josias Creek marsh. As they gazed out over the calm seas and quiet waves all three women were silently wrapped in blankets with a cup of coffee in their mittens. To the left were the fishermen shacks on stilts with garbage underneath, mostly cone topped and copper colored 'Boston Stock Ale' quarts in cans. Brightly colored skiffs and dories were edged up from where the slow moving creek coursed its way through the ice covered marsh grass toward the incoming tide. The smell of the seaweed intermixed with the rotting of the fishermen's traps and nets pervaded their senses until dipping their noses close to the warm mug of coffee they all savored. As the fog began to burn off Holly drew a pronounced shiver when she could make out Dinny's shack, with *DINNY* painted in large weathered red letters on the door, but with the two 'N's printed backwards. It had only been a few days since she saw Dinny while posing and only a week since she broke up with Eben. Dinny could be mistaken for Eben's brother, close cropped dark hair, thin lips with angular features with a perpetual five o'clock shadow as well as a slow easy manner of movement and speech. The difference between the two was that Eben was thoughtful while Dinny was slow witted at best, but both were kind and polite. The only other difference between the two men in their early twenties was that Dinny had a sailor's mouth and could drink himself into oblivion on a moment's notice, while Eben rarely cussed and even more rarely drank alcohol. Dinny went along with life as the seas rolled ashore, but Eben was always tangled up with some semblance of religious or familial guilt that he always eventually qualified in some manner. Dinny always admonished Eben to simply chill out and enjoy life.

Holly figured that if she could combine the two guys into one gent, she might have reconsidered dumping Eben. She whispered to herself, "It seems like a lifetime ago." She kicked herself for offering to screw Dinny that day he showed up delivering alcohol, just to spite Eben, and she was sure she wouldn't have gone through with it. Divine providence had sent the surprising Baroness to accommodate him, luckily, she thought, so she wouldn't have had to confront the issue.

A week ago she was in love and had a boyfriend, but now she concluded that she was all alone and a card carrying prostitute, no longer with any hope of reconciliation with the only man she ever felt love for. Her past dalliances with and for her father meant nothing, for she excused her life then as being the conditions of a childhood, and she didn't consider it too terribly unpleasant, even though if anyone ever found out, they would be summarily horrified.

After servicing her guest last night, escaping without having to screw him, and gazing now at Dinny's shack and the recent past it reminded her of, she suddenly came to grips with her lot, and that it was time to get serious about securing her future. Eben was—and now had to be—gone from her life forever, unless he suddenly got both rich and brave. Her focus now was on securing her position, whatever that was, with Valentine Meadows. Elsa, the Baroness, had twice mentioned last night that both she and Byzar were to be tutored by the older woman in some fashion, and to Holly that sounded like her best option now, as well as a godsend. Holly also concluded that whomever Meadows brought into the picture for Holly's attentions, that she was going to be the most delightful and accommodating woman on the planet, or at least far superior to her roommate and also her new mentor. It was all about Holly now, as far as Holly was now concerned.

As it so happened, Byzar was curled up in her own blanket and thoughts, sipping her coffee while pondering her life in much the same manner as Holly was. What caught Byzar's immediate attention the previous evening was when Elsa hinted that her route to financial comfort was marriage, and that was exactly how Byzar had intended to proceed if she could ever extricate herself from the clutches of her clan, which by great good fortune in the name of Valentine Meadows, she seemingly and surprisingly had. She was thinking, "Here I am sitting on the rocks at this 'beautiful place by the sea', with hundreds of dollars in my purse and about to be tutored by a famous Baroness, how very fortunate am I?" She let out an uncontrolled chuckle to herself and sipped her coffee with a smile. Byzar always considered herself to be very self-centered, and though she was enjoying the pleasure of a newfound friend in Holly, she had no qualms about using her roommate for any advantage possible. This was not inappropriate in Byzar's eyes, and in fact, conduct any reasonable person would expect—self preservation and all. She decided that she would use Holly for whatever advantage she was worth, be friendly enough, but focus her attentions toward the Baroness Elsa and follow the woman's lead; Holly be damned. Byzar decided right then that she was going to be Elsa's favorite.

"Elsa, may I get you another cup?" Byzar asked in her

sweetest tone.

"That is very kind of you Byzar, but I'm okay. Let's stretch a bit and go have a leisurely breakfast, what do you say girls?" Elsa asked, again without the hint of a German accent. "We are going to get to know each other today. The new model, I don't even know her name, is the artists' subject today. We are free to do as we please until dinner. I think she is only here for a few days and she came with one of the students. It looks like it's going to be a nice day and I'll bet the fishermen wouldn't mind gazing at a little fresh meat for a change, you think?" she smirked. "The gal certainly doesn't have the allure that each of you have, and even though she dressed nicely, she really didn't disguise her weight all that well, you think?"

Holly giggled toward Byzar, "I really didn't pay much attention to her, since I was too busy choking on my water last night, you little bitch!" as she playfully slugged Byzar in the arm. They all laughed as they gathered their blankets and rose to go back to the house.

"Just what on earth did you say last night Byzar?" Elsa wondered while smiling broadly.

"Holly asked if I liked my gent, and I simply said he farts a lot," which again brought a round of laughter as the women reached the steps and could smell the warm aromas from the kitchen they were about to enter.

"Elsa, what is Dada? I overheard someone at the dinner table last night say that you were the Queen of Dada," Holly asked as Byzar interjected, "I would like to know also!"

They sat at the kitchen table and Elsa said, "Girls, Dada is a movement, a force in the arts and will soon be in the entire world. In short, the Dada movement, or 'Dadaists' as we are known, endeavor to expose the fraud of society, especially the wealthy and powerful. It celebrates nonsense, disconnection with the societal accepted... well anything, and expresses cynicism about all that the wealthy and powerful celebrate. We shock them and force them to confront all of their silly moral and highbrow conduct. For example, the preachers and priests are universally acknowledged and advertised to be impervious to sin, but we all know they are the worst sinners of the bunch, correct?"

"I hate them because they are supposed to be the ones we trust, but they drink, gamble and screw worse than anybody," Holly interjected, while Byzar added, "All the priests I've ever had the *un*pleasure to date have been very mean. They like to hurt me."

Elsa nodded and waited a moment before continuing, "It is the concept of sin that Dada tries to expose as traits that are in fact human, and normal. Love is normal is it not? Why does it have to be experienced in private? Why not share love, give and receive pleasure when the spirit moves? Why should we women cover ourselves, are we not made of all the same pieces and parts? Why can men go shirtless and wear comfortable clothes, and women cannot? Who decides what art is and what is not? Is there a scorecard? Does the one with the most paintings win, or the one who uses the most paint? Who decides what is beauty? What is societal appropriateness, what is obscene? Is it the same society that builds bombs, guns and bullets for the purpose of killing and maiming people? Why would any sane individual embrace and evaluate personal conduct and its creations based on the morals of a society that builds barbed wire and poison gas?"

By this time both girls were pleasantly dumbfounded and inspired. Elsa went on.

"An industrialist that owns factories employs many

people, and that is wonderful, but at what cost? His employees are treated worse than dogs and work in areas worse than kennels, and yet society treats them as honorable men, all the while knowing the truth. Do you know of the Triangle Shirtwaist fire a few years ago in New York City? The factory owners had all the doors locked from the outside and hundreds of girls your age died because they couldn't get out. The men who owned the building were never punished by society and retained their stations. Why should we honor a society that doesn't punish the worst abusers? Why should we adhere to any part of a society that celebrates such behavior?"

"Dadaists believe we should expose such deceit by demonstrating its maliciousness with… silliness. One of the reasons I came here is because of the art school across the cove: the Woodbury school. You girls see how they operate, what they paint, what they wear, and have seen how accepted and celebrated they are by society, while this school is criticized and scorned, have you not?

"All of those wealthy women who are mostly my age," Elsa smiled, "early forties, but don't tell… are dressed in full length dresses buttoned up to their chins even on the hotter days, all the while wishing that they could strip down and be comfortable as we do, do they not? Of course they do, but their societal morals won't permit such conduct. I can also guarantee you that when they see you girls lounging naked among so many men that they also yearn to somehow trade places with you, especially when you go inside with them! Oh I'm sure that their conversations are scornful, while desperately in silence they wish they could take your places at least once to fulfill their fantasies, if they only would let themselves. That is why I make it a point to wave, smile, and swim and lounge naked in front of them. They are the bastions of society, and I am laughing at them, and they know it. And I love it!

"Live your life with passion, with delight and cast aside or at least examine whether society's directives are for you. But most of all, insist on the freedom to choose how you wish to live. If Dada is for you, we welcome you. If so, I will enjoy taking the journey with you. Open your mind, your heart, and if the spirit moves, your legs, without fear of constraint. However, you must first secure your finances while you are young and sought after, and I will help you with that also."

Byzar and Holly shared a glance and chirped, "Where do I sign up?" and, "You are preaching to the faithful!"

"Are you currently married, Elsa?" Byzar asked, mindful of Elsa's comments the night previous about marriage being, in effect, a first-rate ingredient of any woman's financial portfolio.

"Yes dear, many times in many places. I think currently I am married to three gentlemen, wherever they may be!" Elsa said with a robust chortle. "When I was in my teens, I was an actress and what I called, 'a professional lover'! I was very good at my craft, and enjoyed many lovers, both men and women —sometimes many in one day. My father was a much sought after construction craftsman, and as soon as my woman parts started working, he helped me learn about them. My mother was nothing."

By this time Holly's eyes were swollen with tears, and she blurted out just before sobbing, "My father was my first and then he sold me… again and again… to all the 'respectable' men you spoke of… even our family priest."

Byzar sat back in her chair and was more matter-of-fact, "My clan aunties were my mother, and they sold me since I was about twelve. My father was an old man with many, many children from my aunties; I was nothing but a money earner for him, but I still loved him so much. He always reprimanded me for not growing up fast enough. All he wanted was for me to make him money with my sex. He forced my aunties to start me too young, and my first times really hurt and I remember bleeding a lot. I was always so scared. Now I will make my own money and find a rich old man, whom I will marry and then encourage him to die. Every man I take inside me now will be a means to an end. I don't care. I do not want babies or love, maybe love later, but now I want to meet rich unmarried men for my own purposes. If I ever see my father again, I will kill him... painfully."

Both Holly, who was still wiping her eyes and blowing her nose, and Elsa were staring at Byzar and were struck by her cold resolve.

"How such hard words emerge from such a sweet mouth, young Byzar, but we will make this our summer's goal for you. If we cannot find an old wealthy widower, then at least we'll find a roster of wealthy married ones, from which you will have secured a memento from each. You will have these mementos to threaten to display to their wives, daughters or police, so you can secure your income. You will learn to do this tastefully, as I will show you later. You, I and Holly all have been betrayed by the only men on the planet who never should have, our fathers, and together we will use that betrayal as motivation for our benefit. And you will pay me for teaching you how... ya?" They all laughed hysterically at the fabricated 'Ya' and hugged one another as if lifelong bonds were now formed.

"We are a team now and we must devise our plans," Elsa

stated with a sardonic grin.

"First, we have breakfast, and then I want to read you my poems," said Elsa as she stood to fetch the bowl of eggs off the kitchen counter. "I'll make the eggs, you girls do the rest. It's too early for anyone else to be awake, and we have an exciting day ahead for us."

"You wanted to see me Mr. Jacobs, Sir"

"Dinny, I'd like you to go to room #14 and talk to the guests. As of today I am giving you a raise and you'll be our night watchman. I'd like you to be on duty every evening during our busy months. Perhaps you can share your duties with your friend, Eben, who would also be paid accordingly. Is this acceptable?" said the oft-drunk portly and balding Sparhawk owner.

"I really appreciate yer' thinkin' of me, Mr. Jacobs. What am I supposed to do as a watchman, and what is the deal with the folks in #14? This is my busy season with my responsibilities here and my, uh, deliverin', as you know. I guess I could stay here if'n you have a place for me to bed down, it's a fair piece to hike to and from the cove," declared Dinny, mindful of the thieving ways of the owner. Dinny, as well as many of the Sparhawk employees, gossiped regularly about how the owner would enter rooms as guests headed to the beach for a day of fun and sun. Lots of guests had muttered complaints in the past about lost jewelry and wallets having a little less cash in them than they thought. No one could ever prove anything against the owner, or ever had the guts to confront the gent for that would be unseemly, but the thieving reputation was gaining momentum and more guests were inquiring if they could place valuables at the front desk. At least in this manner repeat guests could protect their valuables from the owner's sticky hands, and many guests would quietly inform new guests to do the same. Dinny figured that Jacobs would never get caught and was to the point that he probably didn't care about his reputation much either. People were going to continue to vacation in Ogunquit, and rent rooms at the Sparhawk Inn regardless.

"Dinny, the guests in #14 claim that they are missing some jewelry. I explained to them that the Sparhawk is not responsible for lost items, and that we would be happy to keep their valuables at the front desk. I also explained that I am the owner of the hotel and have the only other keys to all the rooms on the property, so there must be some sort of mistake. If you present yourself as our night watchman, and tell them that you were on duty all night and didn't see anything, it might mollify them a bit. Would you do that for me? I don't really need you to patrol the grounds except for maybe once a night, but it would be nice to have you accessible in case of emergency. It's more important to be able to inform our guests that we have a night watchman, rather than actually having one, you understand. We don't have to tell them what you actually do, see? How about we convert your gardener shed into a bedroom and you can take your meals here at no cost?"

"Well that sounds fine, Mr. Jacobs, and it does make sense. I keep odd hours for my deliverin' anyway, and havin' a night job alibi here might keep them revenue boys off my back a bit. I'll let Eben know and we'll be sure to have one of us here every night for the rest of the season. I'll go have a chat with the folks in #14, and I really appreciate the raise in pay. Wanna tell me how many tins of hooch you want next week. Local stuff and the good stuff both again?" Dinny asked as he headed out the owners office door.

"No changes Dinny, same as always, and thank you for taking care of the guests in #14," replied Mr. Jacobs as he fuddled with his papers.

Dinny figured he would basically repeat the same advice to the folks in #14 about using the front desk as a repository and be on his way. Whatever was missing couldn't be recovered anyway, so he would just tell the folks that he would keep a special eye on their room. Wasn't much more he could promise them, even if he really did intend to keep an eye on the room; he already knew who the thief was.

"Hey Eben, we got us another job!" Dinny called into his room through the window.

"Just what we need, Din," Eben chuckled as he rolled out of his bed. "I'll be right out, and just what is it that we're doin'?"

Dinny was leaning up against a tree as Eben plodded out the door. "Well ol' son, you and me are the new night watchmen at the Sparhawk, get our meals free, have a place to bed down and don't really have to do nuthin', howz them apples for ya?" Dinny offered. "I'll tell you all about it on our way down to the cove. I saw the Coast Guard boat floatin' around out there earlier this mornin' so I thought we ought to go out there, wave howdy and set some nets jus' for show. You think they're on to us yet, Eben?"

"I think we're doin' okay Din, but I'm still a little queasy about storin' the hooch in my folks barn without them knowin' it. It was fine when we only were supplyin' the Sparhawk, but now we got us a real thing goin' on and we gotta be smart. I was thinkin' that we ought to find us maybe two or three hidey holes, just in case we do get busted. That way we could still meet our orders, ya' know? We're also still at the mercy of the tides to get up into our place on the Josias creek. If we have to off load by trudgin' through the muck when the tide is a'leavin', our tracks will sit there for all to follow until the marsh starts fillin' up again as the tide comes wanderin' in. Anyone could follow them tracks, not jus' the revenue boys, savvy?" Eben pondered as they neared the cove.

Dinny agreed and wondered, "You thought any more about deliverin' over to Meadows' place, knowin' you'll probably run into Holly?"

"I have and I think you better keep doin' it; makes more sense if we keep our routines. I know it's messed up for you to go there, but maybe you can work a deal with Meadows so you can jus' leave his order under the steps in the dark and he can drop off his payment at the Spar? Tell him it's for safety, he'll buy that. He knows that if he is caught buyin' the hooch, he'd be in hot water too. That kinda solves the problem don't it, and keeps you away from all them wierdos," Eben offered hopefully.

"You always are thinkin' right Eben," Dinny agreed. "Now we got to find that little Day kid and set him down for a powwow. I sure hope he's okay. I haven't seen him around much have you?"

"I'm a little worried about that kid, Din. It ain't like him not to be around and the last time I saw him he wasn't lookin' very happy. Talked to his Ma the other day in town and she said she was worried about him a bit. He sleeps a lot she says and is real quiet-like. Maybe I'll wander over to his place when we get back from fishin' and talk to the little fella; see what's what. What time you wanna' pull out to the rum line tonight? We got calm seas and almost no moon," Eben asked as they reached their dory and started loading their nets.

"If that Coast Guard boat is still floatin' about, let's try to start settin' where they'll likely get curious and stop by for a chat. Maybe we can feel em' out a little and see when they're gonna head back into port. Then we'll set our buoys and start anglin' for the rum line. We can tie up over to Boon Island til' the dark comes on, and then make a quick tack out to that first schooner settin' there. I recognize her cut and we've bought outta her before for reasonable money. I figure we can fit thirty tins and that would give us almost a hunnert in store. That stuff is almost pure at 180 proof, and we should cut it in half for the Spar and for Meadows and Dunaway, but everyone else we'll cut it down to about 40 proof, and keep our prices steady. You do the figurin' yet Eben?"

They finished walking their dory through the marsh and out to the edge of the cove where they could climb in and set to rowing.

"Din if we make this haul we're gonna be stinkin' rich. At seventy-five bucks a tin, we'll have seventy-five hundred dollars in stock in the barn. That's why I worried about keepin' it all in one place. At twenty five bucks a gallon, our cost, we sell it now for fifty but I think we can bump up the price to sixty, and also cut it down to about 120 proof. I'm thinkin' we better figure out a better place for our still, but there ain't enough time in the day to work at the Spar, fish, run the still and bottle n' deliver the hooch. We've grown too big for our britches Dinny, so maybe we ought to cut out deliverin' to the shipyards, since we only deliver the crappy stuff there anyway. Maybe we should set down with Henry, Bish and George over to Cap's Al's shack and ask 'em to take over deliverin' to the yards. We don't make much profit there anyway, compared to the risk. They might think us as bein' real neighborly"

"But Eben, what if those fella's don't want that account? The yards will be awful pissed if'n we cut 'em off, not to mention all our pals down there," Dinny worried as he set to paddling away from the cove.

"I'll tell you what we do, Eben. If them boys don't want the account, we'll let the word out that we'll set up a couple gents in the business, and then once they're trained up, we'll walk away. We'll front 'em the money and they can pay us back over time. Better yet, we'll charge em' a small percentage of their profits for as long as they're in the business. We'll make em' think that their payments are really important to us and we'll be like consultants for a fee and give them a couple of our recipes, but if they stop paying us, we'll turn em' in to the Feds and find someone else to take over. We'll never tell 'em enough so even if they get to singin', their tune won't be much. I still think that the fella's at Al's will be mighty impressed with us for given them the accounts, so we might not have anything to lose sleep over anyway." Eben settling in to his rowing.

"In any event, we can let the new guys learn like we did, and keep the sediment in the bottles to a minimum, and not be so spooked when the bottles exploded, like we were," and they both chuckled remembering those early days.

"And Din, now that I'm thinkin' on it, maybe it's time to set my folks down and clue em' in about what we've been doin'. I mean, it's only right to be square with them. I think we should set at the table and hand them a thousand dollars cash money for using their place. If they are agreeable, Pa can help us with the distillin' and Ma can make up the mash n' such. Heck, the thousand bucks might pay off the place, and we can cut em' in on the business for shares. I don't think they've ever seen a thousand bucks cash in one place, ever. What do you think, partner?" Eben asked earnestly.

The Coast Guard boat was already heading back to Portsmouth by the time Dinny and Eben raised the sail on their dory, unique to Ogunquit in its design, for it was built with straighter sides and stouter gunwales than normal Maine dories. This design allowed the fishermen to lean out to fetch their nets without rolling into the drink as a normal bowed-out dory would. The Ogunquit dories were also sleeker than the older standard bathtub style dories, and the Ogunquit dories had a tiller that extended from the keel and a centerboard box which allowed the 20' boat to ride deeper and more stable in the water. Most fishermen sailed out before dawn but Eben and Dinny made it a point to be consistently seen heading out in the late afternoons in the hopes that the Coast Guard and Revenue agents would be duped into thinking that they had a new method of fishing and would leave them alone. They would set nets and buoys, but were really out at sea to be closer to the three mile line where it was still legal for booze laden ships to set as this was the territorial limit at sea. This 'rum line' was where the bootleggers, like Dinny and Eben, would load up their boats with illegal booze and try to make it to shore without getting caught. The big time bootleggers, like the gents who owned the infamous power boat named the Dixie III with its twelve cylinder engine relied on speed to outrun the Coast Guard and Revenue boats, while Eben and Dinny relied on stealth and the concept of hiding in plain sight. They would load up at night and sometimes layup at Boon Island, and then sail into shore after midnight. Any chance they got to visit with the authorities at sea, they made it a point to do so, so that they would become widely known as just a couple of bumpkins scratching out a living from the ocean. Sometimes they would row over to a nearby Coast Guard vessel just to have a chat, even though their dory's bilge was lined with three gallon tins of hooch. So far in the nine months they had been in business, they had never been officially checked, and now that they were well known along their portion of the coast, they likely never would be.

They had also set two moorings off shore where they attached different color buoys every couple weeks. This had been a real chore but they both figured the project was really good insurance. They had bored and cemented steel hook-eyes into two hefty pieces of granite and run a long loop rope through the eyes, each with a stop. They had tied four oak barrels together and managed to roll the large chunk of granite down to the cove. It took three nights of backbreaking work to get each of the granite slabs down to the cove. Once there, they dragged the barrels to a spot where they could roll the granite slab on top of them and wait for the tide to float the contraption. Then they towed the whole mess out to sea, cut the barrels loose and the granite slab sank to the ocean floor. They collected the barrels and repeated the process the following night, only setting the next slab, or mooring in a different spot. They had fashioned a drawstring net which they spliced into each setup so that in a pinch they could stow the cans of hooch in the drawstring pouch and quickly pull it down to the ocean floor and leave it set until it was safe to haul. The slabs were heavy enough to keep the tins from floating to the surface, but not deep enough to blow up the cans. They were both quite proud of their engineering feat. From all appearances it would appear that they were just hauling or setting their nets. They kept changing the buoys to complete the ruse. Now there were only two aspects of their tidy little business that was more exposed than they would like: the storage under Eben's folks' hay barn and their 'hooch cuttin' still, out in the woods. Eben was pondering whether to dig out more of a space under the barn so they could move the still in the new found 'root cellar' and keep the operation under one roof, as it were.

Dinny took a break from rowing, stowed the oars and set back against the nets as the insignificant waves glided through their dory, and their bones. "Eben, let's cut your folks in. Maybe we could give em' a little more cash though."

"You're my best pal forever Din, and that's why I'm proud to know ya', forever," Eben stated with a little blush in his cheeks. Both men leaned forward and earnestly shook hands.

"We'll sit 'em down tomorrow, Din. Assumin' they're agreeable, I'm thinkin' we could deepen the cellar under the barn and bring the still under there also. I know it's risky with the fire n' heat n' chemicals and all, but here's how I got it figured. We'll set a wood stove up where the hay is stored now, and rig it up so the smokepipe from the still comes up underneath the woodstove and joins in its chimney. That way anyone wanderin' by will think we're just heatin' up the barn, see? We'll add on to the barn and move the hay into the addition, and then move my Pa's workshop over next to the stove. Nobody will ever know nothin'. We'll make a new waterin' trough just inside the door so the stock can still drink from 'er, but we'll keep it thawed in winter by closin' the door. We'll run a pipe down into our still from the bottom of the trough so we'll have water year round," Eben concluded.

"You sure been thinkin' on this haven't you Eben?" Dinny allowed.

"Well Din, now that I'm out a woman, I've got lotsa extra

time!" Eben chuckled, even though he wasn't very convincing.

"It's getting' dark, but I don't feel like rowin' out to Boon, let's jus' have a smoke, set and ponder, k?"

"I'm with ya' Din, right on through."

"I love the Ogunquit beach; it's so flat, wide and long. I could dance out there forever!" Byzar chimed.

"I've got cheese, two loaves of fresh French bread, jam, cheese and two bottles of red wine. You have towels and blankets and an umbrella, and Byzar you have, well you have your supple lips and exotic eyes; I could eat you up," Elsa smooched at Byzar and continued. "Let's walk; it is such a gorgeous morning."

By mid-morning the gals were happily lounging on their blanket after Elsa, and Byzar in particular, had drawn stares and appreciative comments from the fifty or so passersby, about not only their expressive dance form but also Elsa's wildly striped full length bathing outfit. Holly lay on the blanket purposefully showing her naked shoulders and legs up to her knees, daring one of the matronly local women to admonish her boldness.

"Girls, I'll be candid with you. Whenever I need money beyond the one thousand dollars I keep with me at all times, I simply write a post card requesting funds from either a husband, or one of the many rich benefactor's of the Dada movement; they would not think of denying my requests, for to be found out would be embarrassing," Elsa began as she took her first sip of wine.

Holly quickly asked, "But Elsa, don't you miss your husband, er husbands?" wondering if her question was as awkward as it just now sounded. "Do you love any of them, truly?"

"Oh Holly, I love them all dearly, and yes there is one in particular, but he has since chosen monogamy and youth, and since I no longer have youth, nor any desire for monogamy, I only contact him if I need a substantial sum. And speaking of monogamy, I have grown to further explore my passions for women; it can be quite delightful, and I hope the three of us will journey together soon. Does this appeal?"

"I find you to be completely fascinating, beautiful and intriguing," Byzar sincerely avowed while reaching over and taking Elsa's forearm, stroking it, and looking deep into the older woman's eyes, which was immediately reciprocated.

As if to shake herself from a slumber of passion, Elsa piped up while still gently holding Byzar's hand in both of hers, "Now listen girls, you know that Meadows gets a 'donation' to the art school every time you are called to host a gentleman; you did know that didn't you?" You two—and others of lesser attributes that he will surely recruit—are how he complements his wallet. I on the other hand, am here because artists from around the world will pay him to be in my presence, mostly their sponsors do, but Meadows makes a lot of money off of my ass too, not that my contribution is anywhere near as enjoyable as your tasks are, farting fat gentlemen excluded," she chortled.

"Are you saying that the 'reknowned' Valentine Meadows is basically a pimp," Holly chided with a smirk.

"That he is young lady, as well as having other devious attributes," Elsa said, "but don't ever sell that man short, for he is an absolute genius. He speaks five languages fluently and likely knows what you are thinking before you do!

"Holly my dear," Elsa continued, "You must attach yourself to Valentine; you are exactly what he needs. An uncommonly beautiful piece of arm candy that is as comfortable in the company of the highest society as she is servicing whomever he directs. You have the opportunity to be his personal and administrative assistant. He has spoken of you to me in the hopes you will aspire and demonstrate such capacity. You can handle his mundane financial and societal chores and he will grow to trust you implicitly, and you'll be paid accordingly. There is a caveat however, as you might already know."

Holly nodded and wondered, "My guess is that he needs someone to act as a buffer when the police or an angry parent learns of his proclivities with young boys, am I close?"

"Spot on young lady. I, and he, know that you are uncommonly bright," Elsa said.

"You two have lost me." Byzar interrupted, "What am I not seeing?"

Returning her affection to Byzar, who appeared a bit hurt by Elsa's attentions toward Holly, she purred, "Byzar, no,no,no,no my darling. It's just that Holly has more experience with Valentine than you do; she's been with him longer than you. We have special designs for you also my dear. Patience my dear, patience," which brought a returned smile of relief on the younger girl's face.

"As Holly well knows," Elsa said turning back toward Holly, "Valentine has some unordinary and somewhat risky affections that can bring undue attentions to him. This anxiety he would like to avoid for many reasons. You can be his siren as well as protector, Holly. You will use your imagination and brilliance, as well as your beauty, to protect him from the outside world. His stuttering problem cannot be helped and it makes people think he is not very smart, but he is just the opposite. You will be his voice and be a comfort for him by doing so. He will pay you a salary and whatever you personally earn through your guiles is yours to keep. Being a courtesan as he directs is part of your position, however. You will have a very comfortable life if you remain loyal," Elsa finished.

Holly was stunned and relieved in the same initial thought. Her worries about going back to college and being basically cast out and abandoned by her mother had now vanished.

"I need to take a walk," Holly said simply. She kicked off her sandals and stepped away from the blanket they were all lounging on. It felt wonderful to walk in bare feet. It was low tide so the full breadth of Ogunquit Beach lay before her. The sand was hard and rippled where the high tide had been, like it always is, and she could see where the beach began its steeper incline three miles up ahead toward where the town of Wells assumed the beach. She whispered to the wind, "It will probably take me getting to there and back for this all to sink in."

How would she pull this off? she wondered. It was quite uncommon for a woman, especially a young woman, to organize and operate a business and household, if that was truly what was going to be required of her. How would she know the limits of her authority? What exactly were her responsibilities? She understood her responsibilities as a hostess, consort and companion quite well, but how could she protect Valentine Meadows from his own actions, and the attacks that would surely come from all corners. In the time Holly had known Meadows—only a few months and most of that time from the distance of a college student taking classes from a visiting professor, or at numerous social engagements she had attended at his request—she had noticed how he dealt with conflict, usually by throwing money at it, like hiring that little French boy's parents instead of being held to legal prosecution for playing with their little boy. He had made an arrangement and the result seemed to satisfy all concerned. He had been taken to task by some people back in Brooklyn for having an affair with the wife of someone important, she knew not who, but he had escaped unscathed by writing a check. She happened to be in his bedroom that evening and heard the entire discussion through the walls, quite heated and threatening initially but the money produced silence and calm. When Meadows had come back into the bedroom that night he was visibly shaken and vomited most of the night, while Holly played nursemaid instead of whore. Maybe that's how she would operate, she thought. She would identify potential problems that Meadows conduct always produced, and she would devise mitigating methods well ahead of time so as to nip them in the bud, so to speak. If Meadows expressed a desire for a particular sexual conquest, she would create the scenario that would allow for such. As she strolled along she began to lighten and quicken her steps, as her future began to emerge in her mind and began to make sense. She now knew she could manage this complicated man's life, enrich herself and live in comfort and style. She smiled and wondered whether she would invite her mother sometime after she became ensconced in her role, just to spite her. "I probably will!" she unknowingly said aloud to no one but the wind and salt air.

"Valentine Meadows will soon be unable to function without me, and I'll have whatever I choose very soon. He may be a genius but he is still a man, so he is no match for the likes of me!"

She wiped a golden strand of hair from her eyes and began to skip in and away from the waves as they reached and retreated back into the sea. She was so lost in thought that she just now realized that she had walked almost out to the Kennebunk Point. She turned back toward Ogunquit to find that she was too far away to see Elsa and Byzar back on the blanket. Holly began to skip her way back the way she had come and thoughtfully noticed how her footprints in the sand had gotten much livelier in the latter part of her walk. "The more I walked, the more I figured things out, and the happier I got!" she said to herself. As she started gaily hopping back toward Elsa and Byzar, and both were soon reassuringly visible, Holly held her chin high with a determined smile and said, "Holly can do anything!"

"That crazy girl is going to walk to the moon, I think!" Elsa said while opening the second bottle of wine.

"I didn't like her much when we first met, but I rarely like any of my competition. Now that I know that she and I aren't competing for attention, I can truly say that I really like her. She's funny and wicked, in a wonderful sort of way. Her father using her like that when she was younger, that was awful. But I think the thing that really hurts her is that her mother was either too dumb to know what was truly going on, or just didn't have the guts to stop it. My guess is that her mother knew all along. What a cruel woman her mother must be!" Byzar said aloud while seeing that out on the horizon, Holly was now heading back.

Elsa said, "Well by the time she gets here, she'll have missed out on this good wine! Refill my sweet?"

"How do you feel about our plans for sweet little Byzar?"

Elsa asked. "Is it not exciting?"

"Sultana Byzar of Crisana! It does have a regal ring to it and I love it! And you are going to help me learn all about this place, Elsa?" Byzar asked. "I am still worried about someone finding out that it is not true."

"Byzar, my dear, it is your heritage," Elsa began. "For all we know you could actually *be* the Sultana. People will not question your title any more than they question my Baroness title. And since I am a Baroness, it is within my rights to name you a Sultana, which I just did. People will ask you what a Sultana is and where Crisana is, and you will be able to answer their questions after some research and training. That part of the world is always changing and is still greatly broken because of the war that just ended, so your claim as a Sultana is just as valid as anyone else's, but no one of any importance will ever challenge such an exotic, lovely and sweet young woman. They'll be much too taken with your bearing and grace. Both you and Holly will be my students and I will teach you how to conduct yourself in accordance with your newfound social stations. When I and Valentine are satisfied with your abilities to move among the elite with grace and ease, we will have a lavish gathering attended by the highest of society in which you will be introduced as the Sultana of Crisana. We will announce that you were secreted here to the United States and hidden as a common waitress at the Sparhawk Hall until your safety—from unknown antagonists from the *old country*—could be assured. You will be a sensation! All very mysterious and that will only heighten the intrigue and attentions for your affections. We will play it up in all of the newspapers and it will be a 'must attend' social event. But we will never announce the purpose of the proceedings until we spring the surprise of your true identity, because we don't want to give inquisitive reporters' time to do research. All everyone will know is that a major announcement will be made, not what the announcement is. We will rent a grand hall or something and charge for attendance. We'll make a mint and your suitors for your hand in marriage will come from only the wealthiest! I will discreetly offer your charms for only the most discerning gentlemen and they will pay dearly for the privilege. You will acquire a morsel of their personal belongings and we'll keep very accurate records. Should one of your suitors reach a level of importance, they will have to purchase our silence about such matters. And if we find a marriage prospect, we'll nurture that also and see where it leads. But for now, your primary tasks are to learn about the Romanian country of Crisana, and of how to conduct yourself as royalty, for that is what you are now, my dear!"

"Welcome back Holly! You look positively radiant! I assume you have life figured out?" Byzar asked with a distinct chuckle.

"I feel wonderful and I can't wait to begin my new life!" Holly said.

Byzar announced with a humorous haughty tone, "While you were walking to Canada, I became royalty, and somewhat drunk!"

"Son, did you really think your Ma and I don't know what you boys are doin'?" Eben's father asked pleasantly, as Eben's mother also smiled. "Truth be told, me n' your Ma have been dippin' into your stock for quite a while, not so much as you would notice though! So if you boys are settin's us down to tell us or been nervous about tellin' Ma n' me, you can relax some."

"Well Pa, we wuz a might worried that you n' Ma might not be real happy about our deliverin' business, but there's more reasons for all of us to have this little powwow." Eben said in his typical methodical manner. "Din, you wanna have a say, you're like family ya' know?"

"I ain't much good at explainin' stuff, you have at 'er. Might'n I give your folks the envelope now?" Dinny asked while lounging in his kitchen chair. He then reached into his back pocket and withdrew a large yellow envelope and slid it over to Eben's folks and smiled, "This is for you and I hope you know I am real thankful for you puttin' up with us. I hope you'll let us hang around a mite."

"Open it Pa, and like Din said, we're real thankful."

Eben's folks were in their mid fifties, both gray-haired and slim like their only son. Eben's mother had miscarried too many times to remember, so they had given up on ever having children of their own until Eben came along unexpectedly. The birth was unpleasant but successful, and Eben's father had been the midwife on that snowbound February morning. Together they had taken care of what needed to be done, and Eben's mother had recovered completely after only a few days. When the weather had thawed a month later they decided to visit a doctor down in Portsmouth, if for nothing else to set their minds at ease about the health of both mother and child. The doctor had advised that having another child might kill Eben's mother based on the difficulty of the birth, so she determined not to do so, and Eben's father did everything in his power to avoid another pregnancy also. They were plain, hardworking and churchgoing folk, and loved each other dearly since they met in school when they were both fifteen. Neither of them had ever strayed elsewhere. They had worked their way to owning two milk cows, had a number of chickens and sold firewood they cut off of their twelve acres they inherited from her folks. Now staring into an envelope stuffed with more cash either of them had ever seen in one place, each of them held their breath at first sight.

"Pa, there is fifteen hundred dollars in there and I want you both to know that I had suggested giving you one thousand, but Dinny insisted that we bump it up," Eben said as he nodded toward his partner. "We have a proposal for you if'n you want to hear it."

The four of them spent the night into the wee hours as Eben, primarily, outlined his designs and plans for both storing the tins of hooch and moving the still into the root cellar that he and Dinny would deepen and expand, working at night so as not to attract attention. While that was being done Eben's father would start building an extension on the barn. Eben's folks agreed to open a bank account down in Portsmouth while only making a minimal deposit in their local bank. It was agreed all around that no substantial purchases were to be made by anyone, at least in the short term. Maybe a new church dress for Eben's mother and some new boots for Eben's father, but nothing much more. Neither made any mention about participating in illegal activities, or expressed any concern for potential morality issues. The only contribution to the discussion from Eben's mother had been that the two protestant preachers of their congregation were widely known to be closet drunks and both thought that their secret was safe. Dinny, who didn't say much either during the night, allowed that he knew for certain that both were drunks, because he and Eben were the ones that sold them hooch in the first place. The table erupted in enormous laughter.

Eben stood up and hugged his mother and shook hands with his father, and then both parents went to Dinny and hugged him also, which brought pronounced tears to his eyes. Dinny had been on his own since he was sixteen, living in his weatherbeaten shack down in the cove, and hadn't had a motherly, or a fatherly hug since he couldn't even remember. While watching this, Eben held the kitchen door open that led into the mudroom, and put his arm around Dinny as he stepped out into the chilly summer air before anyone could see him crying a wee bit.

"Could that have gone any better Din?" Eben wondered knowingly.

"We got enough stored by to cover our deliveries for at least the next few weeks, so we can concentrate on diggin' right off. I'm tired and so is my skull from all that thinkin', but I'm up for getting on the ass end of a shovel right now."

"I'm with ya partner. No time like the present, is there? Let's set to diggin'," Eben declared.

"Aw shit," Dinny muttered as he stopped short. "Ya think I hafta run down to the Spar and make an appearance as the night watchman? I been dropping by the night clerk every night jus' so he can tell Jacobs that he saw me doin' my duties. Shit, I hadn't thought of doin' our diggin' while I'm supposed to be at the Spar."

"You know what Din," Eben interjected, "I just had me a thought about that. That night clerk fella, he just sits by and waits for the sun doesn't he? You wanna bet he's a drinkin' man?"

"Eben, I think I got the smartest partner in the world. We slip him a pint of the good stuff and tell him that he's gonna see one of us each night even if he don't, and we can set to diggin' without worryin' about the Spar at all. That's what you're thinkin', ain't it?" Dinny chuckled while scratching his chin.

"Dinny, you're purely a calculatin' gent you are!" Eben chuckled. "Let's get a pint and take it down there and sound him out. We'll tell him that it is only for a few nights and if Jacobs asks for us, we'll be sure to show up the next night. Heck, we both know that the only sure way to stop stuff from getting' stolen at the hotel is to tie Jacob's hands behind his back anyway!"

"H-H-Holly, this note is for you" Valentine Meadows announced just after everyone had sat down for an informal dinner.

"Please c-c-c-come and sit n-n-next to me, m-m-my dear," he continued.

Holly looked at Elsa and the woman slowly nodded in approval, as Holly stood up, touched Byzar affectionately on the shoulder and stepped to the other side of the table and was quite surprised when Meadows stood and slid the chair out for her. He had never demonstrated that level of respect for her before, and it caught her off guard. To avoid speaking, Meadows always kept a small pad of paper and pencil with him, for his stuttering, high-pitched voice was unpleasant to himself, and likely was to others. For some reason that all of the doctors he had been seen had not been able to explain,

Meadows never stuttered when whispering. In fact, he had a gentle, melodic voice when he spoke softly. In normal conversation he stuttered incurably and when stressed it was worse yet. He put his hand on Holly's arm as the noise at the table of artists and models grew to its normal din, and leaned over to whisper, "Holly, Elsa tells me that you had quite a lovely day at the beach. Isn't Ogunquit Beach such a rarity?"

"It was a wonderful day, Sir. The weather and the company was superb," she offered as she leaned her head toward his while seeking eye contact. She wanted to show him right here and now that all attention was focused squarely on him.

He continued. "Elsa also says that you and she had an informative discussion about my hopes for your, and our futures. Is this accurate my dear?"

"It is Sir, and I hope that I understand exactly what your requirements are. I would never want to disappoint you, Sir."

"Very well Holly. It looks like you got quite a bit of sun. The darkened hue of your face only accentuates your divine eyes of cobalt blue. Will you honor me by addressing me by my given name, unless we happen to be in a business situation? Then, Mr. Meadows is likely most appropriate, and I shall address you as Miss Meadows in kind, or perhaps you wish me to use your family name?"

Holly took a deep breath before speaking and put her right hand on top of his hand that was still grasping her left forearm. She straightened and bore her eyes into his and said, "I would be honored to be known as Holly Meadows from this day forward, er, Valentine. In private we shall be informal, and during other times, we will be Mr. Meadows and Miss Meadows; each of us commanding the respect from others that the Meadows name demands. After dinner I will come up to your bedroom and we can discuss the particulars of my new tasks as well as accommodate any other requirements you may desire," Holly confidently stated while also squeezing his arm in the most suggestive manner. "Now Valentine, let us enjoy dinner with our new family, shall we?" She withdrew her arm and immediately joined the rest of the table conversation.

Meadows sat back in his chair, received a bowl of mashed potatoes as it was being passed around and snuck a peek at Elsa. She gazed at him with questioning concern and he returned her gaze and drew a finger across his pencil thin moustache and smirked in her direction while silently mouthing "perfect". Elsa nodded, smiled broadly and turned her affections toward Byzar, whom she intended to bed as soon as dinner was concluded.

"Holly, your lovely fresh scent preceded you. Don't bother knocking my dear, and you can leave the door open. The scent of the ocean breeze flows through much better with the door open. I was just finishing with Valentine, and I am so excited for the both of you. I just know you will be wonderful for each other, and Valentine my dear, you again have demonstrated your keen eye for talent and potential. Holly is a phenomenal choice!" Elsa concluded as she began to leave the only room on the third floor. She gave Holly a gentle hug and a kiss on the cheek and departed with, "By the way, if you hear unnatural noises from my bedroom do not be alarmed. I have every intention of feasting on some gypsy flesh this evening!" as both Meadows and Holly chuckled.

Meadows third floor lair was wide open with a balcony overlooking the open ocean and a private bathroom with a pull-chain toilet. A queen sized bed and a night stand, a desk with two chairs and the rest of the large room was filled with various easels holding paintings in various stages of completion. In one corner stood a slab of white marble on a very sturdy small table only tall enough so the small boy, Robare, could reach it to work. On an even smaller table was a small figurine made of clay depicting a naked woman like one might find in a European museum. The boy was an art prodigy, and it struck Holly as somewhat of a dichotomy that such an effeminate little boy would be so enthralled with such a seemingly masculine discipline as stone sculpture. The walls were covered with unfinished, unframed paintings mostly depicting the human form is various degrees of undress. On one wall near his desk were far more sedate oil paintings, and Holly noted that most of these were Meadows' own work. All of the others, it seemed, were from his students or of visiting artists of note.

"There is somewhat order in chaos, is there not young lady?" whispered Meadows. Holly was clothed only in light cream colored flowing scarfs that could pass for a robe from a distance. Nothing much was left to the imagination when she stepped before the small electric lights that Meadows had ordered installed earlier in the spring while he was still in Brooklyn. He got up and walked over to Holly and kissed her on the forehead, as he always had done in the past when he was finished with her, and ran his hands all over her body in a most caressing sort of way. He had never demonstrated the kind of appreciation for her form in the manner that he was doing now. When she expected him to enter her he suddenly stopped and grabbed her gently by the arm and invited her to sit in one of the wooden high-backed chairs while he grabbed a pad and pencil from his desk and sat down directly across from her. He handed her the pad and said, "Please take a look at my notations and tell me if this makes sense to you." He then reached over to his desk and grasped a black leather-bound ledger and rested it on his lap while Holly studied the pad he had handed her. His notes described the basic requirements of running a household: food budget, supplies and other basic necessities. It also listed the school employees, of which Holly's name was noted, as well as visitors and paying customers of the art school. Holly thought carefully before speaking, recognizing that this was her first genuine opportunity to demonstrate her acumen of assuming administrative authority for the household and school operations. She had to be bold, she thought.

"Valentine, this is a good beginning, but I will formulate a more precise record, if I may tomorrow. I would like to assume the desk in the sitting room for my office where I can work and receive your guests and vendors. I would also like to move the desk to the corner where I can see whomever is approaching our home from town. I think it would be a good idea to be oriented in this manner. I will also take your ledger and combine it with the operational requirements you have noted here on this pad. You will have to tell me which of these items you wish to continue to manage if any, but from tomorrow forward, I will assume the balance of the responsibilities. These mundane tasks stifle an artist's imagination and freedoms, do they not?" Holly finished.

Meadows sat there in surprised silence for a moment and concluded, "Very well my dear, I see you have given our arrangement considerable and levelheaded thought. Tomorrow afternoon we will visit the bank and the local establishments I have an account with, and I will introduce you as Miss Meadows and authorize you to act and sign on my behalf. You will write the drafts for supplies and payroll, as well as provide receipts for income. You will also have a locked cashbox in your desk with perhaps, five hundred dollars, for petty cash expenditures as may be required. We do pay your friend Dinny in cash for our liquid sunshine, by the way" Meadows said with a smile.

"I will inform Mr. and Mrs. Parent of your new station, and they will report to you rather than to me. Please formulate a food budget so she can organize her kitchen somewhat better, as it seems that we are continually lacking and it is not necessary to go to the market two or three times a day, and keep asking me for money. Organize the food stores and provide her with the necessary funds. Mr. Parent generally needs only paint and cleaning supplies for his maintenance work. This is a good starting point Holly, and my hope is that I can concentrate on my work, and all other tasks will be on your lovely shoulders. Do you think you can handle this, my dear? Because I and Elsa have every confidence in you."

"I am very grateful for your confidences, and I will not fail you Valentine," Holly said. They smiled at each other for long enough for the moment to turn awkward, for Holly now wondered whether she was now expected to perform with her sex, or whether she should excuse herself. So she took the emboldened action of rising and stating matter-of-factly, "Valentine, I am not sure of what you want me to do right now; whether I am to be as I have before, or I should be as you seem to want me now? Am I to be a lover now, or your administrator, or a combination of either? I am open to all, as you will always know."

"For now Holly, let's have Miss Meadows concentrate on her new duties, while I concentrate on my new found freedom! I will continue, however, to introduce you to gentlemen I wish you to entertain."

"I do as you direct Valentine, with great pleasure of course. How much do you charge for Byzar and me, by the way, may I ask? I know I am being bold but I am curious. We are exploring new boundaries of our relationship are we not?" Holly stated with equal directness.

"Actually Holly I think it is better that you know more than less as we move forward, for there are certainly more delicate subjects I will likely have to discuss with you and have you manage. But for now I will say that I would never consider any less than one hundred dollars for your, and Byzar's services. The other girls I bring in might not warrant such extravagance, but you and Byzar set the table, as it were. And as you likely are aware, Byzar's station in life has increased dramatically with her new title of royalty, and I expect that when we hold our reception welcoming the Sultana of Crisana, that you in particular will be quite busy in the weeks that follow. Both Elsa and I will be discreetly representing you and I expect we'll keep your quite busy. I also expect that you will be greatly appreciated by the gentlemen so as to provide you with quite a financial boost also. How many gentlemen can you accommodate in a day do you think?" he boldly wondered.

"Valentine, I am a very healthy woman, and to be candid, I don't think your scheduling could keep up with my appetite," she said in a seductively wicked tone, as she leaned over and pecked Meadows on *his* forehead. She exited the room and began descending the stairs while thinking of how her relationship with Meadows has suddenly flip-flopped completely. She was now the one in position to control his emotions, rather then he, hers. She was particularly proud of kissing *him* on the forehead, and its symbolism.

"Maam, this is always the highlight of my week, coming here to deliver and enjoying the best pie in the county. Is Mr. Meadows available? I need to talk to him." Dinny asked the cook.

In a heavily French accented response the middle-aged, rather frumpy woman stated, "Mr. Dinny, you are always so polite. Is your mother so proud of you?"

"Well Mrs. Parent, I don't really have any folks that I recall. Been on my own since I was a teenager, but somewhere maybe she is," Dinny said.

"That is very sad Mr. Dinny, but you seem to be doing fine. You come visit here anytime and I'll have something for you. My son is wondering where your young friend, Richard has been lately. Is he well?"

"I haven't seen much of him either ma'am, truth be told, but I been so dang busy lately that I ain't been around much neither. Can I see Mr. Meadows please, I'm kinda runnin' around today?" Dinny pressed a bit.

"Actually Mr. Dinny, our household has had a change, Miss Meadows handle all the affairs of the house now, so I'll let her know you're here. I'll be right back," the woman announced as she left the kitchen through the swinging door. A few moments later she stuck her head back into the kitchen and said, "Mr. Dinny, Miss Meadows will see you now, please come with me."

As he followed Mrs. Parent through the dining room he was about to ask whether Mr. Meadows had a daughter no one had heard about but by the time he was ready to ask, Mrs. Parent announced, "Miss Meadows, Mr. Dinny to see you," and she turned to head back to the kitchen.

Dinny stood staring at the woman sitting at her desk with her nose in her ledger, and without looking up, motioned with her hand for Dinny to sit, which he did. He was just about to convince himself that Miss Meadows was actually Holly, but he wasn't quite sure because the woman's hair was tied back and she was wearing wire rim glasses. Just prior to putting her pen down she spoke, "Hello Dinny, it's wonderful to see you again. I'm sorry for my rudeness but I didn't want to lose my place in the ledger."

She got up from behind her desk and stepped around it to take the chair next to Dinny, "How are you my friend?"

Dinny was never very eloquent in front of Holly but he was truly dumbfounded now as she touched his hand and smiled, "I suppose you are here on business? Do you have a delivery with you or are you intending to make one today?"

Dinny finally got his voice and shifted in his chair and said, "Hi Holly, uh, Miss Meadows?" he questioned, and Holly interjected, "Miss Meadows is probably better, so how may I help you Dinny, I am quite busy this morning," the clear implication being for Dinny to state his business before she excused him.

"I'm sorry ma'am, uh, Miss Meadows, but should I be talking to Mr. Meadows about my reason for being here, uh," and again Holly interjected, "Dinny you are here about delivering alcohol and I am well aware of your previous arrangements and prices; has anything changed or will you be delivering tonight as usual?"

Dinny was still quite uncomfortable and said, "Well I guess there is a change and, are you sure this is okay Holl, er I mean Miss Meadows?"

"It's quite fine Dinny, what are the changes, and by the

way I have something else to discuss with you also. Again what are these changes?" she pressed.

"I was wonderin' whether I can start deliverin' at night time and jus' leave the tins under the porch steps? I'm thinkin' it might be safer for Mr. Meadows, uh you folks, as well as for me to deliver at night time, does that make sense?" Dinny said hopefully.

"And then how would we get you paid Dinny? That is the important question is it not?" Holly asked, to Dinny's great surprise.

"Well, uh, yes ma'am, that is what I was thinkin' a bit?" Dinny replied nervously.

Holly got up and went back behind her desk and pulled the top drawer open, reached in and brought out a sealed envelope with 'DINNY' written in exquisite cursive on the front and slid it over to Dinny was a satisfied smile, "Dinny please count it now, if you would. I want to be sure I have the correct amount," she said as she returned to her chair.

Dinny pensively snatched up the envelope and began to open it but stopped and said, "I'm sure it is all there, uh, Miss."

Holly again interrupted, "Dinny please count it now in my presence," which was more of a command than a request.

Dinny did as instructed and said, "You're a little long by ten dollars I think," to which Holly again commanded, "Please count again, Sir."

He again counted and admitted his mistake and tucked the envelope in the front pocket of his jeans and began to rise, when Holly again reached across to grasp Dinny's arm and direct him to sit back down, which he did.

"Dinny, I've been watching you fella's over at your shacks and wonder how you manage to see at night to work on your nets and such. Isn't having all those lanterns and open flames dangerous for you?" she asked.

"We've had our problems in the past to be sure, and if'n a fire does break out in earnest, I expect we'd all be campin' if a fire ever took hold, why do you ask?" Dinny wondered.

"What do you think your neighbors would say to putting up an electric streetlight above your shacks? We could make it bright enough so you can work at night but not so bright so you couldn't get any sleep. A fire at the shacks might set us on fire also, you understand. Would this be a good idea?" Holly asked.

"Yea it would be great and I'm positive that we'd all agree on it. I don't think any of us could afford it though."

"Talk to your friends tonight Dinny, won't you. You gents supply the pole and put it up, and we'll cover the cost of the materials and the monthly expense. At some point we'll all share the electric bill or we'll get the town to take it over. Can you give me an answer by tomorrow? You gents figure out the costs," Holly said in a very direct tone, but with her ever-present smile.

"Is this for real, ma'am, I mean that is awful generous. Can you do this, Holly, er I mean Miss Meadows?"

"We have our reasons to support our neighbors Dinny, as well as making it safer for our clients who may be venturing home after hours. It's just a good idea for all, is it not?" Holly stated as she rose to escort Dinny out toward the kitchen. "Dinny, you make your deliveries and leave them under the porch and it will be our secret. Please don't show anyone else our hiding place, for obvious reasons. You come see me the following day and I will have your payment prepared, and do me another favor will you Dinny?"

"You want me to say howdy to Eben, I expect," Dinny

interrupted confidently.

"No Dinny, I really don't," and Dinny appeared a bit hurt at the firmness of her statement. "What I want is for you to be my friend, actually a friend of this art school, by keeping me informed of any potential problems and concerns that the locals may have about us. If you hear of anything, anything at all that might be trouble, you come see me. Would you do that Din?"

"I will Miss Meadows, I surely will. I think that's a good thing also," Dinny agreed. "By the way, I'm really sorry about you and Eben. I think he made a big mistake by losin' his grip on you."

"Dinny, Eben is a kind and honorable young man; emphasis on being young. His loss. Take care, Dinny," she said as she turned back toward her office.

"Ain't seen much of you lately, ya' little fart!" Eben called out to little Richard Day. "Where ya' been hidin'?"

The boy said nothing, turned his eyes away and continued scratching the dirt where he was sitting back behind his folk's house.

Eben started walking over to the boy while saying, "Saw your Ma, n' she said you ain't been feeling too good, what's up with that?"

Eben put his hand on the boys head to scratch it, like he done hundreds of times before but this time Richard violently slapped it away.

"Whoa there fella, what the heck has got into you?"

"Nothin's got into me. Leave me be!" The boy quickly rose and ran into the woods, while Eben stood there stunned and hurt.

"Hell, everyone is leavin' me these days." He shook his head and moped down toward the cove wondering if he should take a moment and sit down.

"Why am I feelin' so poorly in my guts? I never cuss…Dang I feel like cryin'."

And Eben did.

"It is always better to say much less, than even a little more, Byzar. Remember it is a distinct privilege for anyone, no matter their station, to be in *your* presence, never the other way around. Never forget that. If you learn nothing else from our sessions, learn that. You are the prize; they are not. In public I, even as a Baroness, am in your charge, in a subtle sort of manner. In many cases I will speak for you. I will manage anyone who wishes your audience. You must always defer to my judgment. If you find yourself in a difficult position, you simply be silent and look in my direction, and I will intercede. People will wonder incessantly about why a Baroness is chaperoning a young lady of your title, and we'll let them wonder and speculate. Your job is to carry yourself as royalty at all times, and be sugary sweet in conversation. If someone challenges you in some manner, no matter how snotty, you simply politely smile and defer to me. I will be at your side and the inquisitor will be embarrassed to persist. We use this to our great advantage. If we are at an event with dancing, you must limit yourself to only two or three per hour, and insist that your suitor return you to your chair. When a man asks for a dance and you wish to decline, you simply say 'perhaps later', and nod in my direction. They will get the hint. Above all, never leave the room without me in tow, for any reason. Does this all make sense as to why we operate in this manner? Remember, we are a team and while the other guests are at a social gathering, you and I are working!"

"I do understand," said Byzar attentively. "I am the young Sultana of Crisana, and shall carry myself accordingly."

"In two weeks we will have a reception in your honor in Portsmouth, and from that point forward you will no longer be working at the Sparhawk. When out in public, you must carry yourself as a Sultana, and I encourage you to visit the other art school and get to know the students and other artists there. They will not recognize you as being one of our models right away, but it won't matter. They will be so taken with your beauty and station that they likely will not make the association," Elsa continued.

"I can still dance on the beach, can I not?"

"Of course my dear, it will only add to your attractiveness and mystery. You must also learn how to paint, or at least give it a try. We have a lot of learning to do, so let's start with table manners and then we'll practice some of the more classic dance steps. By the way how is Holly? Are you and she still enjoying being roommates?" inquired Elsa.

"We are fine but she is very busy it seems with her new tasks. I am happy for her though. She really has a good head for figures, you know, though I kid her that she has a good figure to give head!" Both women chuckled.

"It's a mighty fine sunset, ain't it boys?" the fat old

fisherman said to the gathered group. Captain Sunker was as jolly as a fellow could be, for having a last name that all derived good humor from—he being a captain and all. "Only thing that'd make it better is if one of them artist gals would come on down here and let us play with 'er a little bit!" he chortled.

The other six fishermen present didn't say a word nor did they chuckle which struck Sunker quite odd, until he realized that young Eben Ewert was standing behind him.

"Aw shit, I'm sorry Eben. I forgot you had feelins for one of them gals. I really am sorry, mate," Sunker said seriously.

"No worries Cap', it doesn't concern me anymore," Eben said while putting his best face forward. "Let's pull up wickets and have a set afore Edgar gets too uppity," he added, pointing at the pet crow sitting on one of the other gents shoulders.

Good humor restored all around, all those gathered passed around the church key used for popping open the cans of beer each was ready to start in on, except Eben of course. By the time the church key made it back to Captain Sunker, he was already latching on to another can to open.

Hank Decker took a gulp and wiped his sleeve across the bushy blonde moustache that hid most of his face below his nose and said, "So what's up Din, Eben, you boys called this here gatherin'. What's on your mind, if'n it ain't bangin' whores in Portsmouth," he said winking at Eben and Dinny with a knowing smirk. "Hell Eben, yours got the rot yet?" as the group all laughed.

Eben immediately turned beet red and glared over at Dinny, who had obviously told the story of Eben falling off the wagon, as well as his high falutin' God horse, to anyone he could in the past few days. The glare wasn't all that mean-spirited, for Eben joined the hilarity right then also, and retorted, "Well Decker, I ain't too worried about the rot anymore since your sister did some first aid on it the other day. I don't know what that salve is that she uses on every gent in Gunnyquit, but she applies it real nice!"

"Yup you're a funny gent Eben, even if I did have a sister! Now why you gents called us together, I'm in a hurry. My bedbugs are likely getting lonely," he smiled.

"Well gents," Eben started, "Din n' me are deliverin' just like you fellas are, though nowhere near as much, as you know. Din and I just took a night watchman job over to the Spar, and we're jus' runnin' out of hours in the day. So we figured on you fellas with the fast boat and all the cash might want to take over our deliverin' over to the shipyards and the docks. The Spar, Parsons and a few other gents is about all the deliverin' we can handle. Whatja' think?"

Captain Sunker interjected, "Hey Decker, I think ol' Edgar is callin' bullshit on our young fellers, Eben and Dinny, or check that, Edgar is callin' crow shit on that; check the back of your shirt!"

Sure enough, the crow on Deckers shoulder had done the deed but Decker seemed disinterested and said, "Hell that's all right, his shit kills all the bedbugs when I lay down in the bed! I'm just borrowin' Edgar here so ol' Mitch over there don't get crapped on; it's his pet magpie anyhow!"

The fellow named Mitch spoke up from behind his beer, "Hank, it's a crow n' you know it dammit. If it were a magpie it woulda' shit on your head! Now come to papa baby, as the man leaned over, put out his arm and let the bird crawl onto it, and then sidestep up to Mitch's shoulder.

Eben and Dinny sidled next to each other and patiently waited for the gents to get their fill of the playful banter, in hopes that they could extract an answer before too many more cans of Boston Ale got tipped.

Hank Decker spoke up and said, "You fellas don't deliver any of your good stuff over to the yards, do ya?" already knowing the answer in the negative. "I'm guessin' you're just about breakin' even down there, is all?" he said, still fishing for information.

It was Dinny who spoke up, which kind of surprised the group for all knew Eben was obviously the sharpest thorn in the partnership, and that Dinny had always been regarded as a might dull. So when Dinny spoke up, he had their rapt attention, "We do just fine down at the docks, cuz' most of them fellas know that we never short 'em and that we got family all through them docks, or at least Eben does. It's just that they're growing too big for what we can supply, and that's a fact. There's three yards down there now and them boys is working long hours loadin' sand and firewood on to them schooners; that ain't easy work and it makes a fella mighty thirsty. Me n' Eben just can't keep up and that's all there is. Whyn't you boys take 'er over for a spell?"

"Are you ready to leave, Holly," asked Valentine Meadows on this sunny, early summer morning. Tickled that he didn't stutter in his first spoken words of the day, his outlook for the morning turned even brighter. He anticipated a wonderful Monday morning leisurely strolling around the village of Ogunquit introducing Holly to the druggist, banker, grocer and others, all whom he had accounts with, and then hopefully wander down to the Sparhawk to do a little

Greg May

schmoozing with its owner, Nehemiah Jacobs, the thieving rascal that he was. Meadows needed for Jacobs to meet Holly also, and be informed that she was now to be known as Miss Meadows, and that she would be conducting most of his business for him. Meadows was thoroughly positive that Jacobs would be rendered useless due to being in the presence of a beauty like Holly, and Meadows would use this dynamic to his great advantage. The Sparhawk was useful because many of Meadows guests could be situated in the hotel for their short stays in at least the comfort and style they were typically accustomed to. By now, Meadows had already arranged for financial kickbacks for providing so many wealthy visitors to the Sparhawk, substantially increasing its societal standing in the region. He was also intending on installing a few of his 'models' into one or two of the guest rooms so he could arrange for 'visitations' with the many gentlemen Meadows was now inviting to visit his art school, or so they told their wives. Even if the wives accompanied these gentlemen on their visits to Maine, visitations with the models could remain discreet. Holly would handle the details and Meadows would be satisfactorily insulated from repute, both social and legal. Meadows also wanted to encourage Jacobs to form an alliance with Holly so more income could be perhaps produced by his 'models', by having Jacobs attract more gentlemen on vacation to visit his art school, and thereby the special attentions of his 'models'. Also, the nightly 10pm string quartet concerts in the spacious dining room of the Sparhawk would be a wonderful opportunity for recruiting suitors, as most of them were in the bag by that time anyway. Getting the gentlemen down to the cove was the hook, for once inside the home nature would take care of the rest. Gents were 'inspired' by watching beautiful naked young women posing in front of others. These gents would sit in the dining room, out of sight from those outside, wives included, and simply pay for the privilege. If so inclined, Holly or Elsa as the divine hostesses could arrange for short breaks for the models so they could visit with these gentlemen in one of the upstairs private rooms for the appropriate fee. All quiet, tidy and socially acceptable for these 'patrons of the arts'! Meadows School of Art was of course legitimate, but it was also evolving into the most discriminating brothel along the New England coastline. Even the 'models' were able to intrinsically regard their 'work' as part and parcel of broadening their solemn artistic conditions by being in the presence of such noted masters of the craft. Art in itself was self-expressive, critiques be damned. It was, after all, difficult to consider that the tutelage of Baroness Elsa as anything other than a unique and rare experience that would be highly respected in any venue. Their budding careers would be greatly enhanced and opportunities expanded. This only stood to reason. The models were basically students of the Einsteins of the art world. Their families back home would be so proud of their daughters and would no doubt brag about it within their societal circles, mostly from wealth. That they were also generously paid prostitutes was simply part of the training of the mind. It was also well within keeping of the Vassar College dictum of the 'willingness to experiment', that Holly perpetually encouraged of her resident contemporaries. The models, Holly, Elsa and Byzar would often gather out on the early morning rocks and enjoy silly laughter about how their mothers and fathers back home would be bragging—at dinner parties, church gatherings and other activities of higher society—about their daughters studying the fine arts in the presence of such noted citadels of society as found at the art schools in Ogunquit, Maine. Of course the parents would never know about the varied sexual partners and exploits the girls loved to giggle and gab about on the rocks. As time went by, the girls decided to sketch each and every erect penis they serviced and share the sketches with each other. It was all in good fun and a sort of sisterhood bonding. Elsa, a self-professed expert on the subject, was particularly fascinated by the concept of ejaculation and most of her sketches depicted that particular moment. Her fascination extended into her poetry, published in a New York magazine the previous year, that almost got her and the publisher incarcerated for profanity, but only resulted in a fifty dollar fine for the publisher. This court action had only served to enhance Elsa's worldwide reputation as well as the concerted admiration such defiance garnered from the girls enjoying daily breakfasts on the Ogunquit rocks in the summer of 1920.

Of course many of these gents would have to provide explanations to their wives for their sudden interest in the world of art, and Elsa or Holly would encourage a small purchase of some of the resident artists' work as supporting evidence. Lemonade spiked with some of the finest alcohol available in the land would also be served at a healthy price, but as long as Meadows had the number and frequency of visitors regulated so as to be unnoticeable, no one would be the wiser. Meadows activities in Brooklyn provided steady income but not to the level of forestalling his declining familial wealth, and he therefore had been contemplating other methods of producing income. The idea of Holly and Byzar fulfilling their new roles as Miss Meadows and the Sultana of Crisana had been a stroke of genius, even for himself, Meadows thought. His reviews in the art magazines back in New York City were still being acclaimed and revered though the critiques themselves produced little cash on their own. Those artists who had the financial wherewithal or sponsorship to inspire Meadows to write favorably about a certain piece, exhibition or artist always provided a substantial windfall, but the real money in the art world for Meadows was the ability to manipulate the pricing or value of a collection, or single piece, of art work for art collectors or museums via his critiques. As one of the more noted writers and art critics of his generation, his valuations and appraisals were highly sought after by potential purchasers, insurance institutions, museums and collectors. For example, if an oil painting was to be sold via auction, private sale or another avenue, an excessive valuation by Meadows would garner a healthy sum when sold. As long as Meadows and those of his sinister ilk, of which the art world was noted for, gave the initial appraisal, other critics would generally not have the temerity to provide differing appraisals, for it just simply was not how the world of art functioned. Meadows instinctively knew that the business of art appraisal was the ultimate sham, for selling appraisals, which is truly what he often did, was similar to selling, say, air. There was no true method of quantifying an opinion, but the game was to inspire others to consider one's opinion more valid than others, which Meadows was a considered genius at doing. Meadows made a lot of money and acquired a unique collection of very wealthy friends whom his appraisals favored. Meadows was also adept at devaluing pieces of artwork for the benefit of buyers. This was a favorite tactic he utilized when a person with little knowledge of the art world acquired a piece or a collection, perhaps via inheritance, and sought him out for appraisal and possible assistance in selling the work. If the

Greg May

piece or pieces were of substantive value or importance, Meadows was certain to devalue the work while at the same time contacting those friends in his circle whom he knew would be likely to purchase. Meadows would gain possession of the work, so he could display it for buyers, and once sold at an inflated price, with the standard finder's fee attached, he would then contact the owner and present a devalued cash offer to them, knowing that they likely would be ecstatic to get some cash for something they knew absolutely nothing about. Meadows skillfully worked both sides of these transactions and both cherished his efforts on their behalf, even though he had defrauded each.

It was this pool of friends that Meadows invited to his art school in Ogunquit and also to his studio in Brooklyn for the underlying purpose of sampling the charms of his models. This in turn provided a degree of evidence to potentially extort his friends at the appropriate time, if needed. The extortions were never adversarial, but understood nonetheless among polite company of course, and were never in an amount considered to be excessive by any means. Meadows skillfully managed potential difficulties by offering a 'freebie' when the gentleman in question would come to drop off a payment. Should a gentleman be particularly obstinate Meadows would politely offer to send one of his 'models' over to his residence or place of business for a consultation, per se. This proposition typically inspired a timely payment to everyone's satisfaction.

For his part, Meadows was bored by such transactions because he so easily duped those he considered to be his intellectual inferiors, which by rights was mostly all. The transactions that provided substantial financial gains were somewhat inspiring but still and all, they didn't test his calculating machinations to a worthwhile degree. Manipulating humans was simply a game, and not a very challenging one at that. His true enjoyment was derived from making the innocent and overly religious participate in conduct that scared and horrified them. Making young women participate in sexual scenarios that would likely scar them for life had been intoxicating in the recent past, but Byzar and Holly, the two he had endeavored so diligently to completely ruin, had turned out to be the only two girls who seemed impervious to such degradations. In fact, he began to appreciate and gain respect for both, as they seemed to flourish in such situations, and challenged for more. Elsa was like that; nothing was beyond that wonderfully insane woman. Elsa was a creature beyond the realm of reason, but Meadows was confident he could manage her personality by celebrating her various vagaries as the most supremely avant-garde artistry in the world and thereby appeal to her boundless ego. And if that did not work, there was always laudanum, and sometimes opium, which she was entirely addicted to. By natural course and perhaps with slight encouragement, Meadows hoped that Byzar and Holly might also become addicts themselves, though hopefully not to the degree that Elsa was. Elsa's mood swings were miraculous in their range and most of Elsa's most insightful drawings and poems were garnered during her highs. Elsa became as calm as a kitten when she needed or asked for a snort or a smoke, and it was in these vulnerable moments Meadows could get his directives satisfied. He intended to use this same method as a backup plan to control Holly and Byzar if ever the need should arise. Up until now, the inducement of money and self-respect had assured both of the girls' absolute compliance, but drugs were always a wonderful mechanism to rely on should the designed method of control ever fail.

This was one of the primary reasons he wanted Holly to form a relationship with the Ogunquit Apothecary, and its owner, a Mr. Donald Spenser. Spenser had never been overly friendly to Meadows but never shied from accepting his money. Meadows was one of his few customers that paid cash-on-the-barrel, and Meadows expected more pleasant service for being such. Spenser was in his fifties, a tall man with drooped shoulders, wire rim glasses and slicked back gray hair. He was a devout Baptist and extolled the virtues of being a teetotaler to anyone who would listen. His frumpy, drab wife had jowls to match his, and both were as sweet as pie to the locals, tourists and particularly the Woodbury artists. Those known to partake in spirits, or who worked down at the wharves were treated in a curt manner because it was assumed that anyone working at the docks was a drunk, and therefore an unsuitable human being. Mr. Spenser had no qualms about pontificating to dock workers about the perils of drink, lecturing via the use of scripture, especially when the opportunity to do so was in the presence of respectable ladies who happened to be in his store at the same time. Meadows was positive that Spenser was a closet drunk but he cared little, he just wanted his laudanum and opiates dispensed regularly and without drama. Hopefully the presence of Holly would fluster Spenser into some semblance of cordiality and allow the ordering of drugs to be void of any further hassle.

Holly was introduced as Miss Meadows at Edison's Grocery and she was very well received both at the front counter as well as at Mr. Snorer's meat market in the back of the store. Both Mr. Edison and Mr. Snorer insisted that they were not likely to forget Miss Meadows and both her signature, and smile, were better than cash. Holly, as Miss Meadows, would satisfy accounts every two weeks which both found quite satisfactory. Mr. Snorer even allowed that his account could be settled every day even if there was not a balance, if it meant that he could lay eyes on Holly on a daily basis. He said this in an overly appreciative manner that was socially accepted by all, but his leering certainly did not escape Holly. She knew then and there that she could, at any time of her choosing, pocket the money dedicated for the meat department, by simply fucking the man in his ice room. She put this in the back of her mind to ponder later.

Their visit to the bank up in Wells Village went just as famously. A few years previous Meadows had wired the princely sum of twenty-five thousand dollars into the two-teller window bank and since that time all four employees, including the Bank Manager, were at Meadows' complete beck and call. Holly signed a few forms providing her the ability to transact business for Valentine Meadows with a one thousand dollar per month withdrawal restriction. Other than that limit, Holly could do as she pleased simply with her signature.

Meadows purposefully saved the visit to the druggist for last, knowing the potential for unpleasantness from the miserable pair of Spensers. They did not disappoint as soon as Meadows and Holly walked into the small store. Mrs. Spenser simply disregarded the pair, her distaste for Meadows and all he represented quite evident. Mr. Spenser simply stated, "Good day Mr. Meadows, I'll be with you in a moment," even though there was no one else in the store at the time. He was obviously taken with Holly and her radiant smile, but made a concerted effort to avoid eye contact after his first extended glance. His blushing gave him away, as it did with all men. Meadows was about to offer his greetings when Holly interrupted by walking directly over to Spenser's counter and extending her hand saying, "Hello Mr. Spenser, I am Miss Meadows and will be attending to Mr. Meadows' affairs this summer. I am pleased to make your acquaintance."

Spenser was taken aback at now having to gaze into the most stunning pair of eyes he had ever seen, just as his wife piped up from behind with, "I assume that you are one of Meadows little slatterns?"

Spenser was too embarrassed to speak and Meadows stepped back in amusement, awaiting Holly's reaction. Holly slowly turned and bored her eyes into Mrs. Spenser, and gave her an appraising once over and turned back to Mr. Spenser completely ignoring his wife, even though she had no idea what a *slattern* was, but knowing it was not friendly, and again stated, "Mr. Spenser, the bank had us fill out some forms to allow me to transact business on Mr. Meadows' behalf, do you have similar requirements, Sir?"

Mrs. Spenser was having none of it.

"How dare you turn your back on me you... you hussy!" she shouted as she lumbered her way around the front counter.

"Mr. Spenser!" Holly exclaimed, "Is this how all your employees greet new customers? If so it is a very poor reflection on your character, Sir."

"I am not an employee! I am his wife, you little tramp!"

Holly turned on her heel in a very controlled and seemingly unaffected manner and bade Meadows to precede her out the door as she turned back to Mr. Spenser and said, "Sir, I have quite a substantial order for you in my purse if you would like to pick it up at our school in the cove promptly at 3pm. Should we not see you at that time, rest assured you will not have our business ever again… and," as she held her hand up to stifle the next round of bile just about out of Mrs. Spenser's lips, "I will take it as my sole objective to inform all the visitors in Ogunquit of your *lovely* wife's conduct. 3 o'clock, no later… it is solely your choice, Sir" she stated as she majestically strolled out of the small shop under the hateful eyes of the miserable Mrs. Spenser. She looped her arm into Meadows and pleasantly smiled at him and whispered, "Valentine, I believe you mentioned something about lunch, did you not?"

"My dear, you continue to impress me on a daily basis," Meadows volunteered, as they headed down Wharf Lane toward the Sparhawk Inn, and perhaps another difficult conversation with the owner-kleptomaniac, Neahmiah Jacobs.

"What a lovely pair those two are, Valentine, but they certainly have inspired me to consider decreasing their income in a substantive manner," Holly announced.

"And what might you have in mind, my love?" Meadows whispered as they enjoyed the downhill stroll.

"If that jackass doesn't show up this afternoon, I think we will open our own store. Yes I know we do not have a druggist license, nor the knowhow, but we also don't know how to make whiskey or have a license for that either, but we certainly sell enough liquor, do we not? In order for our 'operations' at the school to proceed, we need to continue to place ourselves in a position that the locals, as well as the law, are less than inclined to bother us and our operations. The installation of a streetlight down at the cove won us a great deal of goodwill amongst the locals and it didn't cost much: our girls covered the cost in only two nights. I hear from Dinny complaints all the time about having to go clear up to

Kennebunk for chew and smokes and other items not found in Ogunquit. We know a lot of tourists and locals that also want to buy drugs, so why don't we sell them? We have a captive audience and we can sell the drugs just like a speakeasy sells hooch. If we don't know a person, we don't sell to them until they prove their loyalty. We can worry about that later. Dinny tells me that laudanum and opium in various forms is being sold out on the rum line also, so he can deliver in enough quantity to last us for the entire summer and then some. For that matter, Elsa, Byzar and I can hire a sailboat and get the stuff ourselves. I'll bet we could get a very *fucking* good price!" She playfully needled him in his ribs with her elbow."

"Let's see if Spenser shows up at three," Meadows whispered. "If he does, let's set him down at your desk and once you set him at ease, we'll bring in a couple of the new girls to wrest away that jackasses virtue! That would be very enjoyable. We'll set up our Eastman's Brownie camera and get a snapshot at the appropriate time. I'll certainly appreciate presenting that photo to him then watching the worm squirm, as they say."

"I hope he shows up also, now that I think about it. I'd sure like to have a snapshot of that jackass sucking on my titty so I can show his slob of a wife someday!" Holly commented.

"With you running things, I get a feeling that we'll be able to do anything around here, and as you probably know, I have my eyes set on a couple boys whose rumps need some tending to. You know, most every artist of note that comes to Ogunquit has had their horizons expanded at an early age by some thoughtful gentleman like myself. I consider buggering little boys to be a type of weeding out process, a prerequisite if you will, for any man to develop any artistic talent at all. Robare is a fine example, don't you think?" asked Meadows, who was completely in his own world imagining his conquests yet to come.

Before entering the hotel entrance Holly wondered aloud, even though the thought of raping boys was somewhat distasteful for her to comprehend, "It is always a case of whatever floats your boat, for all of us. I have always been told that pirates were famous for such doings, which I found surprising, and we all know about Catholic priests, but I'm not a guy, so I'll just take it on faith. There are times when I get a kick out of getting my hiney humped also, and that's a fact. I guess that's why God invented drugs anyway! I assume we'll take the corner table facing the ocean?" she said as she led Meadows to their table without waiting for the hostess, who was catching up with menus in her hand.

Meadows motioned for the hostess, one of the drab looking middle-aged Maine girls to come closer as he whispered, "Please inform Neahmiah that I wish to see him if he is available."

She nodded in reply though it was clearly evident that she had no idea who he was, but she would find out as soon as she asked the rest of the staff.

The lunch rush had passed and halfway through their meal Jacobs made his way toward their table, working the room like a cheap politician.

"I'd like to introduce m-m-my niece, Holly," stammered Meadows.

"I had no idea, Valentine, and it is my distinct pleasure ma'am," said Jacobs as he found his chair. "Welcome to Ogunquit young lady, but haven't we met before?"

"We have, but it is of no importance. I am pleased to

finally meet you Mr. Jacobs," Holly said.

"Jacobs, Miss Meadows is going to assume my affairs and I wanted you both to become better acquainted," Meadows whispered. Jacobs knew that when whispering, Meadows rarely stuttered, so he accommodated the condition by leaning closer to him, which Meadows greatly appreciated. "Is this a good time for a conversation, my friend?"

"Well now that Miss Meadows is joining us, I wouldn't think of placing any other task as more important," replied Jacobs.

Holly remained composed, batted her eyelashes and smiled sweetly and rested her chin on her folded hands, even as she rested her elbows on the table.

In her mind she thought, "What a douche bag, I hope I don't have to fuck this asshole," and the conversation about enhanced arrangements with the models at the school and encouraging some of the Sparhawk's male guests to visit the school commenced. After a half an hour all issues were understood and Meadows, clearly noting Jacobs's infatuation with Holly, eyed her with the purpose of instructing her to have him show her the rooms the models would be using to ply their trade.

However, Holly intervened by asking, "Mr. Meadows we do have a 3pm appointment back at home that would be in our best interest to meet, would it not? I am sure that Mr. Jacobs understands our requirements," which was said in hopes that it was more of a statement than a question. Meadows pondered and nodded after a few moments, and then stood to shake Jacobs's hand, which Holly did also, and they left to stroll back to the cove. After a few moments in the slight off-shore breeze, Meadows patted Holly's hand and said, "Well my dear, if I were in your pantalettes I wouldn't want to screw that ignoramus either!" and both chuckled and headed for home.

Holly scampered up the steps to Meadows third floor lair and knocked softly but feverishly, "Valentine, we have an emergency! May I enter?"

"Valentine... Mr. Meadows... please," she said in increasing tones.

"W...W...What is it Holly," he responded in an obviously inebriated and half-asleep tone.

"The police are heading this way, just stay in your room, I'll handle things. You understand, Valentine?" she said through the door in the hopes he would be aware enough to comprehend. "Don't make a noise or come down for any reason, okay?"

"Th-Th-Thank you Holly."

"And keep the boy quiet," she said as she hurried back down the stairs after hearing little Robare begin to whimper as he obviously was waking from Meadows' bed.

"Mrs. Parent, stall the officers while I dress won't you? They are coming up the path now," Holly pleaded as she rushed back upstairs into her room. She was thankful that she had been unable to sleep and had seen the commotion down past the fishermen's shacks just as the sun was making its appearance. She lingered in the window by her desk long enough to realize that the police were bypassing the shacks and heading for the house. Mrs. Parent was busy baking and was equally flustered when Holly came bursting into the kitchen with her instructions. Mrs. Parent's first reaction was that she hoped the police would drag Valentine Meadows to the jail up in Kennebunk and throw away the key. She still wondered why she wasn't poisoning that wicked man for continually assaulting her only son. Unfortunately, it was evident that he truly liked staying with Meadows, and while she refused to accept his inclinations at such a young age, their lot in life had certainly improved because of the situation. She was still lost in thought when she heard the boots tromping up the stairs toward the kitchen door. Before they could rap on the wood, and thereby wake the entire house, Mrs. Parent opened the door and welcomed them in with a smile and a 'shush' as she whispered her compliance.

"We're here to see a Mr. Valentine Meadows, is he about?" the largest of the three green clothed uniformed officers commanded.

She smiled and closed the door after the third officer stepped clear and said in her purposefully enhanced French accent, "Monsieurs, this I do not know, but I will see if Mademoiselle Meadows is available, non? Coffee oui?" to which all three officers declined by motioning their heads. Mrs. Parent left the kitchen and returned after a few minutes with a hand gesture for all three to follow her through the dining room and to where Holly had set up her desk and office. As the officers entered the room they were met with early morning sunbeams streaming through the tall but narrow windows. Before them was a vision in a high-necked, full-sleeved, olive colored yet simple full length dress. Holly had positioned herself so that while she gazed out over the ocean, the sunbeams bore through the flimsy fabric in such a manner that from the officer's perspective they could almost see her buttocks and the space between the hilt of her legs. Holly of course had positioned herself in such a manner to draw exactly the desired effect, and just as Mrs. Parent departed, Holly turned on her heel and looked beyond the obviously rankled officers and said, "Mrs. Parent, tea and Danish if you please.

"Good morning officers, I am Miss Meadows, Mr. Meadows niece and in charge of his affairs here in Ogunquit. Obviously there is a serious matter to attend to that requires your presence here this morning. Please be seated and Sir, please bring one of the dining chairs over to join us, won't you?" Holly already had disarmed them more than if she had taken their pistols out of their holsters herself, and she positioned herself behind her desk, but not before spying many of the fishermen down at the shacks already gathering and wondering about the police visit.

"Ma'am, I am Sergeant Drake, and these are Corporals Couture and Richardson. Thank you for receiving us so early, but we do have a serious matter to discuss, and frankly it is not something I wish to discuss with a lady. Is your uncle about?"

Holly measured the Sergeant as well as appraised both Corporals before she spoke, "I am sorry that you have come all this way, but my uncle has travelled back to New York City, and I don't know the details of his itinerary." She now looked the Sergeant directly in the eyes and said, "May I take it on faith that the reason for your visit is due to something of a sexual nature, Sergeant?" All three men were unsettled and flustered.

"Please be at ease gentlemen, I know such matters are unseemly, but I do know about many of my Uncle's proclivities, and many of which I think we would all find, distasteful, shall we say? I would also point out, as a matter of reference, that my uncle is someone I love dearly and is widely considered to be a genius; he speaks five languages fluently I'll have you know. I recognize your discomfort but perhaps we might forget for a moment that I am a lady, and we can be precise as to the reason for your visit. As you might imagine, there is not much that I have not heard or seen in both knowing my uncle and since my recent arrival to this school of art. Rest assured gentlemen, nothing you say will shock me."

The three men exchanged nervous glances and Holly looked past them and waved Mrs. Parent back into the kitchen with her tray.

Shifting uncomfortably in his seat, Sergeant Drake began, "Well Miss Meadows, this is not pleasant, but we have a complaint about your uncle, ah, accosting a young boy, and we have a witness. We have to bring him to jail for questioning and to answer to these charges, I'm sorry to say."

Holly again appraised the Sergeant, but this time ignored the other two officers, and she tapped her finger on the desk as she delightfully crossed her legs.

"Sergeant Drake, might I propose that our discussion from this point forward be limited to our ears only—no disrespect to your corporals, of course? The less ears matters such as these touches might be best at this time. Since my uncle is not present for you to secure his arrest, perhaps the corporals might visit the kitchen for tea and Danish?" At this point Holly was hoping that no one would stir in the house and as the Sergeant nodded his acquiescence, Holly got up to show the corporals to the kitchen and discreetly waved Mrs. Parent over to her side and quickly whispered, "Go upstairs. Everyone stays in their room—pass the word. Please do so as soon as you can."

Holly came back into her office, closing the double pocket

doors behind her, and instead of returning to her desk she pulled up a chair kiddy-corner to Sergeant Drake's chair. Crossing her legs again, showing her knee as well as a bit beyond it on purpose, she took a deep breath and said, "You know there must be something magical and restorative in the air along the coast of Maine. There is no other quite like it, would you agree?"

"It does a body good, ma'am, that's a fact."

"Tell me, Sergeant," as Holly placed her chin on the back of her hand as her elbow rested on her knee, "was my uncle fucking, giving or getting a blowjob, if I may ask?"

This caught Drake completely by surprise and suddenly realized that Miss Meadows had likely seen and heard everything she claimed she had. Before he replied, Holly said, "Let's dispense with the niceties and deal with realities. Please tell me where we are at this point."

"Well, Miss Meadows I am taken aback a bit, but the reality is that there is a boy whose family was staying at the Sparhawk Hall, or Inn if you prefer, who was seen being molested by Mr. Meadows six nights ago during one of their concerts. One of the dishwashers saw them in the storeroom, and I'm afraid your uncle had bent the boy over some boxes and was molesting him in that manner," Drake stated, still quite uncomfortable with having to have such an unseemly discussion with such an exquisitely beautiful young woman.

"I see," Holly said as she calculated her options. Finally she spoke, "Sergeant Drake, what is your desired outcome of this little visit? Certainly you know that my uncle would be able to provide numerous alibis for his whereabouts on that evening, and the dishwasher's word would be measured against men of finer standing, even if he could be kept around to testify at a trial. Additionally, by the time a trial date could be set, my uncle will likely be somewhere in Europe, and the expense to bring him to Maine, well as you likely know would be prohibitive. Even if he were taken to jail today, I am sure his attorneys would be quite aggressive, wouldn't you think?"

Drake remained seated as hard as stone, "Are you saying that the witness would meet his demise, Miss Meadows?" hoping to entrap her into a foolish response. Holly did not take the bait however. She had learned much too much about the dirty ways of the world, especially the court system, from her father and his pals during her kibitz sessions.

"Of course not Sergeant Drake. What I am saying is that we cannot expect your witness to lollygag around Ogunquit when more perky opportunities likely come along. Without your witness, there is no case, because certainly a young boy is not going to get up in front of a crowd and tell the world he took it in the butt, wouldn't you agree?"

"Miss Meadows, I am beginning not to like you very much," Drake intoned in a very measured voice.

"Oh nonsense Sergeant, I am simply speaking of the realities and of how we should proceed so everyone walks away somewhat satisfied with the outcome."

"And what outcome might that be, Miss Meadows?" Drake asked, getting more disgusted by the minute.

"Well Sergeant," Holly calmly began, "first and foremost, my uncle is never going to sniff the inside of your jailhouse, and that is a fact. Second, you and your department have to demonstrate to the boy's family that you have proceeded in a most dutiful and honorable fashion, and thirdly, the family will likely disappear when the realities of life are explained to them and they receive a cash allotment for their pain, suffering and whatever."

"Is this an attempt at a bribe? You know Miss Meadows, my mates and I were hell bent for leather to come down here to the cove and roust your little pissant of an uncle and haul his slimy ass to jail. We hear all about what happens in this house, and how disgusted the locals are that your uncle and his tribe showed up here. We may be hicks, but that doesn't mean that we're dumb hicks. I hear tell of how your uncle throws his cash around, like for that streetlight, and for community events, and both you and I know why he does it too. He thinks he's protecting his slimy ass by doing so, and it truly seems he is succeeding. But one day he'll slip up and when he does, I will surely be there with my billy club, and after meeting the likes of you Miss Meadows, I'm going to enjoy it. Your uncle has a well earned reputation for being an evil sonofabitch, but you young lady are more dastardly then we ever imagined that shithead could be!" By now Drake was standing and shaking his finger in Holly's face, which though she tried to disguise, quite frankly unnerved her greatly. Still, she did not move beyond the uncontrollable slightly welling of her eyes.

Calmly and somewhat stoically she said, "Now, now *Mr.* Drake, you're accusing me of outlandish behavior, but all I am doing is presenting realities as I see them, am I not? I am a lawyer's daughter and perhaps that is where I derive my perspective. You, Sir, are the only one in this room with a badge, and you can do as you please. All I am saying is that you have been presented with an unwinnable case when you think about it. And *Mr.* Drake, if I wanted to bribe you, your pants would have been around your ankles a long time ago and I can assure you there would have been not a single thing you could have done about it. My charms are irresistible, and *that* Sir, is an undeniable fact. But alas, the house is likely to be waking up any time now so you'll just have to be my guest some other time. As for now, I will write you a check for one thousand dollars, out of which you can deal with the family in any manner you choose, and we'll forget that you ever visited here this morning. I'm either writing you a check right now, or I am going to take a bath, what's it going to be, Sir?"

Holly got up and went behind her desk and pulled out her ledger and began writing, as Sergeant Drake paced and sputtered his disgust. Finally he said with derision, "Make it fifteen hundred, *Miss Meadows*"

Holly got up and put down her pen, having already filled out the draft and said, "The check is for one thousand dollars and is made out to 'Drake', you can fill in the first name."

She placed the check on the front of her desk so he could reach it and as she stepped past the man she cooed, "Why don't you come visit me when you're in a better mood, you handsome devil?" As she did she straightened his lapels and discreetly reached down and ran her finger down the length of his semi erect penis through the fabric. Before he could react she was already opening the pocket doors and gazing in a suggestive manner at the two corporals seated at the dining room table. They had obviously heard every word, and as she began her ascent up the stairs, she announced, "You gents can let yourself out, and please do!"

She lingered up in the second floor window in the bed that Byzar and Elsa shared, and waited until the officers had made their way through the line of fishing shacks without stopping to provide any information to the inquiring minds. By this time the bedroom was filling up with the entire household who had been listening through the floor and hanging on every word. Elsa asked, "What do you think, Holly?

"I think that Sergeant Drake is exactly what he says he is

104

not." Holly stated to the waiting crowd. "And that is that he is most certainly a 'dumb hick'!"

This brought uproarious laughter from the entire household, except up on the third floor, where Meadows was continually vomiting in fear of being brought to jail. Only when he heard the laughter was Meadows able to push his vomit bucket aside and climb back into a fetal position under his covers. Just as he closed his eyes and convinced himself that he was in the clear, his hand brushed the naked buttocks of the sleeping boy in his bed, and he began to masturbate himself to sleep.

"Thank you for stopping by Dinny and thank you for the delivery this morning. I trust you found your envelope?" Holly asked.

"You're welcome ma'am and thank you for the money. What is it that you wanted to see me about?"

"We might be having trouble acquiring our necessities from Mr. Spenser, the druggist. If that should happen, I wonder if you can purchase our requirements out at the rum line. If I understand correctly, those boats lay three miles off shore because that is the limit of the United States territory, and out there they are not constrained by US law, isn't that correct? We need laudanum and opium primarily. Of course we have the required prescriptions, but Mr. Spenser might prove to be difficult to deal with." Holly asked.

"Not surprised about Spenser, he thinks the world of himself, don't he? I can ask around next time we, er, I sail on out there, and yes, you have the rum line figured right. Can you give me a list of the stuff you need?"

"Actually Dinny, I was wondering if you could make a special trip out there, just to ask around? I'll pay you for your time of course. It's getting close to the 4th of July and we intend to have quite a party, so if you can't provide our requirements we're going to have to send a courier down to New York City, you see," Holly said.

"They got me awful busy over to the Spar, Miss," Dinny started before Holly interrupted.

"Dinny, why don't you take my friend Byzar out for a sail and a picnic tomorrow? She'll pack a lunch and I'll give you ten dollars to boot! I know you like her and she has said to me that she thinks you cut quite a site!" To which Dinny shifted nervously in his seat and blushed uncontrollably.

"Geez Holly, er, ma'am, I don't know what I would say to her, I mean she's a city gal ain't she? What would she see in a fella like me? I'm just a small town fisherman, and..."

"Dinny, let me tell you a secret, she is not only a city gal, but she is also royalty!" Holly declared fully knowing that she was about to kill the proverbial two birds by finding out about the availability and cost of pharmaceuticals at the rum line and also initiating the local scuttlebutt about having a Sultana, princess if you prefer, grace the village of Ogunquit, that by the way, already had been graced by a Baroness. In her mind, she could already tabulate the palmed appearance fees at the regional hotels and restaurants. Meadows would be enormously happy at how Holly had managed to advertise Byzar's little ass before he and Elsa had even started their presentation of same. Holly mused to herself that she had already cleverly created a *soft opening* for Byzar's new career!

Dinny was even more reluctant now to go for a sail with a

princess than he was to go with a gypsy, and was wishing he could be somewhere else right at this time, but Holly pressed on, "Dinny, why don't you have a piece of pie and I'll introduce you to Byzar?"

"No ma'am, thank you, but I have to go." Dinny got up without stopping and spirited himself out the door before Holly could protest, but she called after him anyway and hollered, "Dinny, get yourself cleaned up and come back by this afternoon just before dinner so you two can meet, promise?"

Dinny turned and almost tripped off the bottom kitchen step and said, "Holly, do you really think it would be okay?"

"Dinny, you and I are friends. I would never do anything to hurt you. You just be yourself and you'll have a wonderful time. She may be royalty, but she still is just a girl, and she likes you. It can't be any simpler than that, now can it?"

Dinny stopped quivering and looked at Holly as a doe looks at his Momma for the first time and said, "I trust you, please…and if'n you are sure?"

"I am sure, my friend. The worst that can happen is that you and Byzar enjoy a sail together; you make ten bucks and bring me the information I need, that's the worst! As to the best, we'll leave that up to your imagination, correct?" Holly smiled as she leaned against the kitchen door frame.

Dinny just blushed and doffed his cap but before he could speak Holly said as she was retreating back into the kitchen, "Dinny, we'll see you this afternoon and clean the codfish off your hide, will ya'?" and she closed the door. She went straight to her desk window and from there she watched Dinny almost skip toward Featherbed Lane that led from the cove up to Shore Road, which he would take to get back to the Sparhawk. Byzar and Elsa had come into the room and

Elsa chuckled, "We heard the last part of that conversation, does Byzar have a date with that fool?"

Holly turned to both and giggled, "That fool is our new supplier of laudanum, opium and coke! He just doesn't know it yet! I'm also betting that by the time that young man returns here before dinner to meet the Sultana here, the whole town will know that she exists, so you see, I've just made your lives much easier!"

Elsa came over and gave Holly a big surprise kiss with her black lip-sticked lips, a deep tounge sucking kiss at that, and said, "You...young lady, are a real piece of work! You never miss an angle do you?" Elsa complimented, and as she did she stuck her left hand down Holly's underwear and quickly rubbed her vagina and continued, "It is quite evident that your fabulous little twat is only a backup plan in case your marvelously wicked brain happens to fail you!"

Elsa stepped back and touched her finger to her tongue and sniffed it and said, "I just wanted to see if my kiss had any effect, dear child! Oh, and I think it did!" she exclaimed.

"I'm still catching my breath Elsa; you always leak of passion, Madame. However, while the kiss was...interesting, my equipment is always armed and ready, I'll have you know. All a gent has to do is look at me sideways and I am already gushing down there!" She turned to Byzar and said, "Dinny is his name and he is going to take you for a sail tomorrow, so be sweet, please. He is going out to those schooners out there to find out if he can bring in the pharmaceuticals we require and enjoy. Rumor has it that those boats out on the rum line don't sell hooch only, comprende? He didn't want to go out tomorrow so I bribed him with your cute little butt, and no, you don't have to do anything but be your sweet little ol' self, although...we do want to keep that boy loyal to us! I'm sure you can handle things, my princess!" Holly gave her a playful shoulder punch.

Byzar patted the underside of her chin with the back of her hand and in her most regal tone said, "Since you are the slut, er, Madame of the house, this princess will do as you wish!" and Byzar curtsied as they all laughed and went to sit at the kitchen table.

"Hey Din, I had another stroke of genius last night!" Eben said as he emerged from their shed behind the Sparhawk. "I spoke with Mr. Woodbury yesterday and he agreed to let me build a shack out in front of his place on that bluff, ya' know the one I mean?"

"Didn't quite hear ya Eben, what's that you say?" Dinny replied.

Eben looked at his friend and said, "What's with you Din, you look like you've seen a ghost!"

Dinny slowed down his thoughts, put his hands in his coveralls and confessed, "Eben I'm just comin' back from Meadows place, is all."

"What happened this time Din? That place really gets to ya, don't it? Can't say as I blame ya, neither. You run into Holly again, I expect?"

"It ain't that Eben, she goes by Miss Meadows now and she practically runs the place."

"That's what I heard."

"You remember me talkin' about that gypsy gal that's always dancin' on the beach? Well Holly has it rigged up for me to take that gal for a sail tomorrow, on a date-like. I'm supposed to get cleaned up and go back to the cove before dinner and Holly is going to meet us up! I'm nervous as hell about it."

"Are ya' gonna do it Din?"

"I kinda promised I would. Aw, what the hell, Holly is payin' me ten bucks to take that gal; her name is Byzar by the way, for a sail tomorrow out to the rum line. I'm supposed to find out if Holly can buy laudanum n' such drugs out of the schooners. Says she and Meadows knocked heads with ol' Spenser up at the drugstore n' doesn't want to buy from him no more."

"Can't say as I disagree with Holly on that account, he is a kinda' surly gent. They've always been nice to me, though," Eben thought.

"Say Eben, did you know that Byzar was a princess or some such? Holly said she was known as a Sultana from wherever she comes from, and that she's had to hide ever since the war was over. Holly said she was spirited out of her country all secret-like 'cuz people were gonna kill her and her family. They're royalty or some such. Holly said Byzar has had to be kept in hiding but that soon it's going to be safe for her true identity to come out! Heck, Eben, I think I'm about to take a princess for a sail and a picnic! Oh, and Holly said that Byzar said that I was kinda a good lookin' gent. She better not be bullshittin' me or I'll piss in her hooch! Funny thing is, I am beginnin' to trust Holly, even though you n' she split... Me goin' on a date with a princess...,ain't that somethin'?"

Eben stood silent as he waited for his best friend to float back to earth and smiled, "Well don't stand here jawin' with me! You best get yourself over to my folks barn and grab a bar of lye and clean yourself up, so's you look pretty when you head back down to the cove. Heck I'll go with ya' and I'll lay out my Sunday clothes for ya' to wear if'n you want, while you wash your duds in the trough for tomorrow. I'm happy for ya' Din, I hope it works out for you better than it did with me n' Holly! Let's lock up the shed and I'll tell you about my plans to build a shack down by Woodbury's place, I think I got a lot of our deliverin' problems solved."

Mid-morning the next day found Valentine Meadows finally making an appearance out of his lair. He looked more miserable than he felt, but not by much. The little dark, curly-headed Robare had made an appearance last night around dinner and hugged his mother briefly, and had gone straight to bed. The boy's mother, Mrs. Parent, was none too pleased about the relationship between her boy, Meadows and her husband, who had acquiesced to the arrangement in the house, but knew she didn't have too much choice in the matter. Nonetheless, she was pleasant to Meadows in a forced kind of way, and still wondered if she would ever have the courage to start poisoning him for what he was doing to her son. On this morning however, she could truly see for the first time that Meadows was doing a fine job of poisoning himself on occasions that were becoming more and more frequent. She correctly assumed that whatever drugs Meadows was using, they were the likely cause for Robare to also be feeling poorly last night. She vowed to insist that her husband demand that Meadows stop feeding drugs into her son. She already knew however, that her insistence to her husband would be cast aside regardless.

Holly smiled and they both had a cup of tea. Finally Meadows mumbled, "Thank you, for whatever you did. I have truly never been that scared in my life. Am I still at risk?"

"I handled it Valentine. It's over, you can relax. I wrote the cop a check for one thousand dollars. I'll tell you the details when you wish, if you like?" Holly said in a very peaceful tone.

"Should I know, Holly?" Meadows wondered.

"The cop was a fool, of course, and wanted more, of course. But when he cashes the check, and he will, we will have the police in our pocket as long as he is around, and we can do as we wish. We'll manage him just like we do the others. He'll likely show up every now and again, most likely drunk, and one of us will fuck him and all will be right with the world. He really wasn't very bright, Valentine. Like I say, it's handled. You look like the surf drug you in along the rocks; can I bring you something up to your room? Elsa has the school humming along, Byzar has already quietly been announced as a princess around town, and I'll find out tomorrow if we can purchase our drugs from the schooners laying up out on the rum line. I'm going to go to the post office and get your mail and spend the rest of the day reading it," she said with a chuckle. "Once you are back to your loveable wicked old self, I'll show you the reservation list for the rest of the summer at the school. Two new girls are arriving tomorrow, Smithies both, and I'll turn them over to Elsa once they understand and agree to their duties. I've read their letters and think that both seem excited to get out of their pantalettes!"

"I think I'm going to puke...again, excuse me Holly, and please, carry on," Meadows whispered as he rose to gain the stairs with all the unsteadiness in his marrow. Holly thought, "He'll be useless for a couple days at least. And I thought that Sergeant Drake was an idiot! What a fool you are Valentine, what a fool!"

Holly was just finishing her tea when she heard Meadows close his bedroom door. She watched Mrs. Parent cut some onions for the lunch spread for the school. Holly asked, "How is Robare feeling Madame, he did not look well last night?"

The woman, salt and pepper black hair tied into a bun, wearing a simple blue cotton dress that buttoned down the back, stopped her slicing. Her shoulders shook, and tears, helped along by the onions, began to drip from her cheeks.

"He is my only child, I cannot have more. My husband prefers the company of a man. My son is a girl. I am dead inside," the woman said simply.

Holly started to get out of her chair, but the woman, same vintage as Elsa, waved her knife behind her shoulder warning Holly away. Holly sat back down and Mrs. Parent's tears continued to drip on the cutting board, intermingling with the heap of sliced onions. Just then a boy no older than fourteen appeared at the screened kitchen door and peered through, pressing his nose against the screen accidentally, "Good day, is there a Miss Meadows here, please?" Even at such a young age, the boy could sense the emotion in the air, and sheepishly pulled away and stood stock still. Mrs. Parent grabbed her apron in both hands after setting the knife down and wiped her eyes, which was a mistake due to the onion juice, let out a soft whimper and left the kitchen through the back doorway into the small room that she shared with her husband and son, when he wasn't sleeping with Meadows. Holly waved the boy into the kitchen as she got up and reached for a small towel that doubled as an oven mitt and dabbed her welled up eyes with it. Putting on a quick smile, she said, "How may I help you young man, I am Miss Meadows. Who are you?"

The boy nervously stepped just inside the door and barely caught the spring door he had lost grip of just before it slammed.

"Nice catch," smiled Holly, which seemed to put the boy at ease somewhat.

"Uh, Mr. Spenser sent me over from the drugstore. He said to tell you that he is sorry that he couldn't make it yesterday, but that if you give me a list of what you're needin', he'd be happy to fill your order," the boy said in a clearly rehearsed manner.

"Did he now," said Holly, still smiling at the boy who she was sure that was close to wetting his pants out of nervousness. "Please have a seat young man, while I fetch a pad and paper. Help yourself to a piece of pie over there on the counter if you like?"

"Uh no ma'am, thank you ma'am. Mr. Spenser said I should go and come back quick-like," the boy said.

"Did he now," Holly smiled, as she rose from her chair, purposefully letting her white chamois robe part a bit to flash him a bit of breast, a sight he'd likely never before seen. "I'm sure he's not keeping time young man," she said as she tightened her robe and put her hand on his shoulder and continued, "You haven't told me your name yet, and my, my, you surely are a handsome young man."

He could feel her sensuous touch through his shirt even though he had no idea what he was feeling, but Holly's scent also made him noticeably quiver, which Holly could feel under her touch.

"My name is Russell, er, Miss Meadows," he stammered as

114

he looked up at Holly, who was purposefully standing too close for the young man's comfort.

"Well it's very nice to meet you Russell, and I'll be back in a few minutes with my list, and I am glad that you are happy to see me also," she said as she directed her eyes briefly toward the erection evident in Russell's pants, in a manner that the teen instinctively caught on to, and blushed beet red. She seductively removed her hand from his shoulder and appeared to accidently brush his face with her finger as she began to step toward the dining room, calling after, "Russell, if a piece of pie doesn't interest you, why don't you follow me and you can look at some of the paintings our artists produce?" She looked over her shoulder at the red-faced boy and continued, "Are you in Mr. Spenser's congregation, honey?"

"Yes ma'am, he's our preacher when our regular isn't about" he replied.

"That's nice Russell, follow me and tell me what you think of what you see...of the paintings," she coyly suggested. As Holly headed off through the dining room into her open office, she thought to herself, "I wonder if I can make the little turd come in his pants?"

The teenager had made his way into the dining room while Holly took a seat at her desk and began writing. She could see that he was trying to hide his unfortunately persistent erection without much success, and was entirely embarrassed about it, when Holly asked, "Russell, what do you think of that painting of the woman washing her hair?" directing her gaze toward a sketch by one of the new artists to arrive at the school, that the boy was clearly trying not to be caught staring at.

"That sketch was done by a gentleman from France, who is

not much older than you are, do you like it, Russell?" she persisted.

"It's nice...I guess. I, uh, don't know much about paintings, ma'am," he said in as convincing a voice as he could find.

Holly put down her pencil and folded her list as she rose from her chair, while Russell again tried to shift his body away so his erection in his pants wasn't overly obvious, which unfortunately for him, it was. Holly handed the boy her list and deftly moved behind him and grabbed him by the shoulders almost forcing him to stare directly at the painting of the naked woman washing her hair. "I think her hips are too big, and her nipples are too small for the size of her boobies, don't you Russell?"

The boy's dark brown hair was already moist with the discomfort of being in the spot where he found himself, and almost whimpered, "I don't rightly know," and let out a small cough to clear his now waterless throat.

"Well you have been with a girl before haven't you Russell? I mean a young man as handsome as you must be very popular with the girls, aren't you?" Holly said as she dipped her smiling face over the boys shoulder so as to look at him from the side.

"Cat got your tongue? Tell me Russell, does the painting make you uncomfortable in its style, or just because it is of a naked woman? Does that painting of the almost naked man make you uncomfortable also," Holly whispered as she rotated the boy's body to another painting across the room. "It's funny how the world is Russell, isn't it?"

By now the teenager had both hands in his pockets attempting to discreetly relieve the pressure against his zipper so it wouldn't be obvious, except it was far too late for that. Holly continued to torment the boy by matter-of-factly stating, "You know in some places in the world that painting of the woman is so admired that it hangs in a museum, and in some places in the world it is shunned and despised, like it would be in yours and Mr. Spenser's church don't you think?"

"That's true," the boy almost whined, as Holly gently moved him closer to the painting until they were only a few feet away from it.

"Can you feel its texture?" Holly said as she slowly eased the boys hand out of his right pocket. His whole body was boiling red and Holly guided his hand onto the surface of the painting, as she gently rested her chin on the boy's shoulder and said, "How can a person truly appreciate the human form without touching it?" as she slowly guided his smaller hand over the textures that the dried paint formed on the canvas. He was almost crying by this point.

"Does the painting still make you uncomfortable, Russell, or is it my breathing or is it in your pants? You don't want me to stop breathing do you?"

"No ma'am"

"Then why don't you unzip your zipper and be more comfortable?" Holly cooed.

She could see the peach fuzz on his cheeks and he finally turned his head slightly to look at her with an innocent astonishment as she guided his hand down to his zipper. Holly pushed her pelvis into his buttocks with just enough pressure to initiate small uncontrollable gyrations in his hips, when she whispered, "Use both hands Russell, and it looks like you'll need them."

He unzippered himself and let out a distinct sigh as his penis reached for the cool air, as he almost stumbled. He stood there with his hands not knowing what to do, his hips thrusting a little and his pecker flexing and releasing. Holly found his right hand again and slowly made him encircle his penis and encouraged him to begin stroking. Already the first glint of fluid was dripping out of his tip and after a few strokes Holly said, "You probably want me to take over don't you?"

The boy who was leaning most of his weight back against Holly by now, imperceptibly nodded as she grabbed him and had him squirting all over the painting within only a few seconds as he effectually went blind. His gasps and breathing were beyond control and when he regained his composure a few moments later, his first words to Holly were, "Thank you, uh, is the painting ruined?" as he let out a chuckle.

Holly smiled at him again as she wiped her hand on his pants, and said, "I think it is art, what do you think, Russell? I mean, shouldn't every naked woman be covered in a man's come at some point?"

He was about to reply when a voice from behind interrupted, "I most wholeheartedly agree!" as both turned to see Valentine Meadows with his pants around his ankles finishing himself off with a relieved smile. "That was exquisite you two! I'll remember your performance as long as I live! Stay right there," he said as he quickly pulled his feet through his pants and discarded them. He grabbed one of the cloth dinner napkins from the nearby hutch and walked over to Holly, who was still embracing the boy and kissed Holly as he wrapped the napkin around the boys' semi erect penis before the boy could react, and began drying it off. He released Holly and continued to stroke the boy and said, "Young man, do you like girls?"

Russell nodded, still unsure of having a man touch his

118

privates, but what Meadows was doing did feel kind of good.

"Well since this is an afternoon of discovery, you may as well feel the delights of a woman, would you agree?" He nodded for Holly to drop her robe, which she did as she took Russell's hand and brought it to her vagina. This brought an immediate reaction and as the now naked Holly brought her mouth closer to the boy, Meadows immediately dropped to his knees to attend to Russell with his mouth. As soon as the boy was again stiff Meadows reached for Holly to step over and he slid a chair over for Russell to sit on and Holly straddled him as she brought his hands to her chest. While Holly rode him, Meadows brought one of Russell's hands to his own member and stroked himself with it. By this time Russell didn't care if his hand was swimming in a beehive.

He didn't last long.

As soon as Russell was obviously spent, Meadows aimed for the boys' face, which surprisingly did not appear to faze him in the least. Holly stepped off and brought her left breast down to wipe some of the come off Russell's face and feed it to the boy with her nipple, while Meadows brought his mouth back down to the boy's crotch and cleaned him off with his mouth. After a few moments Holly straightened, kissed the boy again and reached down to put her robe back on. Meadows finished what he was doing, stood up and handed Russell the napkin and went back over to the dining table to put his pants back on. Russell in turn, stood up and pulled up his pants also.

Holly tightened the belt of her robe and said, "Do you think you can come back with our order for Mr. Spenser this afternoon, Russell?"

"Order, uh, yea, right, um, yes I will, I mean I'll try, if, um Mr. Spenser will give it to me," he said as his wits were returning. He was all jumbled up inside now.

Meadows walked over to the boy and put his arm around him, which the boy initially shied from but then didn't want to appear unappreciative of what had just happened to him for the past half hour or so.

Holly asked, "Russell, I'll tell you what, if Mr. Spenser can't fill out our complete order today, would you please hurry back here to tell me? That way I can make other arrangements. If he can, ask him to send the bill with the order and I will pay when you bring it, so you can take the money back to Mr. Spenser, and I, of course, will pay the delivery fee also. Does that sound okay by you?" as she and Meadows led him back to the kitchen door.

"Yes ma'am, I think I understand," as he stepped through the door.

"A pleasure to meet you young man," Meadows called out as he extended his hand.

Russell turned quickly to acknowledge, but turned on his heel when he saw Meadows hand in the air, and walked back over to shake it. "My name is Mr. Meadows, and yours is Russell, correct?"

"Yes sir, Russell. A pleasure to meet you also, sir" the boy said with a slight hesitation.

"A distinct and unforgettable pleasure for all of us I hope?" Meadows said as both he and Holly smiled.

"Yes sir, and ma'am, it, uh, was very, uh, thank you, uh, I'll be back as soon as I, uh, can," Russell said as he retreated and nodded, and finally after stumbling on a rock, took off toward the path that led past Oarweed Cove and the fishermen's shacks.

Holly and Meadows stood in the doorway arm in arm and gazed after the retreating boy and then turned their attention to the matronly ladies dressed in full length skirts working at their easels across the cove at the Woodbury school, who quickly averted their glances away from Holly and Meadows and back to their easels.

"They don't all appear to be as engrossed in their work as they'd like to have us think, do they Holly?" Meadows whispered.

"I am sure it is difficult for a woman to concentrate when she is frustrated and perpetually horny," Holly giggled as she purposefully tried to catch the direct eye contact of some of the women across the cove, to no avail.

"That was certainly a surprise and wonderful elixir for me, as you might imagine my dear, I am getting a bit bored with Robare and I was thinking about fresh meat and, voila, you bring a lamb to the barn! I am truly amazed at how smart I was to hire you!" he said while chuckling while closing the kitchen door.

"I'm feeling so much better, so I think I am going to bathe and then make an appearance down at the school. What is your afternoon looking like?" Meadows inquired.

"I think I will clean up also and then spend most of the afternoon at my desk. I have some reservations for the school to confirm, the grocery list to review for Mrs. Parent and our account book to balance while waiting for Russell to come back. Tonight I might go to Portland, I'm thinking," Holly replied.

"Have you ever been to Portland, Holly? I didn't know you had friends up there," Meadows wondered.

"I have never been there, Val, but I am going to take a break for a day and wander around up there and see the sights," Holly said.

"Do you have enough money for your trip? Do you know

which hotel you will stay at? I can certainly write a short letter of introduction for you to some of the houses I am familiar with," Meadows offered.

"Actually Val, I have very limited funds to go with and as to a hotel room, I doubt I'll need the tariff. I need to do some serious, and I mean some serious, fucking—especially after this morning's activities. I intend to find some brute that is insatiable, and then I'm probably good for the next few weeks. What we do here in Ogunquit is fine and for the most part enjoyable, but every now and then a girl wants to be the one that gets pleasured, rather than the other way around all the time. Does that make sense a bit?"

Meadows headed for the stairs and said, "I wish I could be there to watch, you little minx! Enjoy yourself immensely, you have certainly earned it. Take one hundred dollars out of the house account for yourself. Consider it a bonus for doing such a good job!"

Holly legitimately blushed and said, "That really means a lot, Valentine, I mean it really does. Thank you very much."

He smiled and headed up to his lair and Holly dabbed her eyes with the sleeve of her robe and thought, "This is sooo much easier than I ever thought it would be. By the end of the summer I am truly going to own his pathetic little ass, if I don't already!"

By the time Holly got out of the house, the artists, models and students were wandering into the dining room for the evening meal. Holly was dressed in a simple blue gingham dress with an Indian red button down sweater, and carried an oversized purse that contained a fresh set of underwear as well as other essentials. She shared a few words with Mrs. Parent, and nodded toward Byzar who had just strolled into the dining room, who with her eyes, wondered where Holly was going. Holly finished her conversation with the woman, stole another glance toward Byzar, who seemed truly hurt by not knowing where Holly was about, and closed the door behind her. She was already anticipating meeting a new lover and scratching the itch that the earlier encounter with Meadows and the boy had simply teased and frustrated her appetite. It had been almost three weeks since she had serviced a client and she hadn't been this dormant for this long for many years. She stood at the top of the steps and gazed across the cove to see how many of the Woodbury artists remained at that time of the day, and unexpectedly stared straight into the eyes of her ex-boyfriend and lover, Eben. Their eyes held for a few moments but neither of them showed any sign of acknowledgement. Holly thought she detected an imperceptible wave from the shirtless Eben, as he had just laid down a shoulder load of true-dimension eight foot wooden studs destined for his new cabin. She could see the sweat glisten on his trim and fit torso and she smiled and doffed her yellow wide-brimmed summer hat and stepped down the stairs. She picked her way along the trail that led to the shacks and Featherbed Lane and as soon as she found the flat and stable earth she set her bag down as if to adjust its contents, but really doing so to sneak another peek at Eben, just to see if he was looking, which he was.

She thought to wave and was still undecided when thinking, "Hmmm, I wonder if he can tell that I am off to be with another man, and I wonder if that would still make him mad. It probably would, in fact I know it would hurt him, but

I'm not a vindictive gal, so I won't wave; I'm not that mean."

Some of the older fishermen were setting around Cap'n Al's shack repairing nets and splicing lines as she approached, so she boldly took a few steps toward their upturned barrels and traps and said, "My, my, is there always such a collection of handsome gentlemen sitting around here at this time of the day?"

Al piped up, "Lass, if you told us ahead of time when you'd come by for a visit, I could post it on my door and we'd have to find extra chairs for the event! Where you goin' Miss Holly, or do we have to call you Miss Meadows like Dinny does?"

She took a few steps closer to Al and swooped down and planted a huge kiss right on his smacker, to the astonishing delight of the group, and Al almost fell over backwards collecting his wits. As Holly turned to head on her way, she called over her shoulder, "Cap'n Al, you have permission to call me anything you like, mostly because I understand that you already do!" She made an exaggerated wink toward Al and she and the others laughed uproariously as she heard one of them call out, "Missy, by gawd I think you're purely somethin'! No one has ever shut Al's trap as long as I've known im'!" They all guffawed while the crimson continued to pour into Al's jowls.

"Hey girl," the one called Bish shouted after her, "we surely appreciate the light," nodding toward the streetlight.

Holly turned and called out, "It was long overdue, I'll see you gents tomorrow, and Cap'n Al...," she hesitated for effect under their now rapt attention, "you might have gotten a lot more than a kiss if you'd take a bath every now and then!" which brought another round of uproarious laughter from the group, as well as a new shot of crimson up into Cap'n Al's befuddled face. Holly was on a roll and for kicks, and being true to form, she turned on her heel and waved to Eben, knowing he would be watching, and he was.

As Holly disappeared onto Shore Rd., someone in the group of fishermen that spied that brief interplay said, "I don't know whether Eben is the biggest fool on earth for letting that gal go, or the smartest bloke in the world for doing so. That gal is enough to put a good man in an early grave either by screwing him to death or tormenting him to hell, which my bet is that is where that gal is heading anyway."

Cap'n Al's blood pressure was finally settled as he said, "That is a fact. Can't help but feel bad for Eben though, but bein' fucked to death by that gal might be a fine way to go!" and they all nodded in agreement while passing around another round of Boston Ale for all.

"What I can't figure out," Al continued, "is why the heck would Eben build his new place right across the cove where he can see that gal carryin' on with other fellas? Talk about settin' yourself up to be tormented…yeesh!"

The blond mustached Bish said, "Well we all know why he's settin' his place on the bluff. It will make his bootleggin' business a lot easier, in fact, easier for all of us 'cuz he'll be able to keep tabs on the revenue boys! Dinny says that he's gonna rig up a light for all of us to see when the Fed boys are out n' about. That kid is always thinkin' and I'm purely glad he's on our side. I expect he's smart enough that he knew he was settin' himself up for some serious anguish, knowin' he'd be seein' that Holly gal bein' pestered by them men folk over to Meadows place, but he prob'ly weighed that against the business advantage of doing so. Makin' the kind of money he and Din are makin' silent-like prob'ly will take the sting outta seein' his ex-girlfriend continually bent over the porch railing."

"Still gotta hurt some," one of the others contributed, and they all nodded and took another swig.

Holly reached the top of the hill that brought her level with the village and sat down on a boulder for a good cry, making sure no one was paying attention. For a brief moment she considered walking back around the marsh and confronting Eben. She knew she had hurt him by her performance at Al's, and instinctively regretted it before she again hardened herself. She thought, "What am I thinking, dammit! He should be running after me begging me to come back to him. C'mon Holly, get your head right. He had his shot to grow up and be a man, but he just didn't have the balls for it....he does have cute balls though..." She chortled at that thought, took a deep breath and stood up to catch a hack up to Wells and then the train up to Portland. She'd be in the city in a few hours and stroll into any bar or tavern she damn well chose to, despite the laws and society. Then she'd be approached by countless men, and she would make her choice for her own devices. She had no intention of paying for a single drink, meal, nor for a hotel room. She pondered, "Some good looking fool of a man was going to pay dearly for my charms on this night, and I am going to enjoy myself immensely! Damn Eben to hell, he had his chance; now I'm going to get laid right."

As she boarded the hack she shared with a young mother and her son, she breathed in the wafts from the wharfs down along the Ogunquit River and smiled with a great deal of satisfaction.

As the hack pulled out and gained speed to make the first hill out of town, an out-of-breath man broke through the crowd at the station and spied the hack just as it cleared the hill.

It was Eben.

"Plans have changed Elsa, what do you think about Byzar's debutante ball, as it were, being held right here in Ogunquit?" Meadows asked.

"Sooner the better is my thought, darling," Elsa replied.

"It seems that Holly has arranged for the proverbial beans to be spilled and has set the table for quite an event. I spoke with her this afternoon after she returned from Portland and she proposes that the 4th of July dinner at the Sparhawk is the perfect occasion to have some politician or preacher give a speech about how the United States assisted in protecting our young Sultana from the forces of evil back in the old country, and saved her life and honor, blah, blah, blah. Such an event will certainly stoke the nationalistic tendencies of all concerned, and we can invite all the appropriate gentlemen over to our studios for a nightcap, as it were, and keep our models busy 'til dawn. It might be our most financially rewarding night of the year!" Meadows purred.

"Our little Holly came up with this idea on her own, I'll bet. Val, that girl is putting us to shame with her deviousness, and I'm almost scared about it. Not really though, but I tell you that I am surely glad that she is on our side! And she's only beginning! Imagine what she'll have in store for us by the end of the summer!" Elsa exclaimed.

"She has earned my every confidence, but I assure you that I'll keep my tabs on her lusty little soul. As of now I am as at peace with life as I have ever been, and the daily humdrum details not being on my plate anymore has surely helped my bearing. My artistic efforts are reinvigorated for the summer, and I thank Holly for that in some manner. How is your training of our little Sultana progressing?" Meadows inquired.

"Byzar is simply regal. We have had her practicing her table manners and when the two new models showed up last night, Byzar had them both completely in her clutches, genuflecting to the last. All at the table were quite impressed; she'll pull it off just fine. She also took the two girls from Smith College aside, Lesley the bright-eyed one and Lauren the tall slender one, and provided instructions for how they were expected to conduct themselves. Both seemed very excited to explore their womanhood, Lesley by far the more adventurous. Lauren, the tall one is still a virgin but vows to cure that disease before the weekend. I am sure that we can take advantage of her condition at least a dozen times. I'll let Holly know that we have a cherry for sale and it will bring a handsome price."

"Did I hear we have an actual maiden in our midst?" Holly asked as she entered the dining room in a white terrycloth robe, carrying a steaming mug of tea. She had obviously just awakened after sleeping off her adventures in Portland the night before, and though she looked a bit haggard, she had a certain glow about her aura and was obviously refreshed in some manner.

"Well it figures that the only virgin in our island of sluts would be a Smithy," Holly chuckled. Only Meadows recognized the collegial competition amongst the small institutions of the northeast. Elsa just smiled. Holly slid into a chair at the table and caressed her mug as her robe billowed open just enough to reveal her left breast.

"What time did you get in, dear?" Elsa asked.

"I came in just before the sun, so I've had only a few hours of sleep, but I feel quite refreshed. Do we still have all our models aboard for the 4th? It falls a week from Sunday, doesn't it?"

Both Elsa and Valentine nodded.

"Is Byzar ready, Elsa?"

"It's like she was born for the role, Holly. Val and I will have a list of guests for you to contact by this afternoon. You, Byzar and I, and perhaps some of the other gals will get together in the morning and write the invitations, how does that sound?" Elsa asked.

"Sounds like a girl party at sunrise! What fun! I'll track down Byzar after I get dressed and see how her adventure out to the rum line went when she gets back from her big date! I left a note on the druggist's door when I came through town this morning requesting that he make a visit, since our new young boyfriend, Russell, didn't make it back yesterday afternoon. We should have our happy juice issue resolved by this afternoon, then I can put my full attention towards next weekend's festivities for the 4th of July, unless either of you have other tasks for me?"

"No Holly, I think the 4th should be our focus, don't you Elsa?" Meadows inquired.

"I agree. My focus will be getting our models in top form for the extended weekend. I will pay particular attention to our new maiden, so she'll be most accommodating by the weekend. I might have to recruit some of the local boys for a few freebies, but opium works wonders for a young woman's virtue!" Elsa mused.

"Always worked for me," Holly contributed, "and

Valentine, did you ever hire that little local boy Richard; the one who hangs around with Robare?"

"Little Richard was not very compliant, I'm afraid, which of course only heightens my focus. He ran off before I could get him into his skivvies, but I have full faith in candy, human nature and opium. He'll wander back in time. He has a sweet mouth, that one, indeed," Meadows opined.

"Do you think it wise, Valentine?" Holly asked with due caution for her newfound position vying with genuine concern for the little boy whom she truly liked. "I mean messing with a local child carries much more risk than a one night poke with some kid who is only here for a few days with his parents, don't you think?" Holly said, hoping that Meadows would consider her statement without emotion.

"Are you overstepping your bounds young lady?" Meadows stated as tension immediately filled the room.

"Of course not Val, I meant nothing of the kind!" Holly said with a hopeful chuckle. "We operate here on a very thin tightrope with both the law and the community, and you well know the waters are treacherous. All I am asking, repeat asking, is to let us consider our course that we sail. I handled the cops the other day, but like you, it scared me to the point of puking just after they left, though I hid it well. Ass is ass, to a degree, is it not?" she wondered.

Meadows exploded away from the table in a violent fit never witnessed by neither Elsa, nor Holly, and it scared them both to the point of welled up eyes. Holly was sure she had crossed the proverbial line, and her life that had just been greatly improved with her new position, was now likely terminated. The scowl that the red-faced Meadows directed at Holly was murderous, and he maintained it for a few seconds while neither Holly, nor Elsa, dared to breathe. Meadows vacant, icy blue eyes bored holes into her being. He turned and stepped to the staircase and as he put his hand on the banister, his shoulders slumped a bit as he looked at his feet for a moment before whispering, "Please forgive me, ladies, especially you Holly. You are of course correct, but I am afraid the deed has already been done, twice. If the boy comes around again, well then he does. I won't make further entreaties toward that end however, and we'll hope that it passes without any disruption from the locals."

Both women, almost sobbing, rose to join Meadows with a group hug, and Meadows kissed them both on their foreheads and apologized again, especially to Holly who was visibly shaking by this point.

"You are both doing wonderful work, and I don't want to consider life without either of you," Meadows whispered as he began to climb the stairs. He stopped after the first few steps and said without turning his head, "I'll have you know, that I never buggered the little fellow, though I almost tried. I gave both boys the same dosage of laudanum in their lemonade and Robare was a fine instructor for little Richard in the art of fellatio, so I couldn't resist. Perhaps Holly, you can begin to secure some young talent from the tourist trade?" Meadows wondered as he again began to climb the stairs to his lair.

Holly called after him, declaring, "You can count on it, Sir Meadows."

Holly went back to the table and let out a sob of relief as Elsa rubbed her shoulders from behind while kissing the top of her head with motherly comfort.

"I almost blew it, didn't I Elsa?" she questioned.

"It had to be said, my dear, and you were very brave to do so. I'll be sure to emphasize that fact when the time is right with Valentine. He and I go back quite a ways and I know he realizes that you are correct. Sometimes I guess like all addicts, he just can't stop himself even if it means his own destruction. That said, and while we are on such a subject, we might have another problem with the police," Elsa cautioned.

"Oh shit," Holly said as she was drying her eyes. "Now what?"

Elsa smiled and sat down across from Holly and began, "Well dear, our young Japanese painter, the one we call YaYa, seems to have found himself a young local girl he paid to pose for him without most of her clothes in her family's barn. To make a long story short he was discovered by some of the girl's family and our young man barely made it back here with his life. His easel, paint and brushes I imagine are all with the police, and God knows how far he got on his canvas. If he got too far, they are going to come for him, and I am not sure we can protect him at this point. He is hiding in his room but I doubt that will do him much good. Do you want to talk to him?"

"No, I doubt if there is anything I could say at this point. Does Val know?" Holly asked.

"Well if he doesn't, I'm sure he will be told sometime today," Elsa said.

"Is somebody with him, he is a horny little gent isn't he?"

"Oh he most certainly is. He is insatiable, but then again what 20 year old boy isn't; homo or otherwise?" Elsa chuckled.

"All right, I'll think of something. I might have to actually have to flop around with that Sergeant Drake after all, dammit. Does anyone know where the girl lives, maybe a visit to the family might be the angle to take the coppers out of it? I'll bet Dinny will know. Have he and Byzar already left on their date?"

"Yes. They left before you awakened. Anyway I have to head down to the studios and put in an appearance. I'm quite glad that I am not you on this day, my sweet, and don't worry, I'll have a chat with Valentine about his proclivities, okay love?" Elsa said as she rose.

Holly grabbed Elsa's hand and kissed the back of it in earnest and looked deep into the woman's eyes and said, "Thank you Elsa, so very much." Elsa nodded and smiled as she headed for the kitchen, leaving Holly with her thoughts of both relief of the stress of potentially sabotaging her position with Meadows, but also knowing that if the police showed, there was likely nothing she could do to stop them from searching the entire facility. Holly knew that they would turn up enough alcohol and drugs to close the school and put Meadows, and whoever else they chose to, behind bars for long enough to ruin everyone's dreams. She stared into her cold, half filled tea mug and vowed to herself, "I've got to get to them before they get to here, and I can't wait on Byzar."

Holly hurried up to her room to get changed and just before getting to the stairs, quickly went to her desk and peered out her window toward the fishing shacks to see if anyone was about, and thankfully there was some activity. She needed to speak with Captain Sunker before she left and reminded herself to grab a pint of the good stuff from the storeroom.

"Good afternoon, my handsome Captain!" Holly exclaimed as she approached the portly, scruffy-faced gent.

"Here comes trouble fer sure," the smirking Captain announced to the cool breeze, as well as any of the fishermen lounging around fixing their nets or splicing rope.

"Trouble never looked so fine," someone called out.

Holly never broke stride as she slid over an overturned bucket to sit on. She was wearing a simple blue bib style dress that buttoned down the back and reached to her lower calf just above her socks. Under the dress she wore a light brown long sleeve cotton shirt with buttons down the front. Her wide brimmed hat was made of simple straw with a blue sash. The Captain wore his wash-once-a-month outfit of a stained olive nightshirt tucked into his black jeans with a broken zipper, held up by overtaxed black suspenders. His small ivory pipe was never far from his remaining tobacco stained teeth, and his brown sweat stained Irish paddy cap was glued to his scalp.

"I'm glad you are here Captain, might we have a chat?" Holly said as she sat down after knocking the dust off the bottom of the pail by clanging the edge on the ground.

"Sure Missy. How come we don't see you posin' on the rocks anymore? That's somethin' I could sell tickets for ya' know?" he chuckled.

"What would be my cut?" Holly countered, not missing a beat. "Are you going to be here for the rest of the day, neighbor?" she asked.

"I expect so, Missy, why do you ask?"

"How about calling me Holly? Every time you call me Missy, I wonder if there is a gal behind me, fair enough?" Holly cooed.

"Fair enough Holly darlin'. What's on yer mind?"

Not letting on that the police could come marching down the lane at any moment, Holly steadied herself and asked, "I'm thinking of opening a small shop, Captain, one that sells tobacco, among other things. Do you think it would be profitable?"

Sunker replied, "Well I don't think you'd make a million,

but as long as the prices weren't too dear, I think you'd make a go of er'! Especially if you staffed it with your lounging beauties—different one each day!"

"Why Captain, what a famous idea! You've won first prize!" Holly exclaimed as she reached into her purse and handed the portly man a small corked bottle of high-grade moonshine. "I was thinking we might sell some of this stuff under the table whilst we were at it!"

The Captain shifted his straddled feet just a bit so as to split his butt cheeks a little more and appraised the young woman for a few moments before stating in a knowing, amused tone, "Okay Holly, you threw out the bait, and I'm hooked right through the eye. Dang but aren't you a clever one. What do you really want of me, now that I'm danglin' off yer' stringer?"

Holly paused for a moment and grinned, "Aw Captain, you are much too wise, but the store is really an idea that I think we'll do. However, I do have a situation that I need your help with. I am on my way up to Wells to visit the police, but if they should come by before I get there, could you intercept them and tell them that I have everything they seek with me. I am meeting a gent in town and accompanying him to the station," Holly lied, but continued. "My hope is that our school will not be disrupted during my absence."

"I'm happy to relay the message should the greenies wander by, but I doubt if I can stop them if they're determined," the Captain stated earnestly.

"I know Cap, but if you relay the information as I've described, they might turn around and meet me there, for I will wait for their return if I happen to miss them. Please relay that information also, would you?" Holly asked as she got up to leave.

135

"I'll do my best Holly, and thanks for the, uh, bait," Sunker said as he raised and fingered the little bottle. As Holly turned to leave Sunker cleared his throat and nervously called after her, "Hey Holly, please wait for a moment." Holly paused as Captain Sunker rose from his seat and stepped toward the girl kind of sheepishly and nervously cleared his throat and said, "Uh Holly, ya' know, uh, watchin' you gals out there on the rocks can get to a fella, uh, I mean, uh, I'm a wonderin', if, uh…"

"Captain, say no more, I'll arrange it if you promise to clean yourself up, no offense intended, understand?" Holly said. "Let me deal with my little police issue first and I'll see what I can do. We'll keep this our little secret, agreed?"

Holly playfully poked the man in the belly and turned to head toward town, but not before peeking across the cove to see if Eben was working on his cabin, but he wasn't.

"How long does it usually take to reach those beautiful ships in the distance, Mr. Dinny?" Byzar asked as she arranged her dress while sitting in the stern of the freshly washed dory.

"Well ma'am it depends on the tide, the current and the winds, as well as if we row or sail the whole way," Dinny nervously replied. Byzar had met Dinny on the porch the night previous for a few moments while everyone was gathering for the evening meal. Byzar had asked if Dinny would like to join the group for dinner but he had quickly declined, stating that he had to be at work as the security guard at the Sparhawk, which was a lie. He was just too nervous around females, especially one as attractive as this little bundle of energy of a Sultana, which he considered on the level of being a princess. He was not far off, if Byzar actually were a Sultana, rather than an entity conjured up by Meadows and the Baroness. The hicks from Maine would never know, nor would any have the gumption to do any research on the matter.

Dinny half stumbled off the porch after agreeing to bring his dory by at whichever time Byzar had chosen, which was anytime between 7-9am, Sultana standard time. Byzar was learning her new craft, and being appropriately late was part of the charade. Dinny had his dory drug up the rocks as far as the tide continually would allow. He had been there for almost forty-five minutes before Byzar appeared on the landing of the kitchen steps holding a small lunch basket in one hand, and a frilly off-white parasol in the other. She wore a small blue bonnet tied under her hair, which matched the simple blue dress over full-length white pantaloons. Dinny scrambled up the rocks to meet her and said, "Good morning Miss Sultana Byzar," at which Byzar let out a small giggle while thinking to herself, 'what a boob. He's probably a crappy fuck also, but at least it is a beautiful, clear day.'

"Good morning Dinny, you look very handsome today!" To which Dinny clearly blushed.

She held out the basket and kept her hand in place as he grabbed the basket and turned toward the dory, only to catch himself before stepping and saying, "Sorry Ma'am," as he then joined her hand and led her off the steps.

Dinny was incredibly nervous, and was carefully measuring each step in the hopes he would not stumble, which unfortunately, he did often. As they neared the dory, which was now in the dry due to the receding tide, Byzar spoke up with a reassuring smile, "Dinny, please, take a breath will you? My name is Byzar, yours is Dinny. I am a woman, you are a man. We have a beautiful boat, calm seas and a bright sunny day. Mrs. Parent packed us a fine lunch and we'll have a splendid morning at the very worst. Is this worth all your fretting, you handsome devil?"

Dinny was completely disarmed and let out a substantial breath of air. He actually bent over and hung his head for a moment before smiling up at Byzar as he stowed the basket.

"Thank you Byzar. I don't know when I've ever been so nervous. That was very kind of you. Let me get the boat in the water and we'll figure out how to get you in. You mind getting your feet wet?" he asked.

"Actually Dinny I'd prefer to stay dry for now. Would you be a gentleman and carry me, you sure look to be strong enough!"

Dinny pushed the bow into the water, stowed the oars and raised the mast and laid the boom lashed with the sail to the side. He stowed the tiller in the bow and lashed the rudder so it couldn't sway. He approached Byzar expecting her to jump on his back as was customary, but she would have none of that. As soon as Dinny got close enough she wrapped her left arm around his neck and snuggled her face into the crook of his neck, and proceeded to jump into his chest, forcing him to catch her with his hand under the back of her knees. This flustered Dinny greatly and as he stumbled along the twenty foot length to the dory, he was overwhelmed by her feminine scent and hormonal aura. He gently set her feet down in the stern in front of the bench seat just forward of the transom and waited a few moments until it was clear that she was settled. Byzar kept her parasol closed and smiled at Dinny and remarked, "Well that was fun, wasn't it?"

Dinny, feeling somewhat more emboldened nodded, and chuckled to the wind, "All aboard!" hoping that Byzar would at least giggle, and was quite relieved when she did so in earnest. He gave a final push that brought the dory barely afloat and nimbly hopped in without getting so much as a toenail wet, like he had been doing for years. Once in the slight current of the intermixed Josias Creek and the salt water, Dinny cleated the oars and proceeded to head around the corner into the gentle waves. Fifteen minutes of gentle rowing brought them away from the waves and into the gentle rolling sea.

"Would you like to sail or have me keep rowing, Byzar?" he asked.

"Actually I like the rowing for now, if you don't mind," as Byzar rolled over the gunwale to stare into the crystal clear water. "It is amazing!" she exclaimed. "I can see all the way to the bottom, Dinny! How deep is it here, I wonder?"

"I can tell you exactly if you want, Byzar?"

"How can you do that?"

Dinny smiled and stowed the oars and reached under his seat for a small spool of fishing line that had a weight tied to it. "Here's how, Byzar. This line has a mark every yard and we just count the marks until we feel the weight disappear. How deep do you think it is, take a guess?"

"I'm guessing 10 feet, maybe?" she replied.

"I'm guessing it's about 24-26 feet, but let's give er' a try. You count and we'll see, okay?"

She began counting as he slowly unrolled the spool.

"Almost nine marks by my count, you were right on Dinny. I'm impressed! Can I try?"

"Sure Byzar. The trick is to go slow and pretend you can't see the bottom. Pay close attention to the string and see if you can tell when the weight hits the bottom. Try closing your eyes, it makes you concentrate more."

Byzar started and closed her eyes, but then opened them and asked, "If my eyes are closed, how can I see the marks?"

Dinny looked at Byzar for a moment and thought to make a snide remark, but caught himself in time. He gently said, "When you think you've hit bottom, open your eyes and count the marks as you haul it in."

Byzar examined Dinny's face for a moment and pondered, and then exclaimed with a big smile, almost blushing, "Ach, what a dummy I am!" and they both enjoyed a good laugh.

"Actually Byzar, if you feel the line real careful, every mark on the line is roughed up a bit, so you can count that way also," Dinny advised.

"Well that is kind of smart, isn't it? Can you teach me to row?" she asked.

"I'll tell you what, Byzar, why don't we do our business out at the rum line, and lollygag about on the way back. You can never be sure when the sea decides to get angry or when those boats out there decide to haul anchor," Dinny explained as he set the oars back out into the water. "Roll that spool up neat like, if you will, so that the line doesn't get crossed. Here's the leather strap that holds it in place, okay?"

Byzar looked at Dinny suddenly in a different light and said, "Of course you are right, I am not thinking this morning am I?" she wondered.

"You're doing fine Byzar, this is all just new to you. I've been asea since, well, forever, and I'm learning new tricks every day!" Dinny said seriously.

"You really are quite smart, aren't you Dinny?" Byzar said respectfully.

Dinny smiled, "I have my moments, lass, but don't tell

anybody!"

"Good afternoon, officer, is Sergeant Drake available?" Holly inquired at the desk directly opposite the brown framed front door that was badly in need of another coat of paint.

The officer behind the desk was obviously fast approaching retirement and had not yet looked up from his newspaper. His white mutton-chopped sideburns and moustache still had bits of his lunch ensnared around his mouth.

"State your business and name for the record..." he began before raising his head to see the most beautiful woman he had ever seen smiling at him not more than three feet away. He blushed, and forced himself to continue. "...Uh, er Miss, ahem, that is please tell me why you wish to see the Sergeant."

"Sir, my name is Holly Meadows from Ogunquit, and I have a matter to discuss with the Sergeant, is he available? He knows who I am, sir" Holly spoke in earnest.

"I see. I'll see if he is about. Please have a seat," as the man pointed to a wooden bench against the wall.

Holly could feel all the eyes in the building upon her, and she thought she recognized one of the corporals that had visited the cove a couple weeks ago. She mulled over her strategy as she gazed out the etched windows toward nothing in particular. Even while in the hack she had rented in Ogunquit for the ride to Wells, she still had no idea as to what she planned to say, other than YaYa was a Japanese national in his late twenties and already quite a well known artist. He barely weighed more than Holly dripping wet, and was quite innocent and entirely focused on his art. She was absolutely sure that he would never accost a young girl. Out of nowhere Drake appeared beside her either by purposeful stealth or by Holly being entranced in her own thoughts. He hovered with his zipper too close to her face than was decent, and Holly shivered and adjusted her seat.

"Sergeant Drake, I am glad you are here. I was hopeful that I'd find you in," Holly stated as she looked up at the overbearing man. Her eyes welled a bit but she did not let that belie her purpose.

She held his eyes in a stern but pleasant manner, and finally he spoke, "What brings you to headquarters, Miss Meadows, as if I didn't know?" he smirked.

"Well Sergeant, since you already seem to know the purpose of my visit, perhaps the courtesy of a discussion is warranted? If not, then I'll take my leave," she challenged.

"Come with me, ma'am," he ordered.

He led her to the door behind the desk officer and once through directed her to walk in front of him, all the while under the hard and somewhat lustful gazes of the half dozen men at their desks. All had stopped what they were doing for a moment, until Drake ordered, "Sit here," as they got to what was obviously his desk. Drake proceeded past her to an office door about ten feet away, and lightly knocked before entering and closing the door behind him. Holly caught a quick glance into the office and spied Yaya's easel leaning up against a corner, just before the door closed. Above the door was stenciled 'Captain'. Holly already regretted having made the trip and she could not remember if she had ever been so nervous and downright scared. But she was here and there was no turning back. What seemed like an eternity, but in actuality was only a few minutes later, Drake opened the door and motioned for Holly to enter, which she did.

The Captain was a man with a bushy blonde moustache that was losing its color to age, and was about as tall as Drake: a few inches over six feet. As Holly entered the man stood up and held out his hand and smiled with warm eyes that immediately set Holly somewhat at ease.

"Miss Meadows, I understand," to which Holly nodded.

"I am Captain Duvalier and I think we all know why you are here. Firstly, this office appreciates the fact that you have come here on your own volition. This must be a very intimidating place for a young woman to enter."

Holly's shoulders slumped a bit and she let out a substantial sigh while dabbed her eyes before whispering, "Thank you, sir. This is not the easiest task I have assumed for the School of Art, nor for my employer."

She shot a quick side-long glance at Sergeant Drake who was still hovering and the Captain recognized her discomfort before commenting, "Let's give the girl some room, shall we Drake?" as he subtly motioned for the man to step away.

Holly's first thought was that this was a well-practiced routine by the two men, but dismissed the 'good cop-bad cop' scenario until the men distinctly proved otherwise. The kind eyes and manner of the Captain had earned the benefit of the doubt.

"Miss Meadows, I understand from the Sergeant here that you have a great deal of responsibility on your shoulders down at the Cove, some aspects none too pleasant if I may be so bold," the Captain offered.

Holly replied, "Sir, I am challenged every day more than you can imagine, and my uncle installed me in my current position only about a month ago."

"Tell me about yourself, if you please, young lady," the captain asked in a polite yet determined manner.

"Not much to tell really, I am a student at Vassar College, and my recently deceased father was an attorney. I am majoring in art history with a minor in mathematics."

"Mathematics! That is quite rare for a woman in this day and age, is it not? How are your grades if I may inquire?"

"There are less than ten math majors at Vassar, and I agree it is somewhat rare for women to be in the field, but who knows where such disciplines lead? I am fortunate to record perfect scores so far in my studies, and frankly, schoolwork at college is much less stressful than my first summer working for my uncle!" Holly chortled in hopes of relieving some of the tension in the room, which it did.

The Captain smiled brightly and let out a small guffaw, which was soon followed by a forced snigger from Drake, who continued standing nearby. 'How smarmy' Holly thought.

"I am suitably impressed Miss Meadows, and would you mind providing a couple of references from Vassar? Not to be unseemly but it is part of the package when toting a badge, as I'm sure you understand."

"Completely Sir, and I'll feel better about doing so also," Holly agreed.

"Very well. Let's get down to business shall we? It was reported to us by the family of a sixteen year old girl that an artist at your school kidnapped said child and commanded her to take her clothes off while he, uh, painted her." He held his hand up before Holly could protest and continued, "Understandably the family is up in arms and making all sorts of threats, as you might imagine. They promised me, however, that they would allow the police a few days to bring the man in for questioning, which we intend to do either with your assistance or without. Obviously you have a decision to make young lady."

Holly felt entirely trapped and finally spoke before dabbing her eyes for effect, "Captain, I will escort him here tomorrow. You have my word," at which the Captain smiled.

"May I ask a few questions, Sir?" Holly asked.

"You can ask, but I might not be able to answer from a legal standpoint, okay?"

"I understand, Sir. YaYa—as we call him—is in our country and, as I understand the situation, is under sponsorship from my uncle, which I guess that means me, to some degree. I will be sure to bring all of the appropriate documents, as well as a report from the Japanese Consulate in New York, whom I have already contacted regarding this matter. To be blunt, Sir, and knowing YaYa, as well as seeing the evidence in the corner over there, I don't believe the girls story for a single second, do you?"

The Captain glanced up at Drake, who imperceptibly shrugged and said, "Please continue."

"Well YaYa has no bruises or scratch marks that I could see when I visited him this morning, and his easel, canvas, paint and brushes all seem to be in good order and unbroken. No one has mentioned anything about the girl's clothes being torn or any bruises on her person, so I conclude that she was a willing subject, age notwithstanding," Holly stated before rallying to the task in earnest.

"For all we know, she could have recruited YaYa to draw her, and perhaps our school bears some responsibility for that because many children spy on our artists and models while they are working. If she was forced to comply by YaYa in any way, there would be evidence on display for all to see, and I simply don't see anything to lead me to believe that our YaYa was somehow lurking in the bushes with his easel and brushes waiting to pounce on the first female that happened to pass by. In YaYa's culture painting young girls is natural. He has no idea that he is breaking any laws, even though it is his responsibility to know the laws of our country. And being the daughter of a lawyer, yet not a lawyer by any stretch, I simply don't see where any law whatsoever has been broken in this case. It just doesn't pass the sniff test, in my eyes, does it yours Captain?" she concluded.

The Captain again glance up at Drake who seemed to ache to speak, so the Captain nodded and said, "Well Drake, spit it out before you choke on it," to which the Sergeant shook his head slightly in the negative before the Captain said, "Never mind, I know what you want to say anyway."

This exchange had Holly completely confused, but she was still emboldened and curious as to how her speech was going to be received.

The Captain stared at Holly as if to measure her resolve, but was only met with the loveliest face he had ever laid eyes on. Holly was very nervous, he could tell, but she was smiling as well as good-natured, and exceedingly bright, he concluded. He leaned back in his chair and put his hands behind his head before speaking, without once releasing his stare into Holly's eyes.

"Drake, please have one of our young men come in and load these supplies into one of our hacks, and draw straws to see who gets to escort Miss Meadows back to Ogunquit. Now young lady, I am going to hold you to your word about delivering your Mr. YaYa to this station in the morning. I will want to have a chat with the lad, and read him the riot act about placing his little ass in a sling on foreign soil. Nothing too scary mind you, but it will be enough to make sure he keeps to the straight and narrow. In this way I can also talk to the girl's family and demonstrate to them that their little darling isn't being as truthful as she might be. Hopefully this will all blow over by the 4th and we'll hear no more about it. What I am requesting is that you keep our local kids away from gazing at your models while they are, well, posing in various degrees of undress, am I making myself clear?"

"You most certainly are Captain, and I will bring our young Japanese friend here before lunch tomorrow if that will be acceptable."

"That will be fine young lady, and if I may ask, what is it about mathematics that would make you bury your head in numbers, when you obviously have quite a knack for the law? Frankly I'd like to see women lawyers, always said so, and you certainly would make a worthy adversary in a courtroom," he said with a smile.

"I don't know what to say, Sir," Holly blushed with tears welling up again. "I truly don't know what to say Captain. You are very kind to compliment me so," she said with all sincerity.

The Captain stood and held out his hand and Holly shook it firmly before practically floating out of the office, while the men quickly shuffled papers to appear busy to their boss. Outside the hack was loaded and one of the uniformed officers who had been to the cove was waiting to assist Holly into the seat.

"Corporal Richardson, isn't it?" Holly asked.

"I'm surprised you remembered, ma'am," the young man replied.

"I never forget a handsome face, Sir!" Holly playfully giggled as she boldly elbowed the officer in the ribs.

Richardson had all he could do to keep his composure and blushed emphatically, while assuming that his fellow cops were staring out the window at them, which they were.

Holly climbed into the seat feeling beautiful, fortunate but most of all, smart.

Eben was making good progress on his new shack, which from outside appearances it would be, but inside it would be his home. He had always got along well with the Woodbury's, and Charles well understood the need for Eben to locate his shack at the head of the Perkins Cove Harbor, so the subject was not necessary to discuss. Eben had worked for the Woodbury's doing odd jobs since his early teens, and was a favorite of Charles' deceased wife, Marcia, back when she was alive. His School of Art had been consistently successful since it's inception just over twenty years previous, and had gained a most loyal and respected following. Woodbury was a serious, quiet and congenial sort, and whatever thoughts he had about the wickedness on display across the cove at Meadows School of Art, he kept to himself. On those occasions that he happened to cross paths with Meadows, he was always courteous but remained disengaged. Meadows at one point elicited Woodbury's inclusion in an attempt to fortify Ogunquit's, and thereby Meadows', renown position in the modern art world, but Woodbury had politely declined by explaining that he enjoyed his little niche in the world and preferred not to expand in any manner. Meadows often attempted to engage Woodbury in conversation about differing influences in the world of art, particularly the more modernistic fringes such as those that were attracted to the

Meadows school, but Woodbury always declined to engage, preferring to state that the world of art was an ever-expanding sphere while wishing Meadows all the best.

Eben was convinced that privately, Woodbury considered Meadows to be a complete jackass.

Woodbury refused to accept cash for the small bit of land he sold Eben, preferring a handshake agreement that Eben would continually provide a security presence during Woodbury's absences, which were generally increasing as Woodbury approached his sixties. Woodbury was a soft-spoken, slightly built gentleman, but his words resonated careful thought and were generally well considered.

The shell of the shack was starting to take shape, as framing was the kind of task that always showed results at the end of the day. Along about noon Eben had just finished bracing a newly raised wall when he spied Dinny rowing into the cove with the gypsy girl he had made a date with. He could see that both the girl and Dinny were soaking wet and they seemed to be enjoying themselves immensely. This brought a satisfied smile to Eben's face, for he had always hoped that Dinny would find a gal that liked him for him, rather than the cash he sometimes proffered on the Portsmouth harbor whores. As they rode by both flashed delighted smiles and waved up at Eben, who shook his head with a smile and feigned returning to work. He peeked again a few moments later at the pair in the dory, and by this time Dinny had run it up to shore below the kitchen entrance to Meadows' house, and Byzar scampered out and quickly threw her dress over her shoulders, as she seemed to forget that she was only wearing her pantaloons. She grabbed her parasol had sloppily thrust her hat on her head, grabbed the basket and leaned down and quickly kissed Dinny on the cheek before scampering up to the door. At the door, Eben could see that she said something to Dinny and then disappeared into the house. Dinny immediately turned to look for Eben and flashed the biggest smile Eben had ever seen on Dinny, and again waved. Eben was sure he would get all the juicy details of their 'date', as soon as Dinny moored the dory and hotfooted up to the building site to help for the rest of the day.

About a half hour later Eben heard whistling and knew Dinny was approaching. There were about a dozen art students huddled in the shade under Woodbury's deck to get out of the mid-afternoon sun, sharing lemonade and quietly reviewing each others' progress for the day by exchanging canvases. They didn't seem to mind the noise Eben's hammer and saw made and a few had even turned their attention toward Eben's construction project and began to draw him in action. Dinny sauntered around the pile of true dimension studs, and said, "Howdy pard!"

"Are ya' gonna see her again, Din?" Eben asked, dispensing with the usual, 'How was your date' question, because he already knew the answer by watching the two of them enter the cove earlier.

"She says I'm smart and hopes I'll ask her out for a sail after the 4th, 'cuz she says she's real busy until after that," Dinny bubbled.

"I'm glad you had a good time, Dinny. Just keep your wits about you, okay. I don't want to see you get hurt like with me and Holly," Eben cautioned matter-of-factly, but with obvious concern for his friend.

Dinny pondered for a moment before quietly saying, "I'll go for the ride, Eben, fer sure, but I'll be mindful of what yer sayin', but dang, she sure is a sweetheart of a gal. After leavin' the rum line we sailed over to Boon Island and went for a swim, and I taught her how to row and sail. She said it's the best time she's ever had! As fer me, I can't remember ever feelin' so natural around such a pretty gal, let alone royalty fer' chrissakes!"

"I'm happy for ya' Din, really am. When you come off of that cloud yer floating on," Eben chided, "how about helpin' me nail up some one-bys, so we can start shinglin' the place?"

He went on, "I think some of Woodbury's virginal wayfarers are startin' to take more of a passing interest in my doin's, prob'ly inspired by the gals loungin' around across the cove, so what say we shuck our shirts and give 'em a bit of a show, jus' to be neighborly a' course!"

"You're getting' kinda randy your own self for a church goin' gent ain't ya', Eben? We need to make a run to Portsmouth so you can have another go at that gruesome creature that threatened to cut off your wanger?" snickered Dinny.

"Portsmouth maybe, but we'll stay clear of that pub, thank you very much! Now let's get to work Romeo!"

"How long have you been on the police force, Corporal?" Holly asked as the hack rolled along to the sing-song beats of the horses hooves. "We can slow down a bit if you like. I'm still recovering from my visit to your station"

"We all thought you handled yourself quite well, Miss Meadows. The walls in the station are paper thin, you see. By the way, we had already figured out that your Japanese friend was innocent of any real wrongdoing, but we were going to bring him in anyway, just so you know," the young man offered. "You did a fine thing by coming in on your own accord, Ma'am, and you certainly earned all of our respect, if you don't mind me saying."

"Thank you Corporal, that's very nice of you to say. I sure wish I knew that YaYa was basically in the clear before I met with your captain. I was scared, especially of Sergeant Drake. He doesn't look at me in a very comfortable manner, if you know what I mean," Holly stated.

"He's a brother officer, and I guess we all have our different ways of doing our job, but in the almost three years that I have been on the force, he has earned our respect. He is not a gent to trifle with, I can tell you that."

"He still gives me the willies. Would you mind if we made a quick stop at the drugstore, I need to get something to settle my stomach and have a quick chat with Mr. Spenser. Do you know him Corporal?" Holly asked.

"I've had a few dealings with him. We are in different churches," the young man replied. "I'd be happy to make a quick stop, I'm sure the Captain would understand."

They pulled up in front of the drugstore and the Corporal set the brake and tied the lines to the loop in front of the seat before offering his hand for Holly to get down. She clutched his arm as he led her to the door and stepped into the door before holding it so Holly could enter. Both Mr. & Mrs. Spenser straightened somewhat nervously when seeing the imposing uniformed man enter their store, and were further unsettled to see that it was Miss Meadows whom he was obviously escorting in on some official duty. The corporal removed his hat and said officiously, "Good afternoon Sir, Ma'am", as Holly whisked by Mrs. Spenser's station without so much as a glance and strode directly over to the druggist while the corporal stood by the door.

"Might you have a moment to speak in private, Mr. Spenser?"

"Of course Miss Meadows, please come around the counter."

"Thank you, sir." Once behind the chest-high counter Holly whispered, "Don't mind the officer; he is just escorting me home from my visit to the police station and I thought I'd make a quick stop to see what you have come up with. All is well. Were you able to fill our order and produce a price list, Sir? I was out of town so I may have missed your young man, Russell. He is very polite and dependable, by the way," Holly stated sweetly.

"I was a little nervous about sending Russell but he said that you and Mr. Meadows were very kind to him, and for that I am grateful. Here is our price list and all of the items you requested are available. We rarely run out of stock. Perhaps it is best if you pick up your order in the morning?" The druggist said nodding to the officer who was at the time in a deep conversation with his wife.

"Perhaps that is best Mr. Spenser. I'll review your list this evening and I have to return to Wells sometime in the morning, so I can stop by then, if that is acceptable?" she asked.

"Of course Miss Meadows. I hope your situation with the police is not too serious," Spenser said, obviously in hopes of pumping Holly for information he could use to bolster his salacious rumors about Meadows' art colony. Holly recognized this immediately and used the opportunity to full advantage.

"Actually Mr. Spenser," appearing to confide in the man, "it is quite important matters of State with the Japanese

Consulate as well as eastern Europe government spies, as I understand things. Very important issues. Will you and your wife be at the Sparhawk for next weekend's activities? The guest list will include numerous senators and judges, for on the fourth a significant announcement—which I cannot divulge—will be made. It will truly be a great day for America, I can tell you!" Holly concluded.

"This sounds very exciting Miss Meadows. I would certainly like to know more so I can pass the news along to my, er, our congregation," he practically pleaded.

"Perhaps I'll have more time tomorrow, but I've already kept the officer waiting longer than I should have. Do you have a lozenge to settle a girl's tummy?"

"Of course Miss Meadows, take as many as you need." He handed her a basket full of wafers. She delicately grasped two and somewhat seductively placed them on her tongue as she reached for her purse. Spenser put his hands on hers rather boldly implying that there was no need to pay, and quickly caught himself for his hands lingering a little too long, and smiled, "Tomorrow then, ma'am?"

Holly came around the counter and called a 'thank you' over her shoulder and interrupted the corporal and Mrs. Spenser's discussion by saying, "Oh, please forgive me Mrs. Spenser, for interrupting, I'm sorry for my delay corporal. This certainly is a 'chamber of commerce day' is it not Mrs. Spenser? Simply delightful weather today!" as she stepped through the door the corporal was holding for her.

As soon as they were back in the hack, Holly could see Mrs. Spenser quizzing her husband through the window, and smiled yet again. 'This day has gone famously' she thought.

Mr. Spenser peered over his glasses at his frumpy wife of more than thirty years and knew the look on her face quite well. Before she started in on him he asked, "What did the officer have to say?"

"Well I dare say that it appears that the police department in Wells thinks very highly of Miss Meadows, but thankfully not much of her uncle and the obscene conduct down at the cove. He said that their investigation reveals that Miss Meadows is quite an accomplished and well respected student in college, and is somehow fulfilling her familial responsibility by managing her uncle's affairs. What did she want with you?"

"Very businesslike, and I think that we perhaps have misjudged her, dear. I think we ought to give her a chance. She certainly seems to have a bright head on her shoulders. She spoke of some senators and judges, coming here to the Sparhawk on the 4th for some special announcements about the United States, and that somehow their art school is involved. She also said that she hoped to stop by tomorrow on her way back from the police station, where she was today, and introduce us to a Japanese gentleman from the consulate in New York City! Imagine that!" Spenser said beaming with civic pride.

"Perhaps it is in our best interest to hear the young woman out," Mrs. Spenser agreed. "I hear that she and Eben Ramsdell are good friends, and we know the fine character of Eben. I'm sure that he would not be mixed up with anything untoward or unchristian-like. He's a fine young man, so if he approves of the girl, perhaps we should too."

"That's a fine attitude to take dear, and I agree wholeheartedly. Let's close up shop, it's getting on near to five."

"It's been a long day for me Corporal, but I really appreciate your courtesy, and this has been a most enjoyable ride with you, Sir," Holly said as the hack approached the end of the lane leading to the cove. The smell of the ocean, intermixed with the stale stench of the fishing shacks, reached them before sighting the idyllic setting.

"It has been my pleasure, Ma'am. I look forward to seeing you tomorrow, if that is not too forward."

"Of course not, Sir. I enjoy your company and hope to see you again also," Holly replied, just as the corporal brought the hack to a stop.

"May I help you with this equipment Ma'am?" Richardson said as he helped Holly out of the seat and reached in the back for YaYa's easel and supplies.

"Thank you, no. We can just set these supplies by this tree and I'll send someone up from the school to retrieve them. She reached out her hand and as soon as his burly palm wrapped itself around hers, Holly unexpectedly leaned forward on her tippy toes and pecked the corporal on the cheek, which embarrassed him to the point of unabashed blushing.

"Thank you again, Corporal Richardson. Perhaps we'll see each other tomorrow?" Holly smiled and gathered her things and strolled toward the fishing shacks and beyond those, her home.

The Corporal tipped his cap in kind, stole a glance at all the fishermen watching from their seats around Sunker's shack, and led the horse in a circle before mounting the hack and driving away. Holly, of course knew that her demonstration of affection for the police officer would garner more rumors from the fishermen, and that was very advantageous on a number of levels. She walked audaciously toward the group of fishermen, who were by now accustomed to Holly's boldness, and just before reaching the group she stole a gaze toward Eben's construction site and noticed that Eben did not miss the performance either, nor did Dinny, and she smiled inwardly while thinking, 'yes Holly, it is a very good day!'

"The last time the cops came to the cove they were gonna haul you off to jail, now you're kissin' em on the cheek! By Gawd Missy, you surely must cast a spell. Be careful here in New England, we've been known to hang witches!" Sunker bellowed in good humor.

"So I've heard," Holly said as she unabashedly plopped down right on Sunker's knee. "And for Christmas, Santa, I want a wagon, and a dolly...!" which drew riotous guffaws from the group.

Sunker slid his hand down onto Holly's rump, fully expecting to be slapped by Holly, but instead Holly piped up, "Why Santa, be careful: here in New England, we've been known to castrate child molesters," at which Sunker immediately pulled both hands away with exaggerated mirth, which everyone enjoyed.

"Captain," Holly said loudly for all to hear, "It seems you actually bathed today! I guess you remembered our dinner date tonight after all?" which set Sunker back a bit, though remembering their conversation earlier in the day. "When you come, say in about an hour, would you be a pal and bring the supplies that handsome officer leaned against the tree?" she said as she rose to leave.

"You can bring them into the kitchen door if you please, everyone is excited to meet you, okay?" to which the Captain recovered in time to say, "Of course Holly, I'd never forget a date with the likes of you. See you before an hour is up. Thanks!"

Holly stepped into the kitchen and saw Byzar, Mrs. Parent and the two new models standing around and chatting while helping arrange serving dishes and such.

"Bonjour Madame," Holly said to Mrs. Parent, who smiled and nodded. "I see you were not lost at sea, our little princess!" she giggled at Byzar, who sat in her satin robe with her hair wrapped up in a towel.

Byzar giggled back, "Well it was worrysome at first, but we had a wonderful day. I hope to do it again; it was a lot of fun!"

"Love on the water, how romantic! Have you set a wedding date with our friend Dinny?" Holly teased.

"I could do a lot worse, I'll tell you that," Byzar said, surprising all.

"I can't wait for the kiss and tell part, but were you successful out at the rum-line?" Holly queried.

"I left all the information on your desk, and yes, they have everything we require," Byzar said.

"Wonderful and thank you. Has YaYa made an appearance or is he still hiding in a closet somewhere?" Holly asked aloud.

Mrs. Parent spoke up and said, "I'll go find him. He is still terrified."

"Thank you Ma'am. Please tell him that everything is okay, and I'll chat with him later."

"Oh he'll be so relieved, as am I. I like him very much. Thank you," the older woman said as she headed for the stairs.

"Oh, and Mrs. Parent, one of the fishermen is joining us for dinner. He should be by shortly with YaYa's easel and supplies. His name is Captain Sunker, and we want to be sure that he feels most welcome."

"I'll see to it Miss Meadows," she said as she climbed the stairs.

Holly turned her attention to the two new models, Lesley and Lauren, and said, "And who might we have here?" as both girls nervously stood and slightly bowed while offering their hands.

"I am Lesley, and this is Lauren. How do you do, Miss Meadows. It is very nice to finally meet you!"

"Likewise. And it's Holly when we're in private, please. I understand one of you has a condition in need of immediate therapy, my guess it's you, Lauren," which immediately concerned both girls, while Byzar tittered.

The new girls shared a glance before Holly smiled at Lauren and said, "You have been here almost two days and still haven't gotten laid? That's got to be a record!" and they all laughed while Lauren turned beet red.

"No ma'am, er, Holly, Miss Elsa arranged for my 'cure' last night over at the Sparhawk Inn," the girl replied.

"And?" Holly queried.

"It was wonderful, and quite a relief…both times!" Lauren laughed.

"Well welcome to our humble home ladies. I hope you both have an adventurous spirit. Do you?"

Both girls smiled brightly and giggled. Lesley said, "As long as we don't get pregnant, we're game!" to which Lauren nodded in agreement.

"Do you have assignments from Elsa for tonight, yet?" Holly inquired.

Lauren spoke first this time and said, "Miss Elsa said for

us to take it easy until about 9:30, and she'd let us know if, er, something will come up!" All the girls giggled at the phrase.

"Well I'll speak to Elsa, but in the meantime I'd like you to do me a favor. A very fat, funny neighbor is coming here for dinner. You may have seen him over at the fishing shacks. His name is Captain Sunker and his alliance with this school is imperative to our success. I'd like you to take him up to the clawfoot tub after dinner and scrub every inch of his body, and be sure that he is treated with a once-in-a-lifetime experience. I doubt he's touched a woman in decades and probably only been with lovelies like you in his dreams, so let's fulfill them, please. Do you understand, girls?" Holly asked seriously but with her ever-present smile.

Lauren and Lesley looked at each other smiling and Lesley said, "We'll do our best to give him a heart attack, Holly!"

"Oh dear, don't go that far. We'd never be able to lift him out of the tub!" Holly said to giggles all around. "Welcome girls, and nice to meet you both!"

Holly headed up the stairs to get cleaned up for dinner. Just before she reached the top step, Meadows and Elsa appeared on the next staircase on their way down.

"Holly dear!" Meadows exclaimed with a brightened face, as did Elsa. "You look like you've had a day of days!"

Holly hugged them both and said, "I need to jump in the tub, but briefly, YaYa is in the clear, though I have to bring him to the police station in Wells in the morning with all his papers. Between the Spenser's and the rum-line we can acquire whatever supplies we need, though I have not had time to compare prices. Captain Sunker is joining us for dinner, and the new girls are going to give him a bath he'll never forget after dinner, if that is all right with you Elsa. The police will contact me if there are any future concerns here at the school. The rumors have started around town about the dignitaries that are scheduled to visit the festivities at the Spar for the Sultana's announcement to society, and, um, oh yes, the fishermen will help build and acquire supplies, and tobacco, for our new store. There is probably something I've forgotten but I can't remember right now. What did you folks do today?" she asked with an innocent-appearing, ever-smiling face.

Both were stunned by Holly's accomplishments and smiled very approvingly before Elsa said, 'That is a wonderful idea to have Captain Sunker over for dinner, and an even better idea to have him bathed," Elsa laughed. "I hope he doesn't drop dead with delight, we'll have to hire a crew to lift him!"

"We cautioned the girls about that very thing also, Elsa!" Holly laughed.

"I am very relieved that YaYa's situation has been resolved. Thank you very much Holly, and I look forward to learning of all the details, but for now, take your well earned bath and we'll chat after dinner," Meadows whispered.

"A good plan, Sir, and I think tonight I'll sleep for three days!" she said as she headed for her room while unbuttoning her dress in the same motion.

A commotion greeted Elsa and Meadows as they reached the bottom of the steps that led into the kitchen. YaYa was close on their heels, as they saw Capt. Sunker, as clean as they had ever seen him, setting an armful of supplies in the kitchen table with Mrs. Parent's dutiful and good natured assistance. YaYa recognized his easel and supplies and almost leaped over the railing, much to the amazement of both Meadows and Elsa who were basically shoved out of the way, and went immediately over to his canvas to inspect for damage, of which none was evident. He began weeping while clutching his canvas like a long lost child, which in effect it was, since the unfinished painting was that of the young girl in the barn that had brought him so much terror and anguish. YaYa had been told briefly by Mrs. Parent that he was not being sought by the police anymore, so he naturally assumed that his salvation was due to the efforts of the obese man who had brought his supplies back to him. YaYa began bowing and hugging Sunker and thanking him profusely in words no one in the room understood, and Sunker simply had no idea what had brought such a reaction from the very slight of build Japanese fellow. Sunker looked pleadingly about for an explanation but all his eyes were met with was happy, tear-filled eyes of the burgeoning collection of artists who were entering the kitchen to see what all the excitement was about. Elsa stepped forward and put her hand on YaYa's shoulder and gently brought him away from the Captain while nodding for Byzar to take him into the dining room so he could compose himself while she explained that Holly was his savior, not the large man in the doorway. Elsa turned back to the still astonished Captain and took him by the arm and said to all in full baroque tone, "Vee velcome our friend Captain Sunker, ya?" as she led him through to the dining room while everyone expressed their personal greetings with great resonance. The Captain was increasingly at ease and Lesley asked if she might get him a drink before dinner, to which he stated, "That would be very nice of you, and your name is, Ma'am?"

"My name is Lesley and this..." motioning for Lauren to join her, "is Lauren. We are your private hostesses this evening Captain, so if there is anything we can provide for you, please let us know. Now what is your pleasure, sir, to drink I mean?" Lesley said while Lauren rested her hand on the man's shoulder, soon followed by her chin, which was then followed by her lips on his ear.

Lesley moved in front of the Captain while the others began to bring in dishes of food to the dining room, and said, "Have you ever enjoyed iced tea, Captain?" to which he nodded just as Lesley ran her hand down the man's rotund belly and into the gap created by his suspenders, and clutched around his shriveled penis. "I mean have you ever enjoyed Long Island *Hard* Iced Tea, Sir," she cooed as she fondled.

Lauren interjected, "Now Lesley, let this handsome brute have a little air before dinner, shall we, and fetch him a glass of tea?" to which the still speechless Captain nodded somewhat embarrassed.

"Yes Lauren, that is more neighborly. Captain, you be sure to save the chairs on either side of you at the table for us, won't you? And I'll bring you your *hard* iced tea," and she playfully gave his penis a final squeeze just as she said *hard*. "Lauren will introduce you around".

Dinner was in full swing and Captain Sunker was the star of the evening, bringing forth his jovial, quick wit and larger than life presence. He was on his best behavior until the spiked iced tea that the girls had been feeding him began to slur both his speech and language, but not to the bawdy stage just yet. His cheeks were rosy while his stories of the sea, and ports, became increasingly randy, which delighted all who remained at the table, which was most. Even Mrs. Parent had joined the table, which was quite a rarity, and laughed to the point of tears on more than one occasion, even if she didn't quite understand much of the language. The weight of the world was lifted off of YaYa's shoulders, and the usually reserved man was laughing unabashedly right along with everyone else.

All through dinner the captain's hands were discreetly encouraged to stroke the inner thighs of both the Smith College gals sitting on either side of him. Sunker had been mostly impotent due to his weight for the better part of the past decade, but had spent the entire dinner with a steady, somewhat erect penis, and that encouraged and relieved him greatly, if the two girls were actually going to let him dally with them. At some point during the last part of dinner Holly had silently sat on the stairs sideways, watching and listening to the festivities, dressed in a short, white terry cloth robe that barely covered her knees, which she had tucked up to her chest. Sunker could see clear up to her nakedness through the railings, but after the first few peeks he lost interest in favor of the charms sitting on either side of him. At one point Meadows finally noticed Holly and spoke aloud without stuttering—drink helped his condition immensely—"My dear Holly, we have missed you, why are you not joining us?"

"I'm sorry everyone, I fell asleep after my bath, but I have truly enjoyed watching from afar, please continue, and of course, I'm not properly dressed," she said.

Elsa, as under the influence as the rest, spoke up and said, "Holly, please stand up, and toss me your robe, would you?" as the room filled with silence.

Holly smiled a bit nervously, but was ever game and said, "Why of course Madame Baroness," as she untied the sash and deftly tossed it over the railing into Elsa's waiting arms.

"Now let everyone decide if you are properly dressed!" to which all applauded and whistled as Holly did her best burlesque imitation as she seductively marched up the stairs. At the top of the stairs she stood like a hipshot horse and explained, "Always leave them wanting more, right Captain?" she announced as she slapped her left butt cheek and disappeared into her room, to the rousing applause and cheers from all.

Lesley motioned to Lauren and both stood up and placed their hands on Sunker's shoulders, as Lesley cooed, "It's time to come with us, Captain," which kind of signified that the dinner hour was over after the Holly's rousing performance. As Sunker tried to find his balance as he stood, Elsa said, "Captain, we would like you to pose for us tomorrow. We all think that you would make a unique and interesting subject," to which all the remaining artists mutually agreed and nodded.

"You mean lounge around on those rocks like your gals do? I'd be the laughing stock!" he replied.

Meadows interjected, "Ah Captain, we have a place that is out of sight, you'll do us a great honor, and if you are hedging, please inform your hostesses of your decision, but I expect they will do everything they can secure your agreement. They can be quite convincing you know. It's been a wonderful evening, thanks to you sir. Now please, the girls will enjoy the rest of it with you, and I hope to see you in the morning."

"Thank you to all! I've had more fun than a barrel full of jellyfish! Off we go lasses, I hope when you're done with me I still be breathin', though even if I'm not, I doubt I'll care...Off we go!"

"YaYa, it's time to wake up, Sir" Holly said as she gently shook the 27-year-old artist awake.

"Ya ya ya," he said as he fumbled around on his night table for his glasses.

Holly made the motions signifying 'to eat', and he understood and nodded while Holly left his bedroom. It seemed like she and YaYa had been the only two people in the entire house that had slept by themselves that night. Every bed and couch that Holly could see through the doors, or in the common areas, was occupied by two or more bodies still asleep at this early hour of the day. The free dispensation of last evening's drugs was clearly evident. Holly had declined participation for she was so very tired and slept quite soundly and deeply, foregoing any dinner, and was already dressed and fixing some breakfast for both she and YaYa. She had awakened when the seagulls started chirping in earnest outside her open window, and remembered being lulled to sleep by the monotonous groans of pleasure emanating from Captain Sunker in the large bathroom next to her room. She was thankful that the bathroom was vacant when she needed to use it in the morning, but the floor was covered with wet towels and clothes from the obviously overloaded and active bathtub last night. She had delved into the pile of handwritten invitations to the upcoming 4th of July festivities, and addressed one to Captain DuValier, Sergeant Drake, Mr. & Mrs. Spenser as well as a personal one to Mr. Dalton Richardson. She would hold on to the Richardson invitation until she was sure that he was not married, but cared little if he happened to be involved in a relationship. If he happened to show up by himself, she had already decided that she would bed him out on the beach after midnight, if the tide cooperated. He was a big, powerful young man and if she was able to get some alcohol in him, he might turn out to be a voracious lover.

YaYa came down the stairs clutching his recently returned canvas and set it on the kitchen table as Holly was just finishing scrambling some eggs in the cast iron skillet that never left the stove. She already had some toast and marmalade on a plate covered by a white napkin, and as she was dishing out the eggs into a bowl, she motioned toward the icebox for YaYa to fetch a pitcher of orange juice, which he understood and did. She pulled up a chair and slid a plate and a spoon toward YaYa and spooned some eggs on her plate while nodding for the man to get his own toast. Breakfast was always casual at the house, while dinner was a more formal affair in which everyone was encouraged to sit together.

"How are you feeling Ya?" Holly asked.

"Still nervous. I thank you so very much for all you have done. Why do I have to talk to the police?"

"The Captain is a nice man, and he wants to be satisfied that you know the laws of our country and town. He wants to be sure that you will be safe and feel welcome here. He doesn't see too many people from your country, and he needs to check your papers," Holly explained. "Bringing you to the station is part of the bargain for you not being put in jail. Just consider our morning together to be a pleasant outing. If there was something for you to be worried about, I would tell you. Just say as little as possible, be polite, and never tell anyone about our lifestyle here at the school. Just say we are an art school. We paint, sculpt and learn. Period. Is that understood, YaYa?"

"Yes, yes, Miss Holly," the man said with newly found deference.

"If you give out any information at all about our home life here, some people will twist your words and turn it into '*talk-talk*', people are like that everywhere as you know, but in a small community such as this, sometimes rumors take on a life of their own, especially given the nature of our school and naked women floating about. I am also going to introduce you to the drugstore owners, or the 'chemists' as you might know them. A brief stop that I have my reasons for, but please feign that you understand less English than you do, and we'll be in and out of there quickly, okay?" she said as she offered her hand to take his empty plate.

"I just follow your lead," he said meekly.

"Why did you bring your canvas down with you?" she asked.

"I wanted you to see that I wasn't taking advantage of that girl. Here is what I was drawing." He he showed the beginning of a painting of a fully clothed girl in a barnyard, in the YaYa style of distortion of scale and random thought. The girl's neck, forearms and shins were the only body parts exposed. 'Hardly obscene by any standards,' she thought.

"YaYa, I knew that, you don't need to prove anything. You are an artist extraordinaire, we all consider you to be such. We also know that you start your paintings, and then leave them for a while to let your imagination work its magic, and then return to your work later. Now let's clean up and get going!"

"Wait, wait, I have something to show you!" he said excitedly as he took his canvas and bounded back up the stairs to his room.

"Don't forget your documents!" she called after him just like a schoolmarm would, and she turned to finish cleaning up the kitchen. She went through the dining room and over to her desk to quickly glance at the price list that Byzar had left for her, and placed that list in the envelope provided by the druggist, which was perhaps humorously labeled on the front as *Mr. D. Spenser.* Holly let out a short giggle and wondered if there wasn't a reasonable gent inside the surly druggist after all. She thought, 'Well if I were tied to that ugly hag of a wife for that long, I'd probably be a miserable guy also'. She grabbed the invitations and put them in her purse, along with the addresses for Vassar she would provide for the Captain, and retrieved fifty dollars from her cash box and stood in momentary thought to be sure she had remembered everything. She turned to head toward the kitchen, only to be met by a smiling YaYa who was quietly standing in the doorway holding a large canvas with a towel over it. They held eyes for a moment and just as Holly opened her mouth to speak, the artist let go of the towel, and the image appeared.

"I call this one, 'Lay Figure', and this is of course, you," he smiled.

Holly put her hands over her mouth and turned as pale as the white towel that YaYa had let fall to the floor. Tears emerged from her eyes and YaYa could visibly see her knees shake behind her cream colored dress. YaYa walked over to one of the chairs and leaned the canvas on the arms, and quickly slid another chair only a few feet in front of it, and helped Holly to sit down. He stepped behind Holly's chair and placed his hands gently on her shoulders. She reached for the hand on her right shoulder, and brought it to her lips and cheek and caressed it in both of hers. She turned and looked up into YaYa's eyes only briefly, before breaking down into an uncontrollable sobbing. She couldn't take her eyes off the simple beauty of the painting: an exquisitely beautiful young woman lounging sideways in a bamboo summer chair, encased in a sheer black negligee, with her arms clasped behind her head, and most importantly, seeming completely at peace. It was the first painting of a woman she had ever seen by YaYa in which the human form was accurately portrayed without his typical distortion of scale, as well as not depicting a woman's 'special' places.

Her sobbing evolved into a simple steady, yet light stream of tears, but she wouldn't release her grip on his hand. She looked up at him again and innocently said, "May I touch it, YaYa?"

YaYa leaned over and kissed her on the top of her head and said, "Of course you may, Holly, for it is yours," which brought another pleading gaze from the girl, as she tentatively reached out with the fingertips of her right hand, and felt the texture of the brushstrokes, especially those that depicted her face. She was enthralled that he seemed to have captured her soul by bringing it into his own, and let it flow through his brush and made her come alive on the canvas. She sensed a slight scuff from the doorway and she turned to see Valentine Meadows and Baroness Elsa standing in their nightclothes arm in arm, both also just finishing a good cry. Meadows walked over to Holly and squatted down on his heels next to, and below her eye level, and looked up into hers and whispered, "I see that you've noticed that he has painted you as you are, rather than in his usual style. We also don't see any of your charms on the canvas, as he also usually does. Do you know why that is, Holly?" To which the girl, still weepy-eyed, shook her head no.

"It is because he, like all of us," he whispered as Elsa moved over beside him, "respect and admire you so very much!"

Holly let out an uncontrollable sobbing gasp, and again buried her face into YaYa's hand, as a new round of tears escaped her emblazoned wolf-like eyes.

"This is what art can do to a soul; this is how the emotions it stirs can change lives. You feel it now in your marrow, don't you?" as she nodded. "Elsa and I are as fortunate as you are in this moment, for you see how moved we are also, not so much by the painting as you are, but witnessing in person your reaction to it. What a special day!" he smiled. "And by the way, and without realizing it, you have paid YaYa the highest compliment an artist can ever receive, simply by showing him how your heart has forever been changed by his work. Now, young lady, you better let go of his hand or he will have to learn how to paint left handed for the rest of his days!" he said as everyone let out a comedic breath of laughter.

Holly motioned for Elsa to hand her the towel that she had picked up off the floor, and Holly began to rise before stealing one more glance at the painting, only to find that she was not quite ready to leave the moment, and sat back down and buried her face into the towel as a new round of sobbing wracked her shoulders. Meadows put his arm around YaYa and said, "Let's head into the kitchen, and Holly, you join us when you are ready," to which he saw her nod her head while still buried in the towel.

Holly found herself alone in the room with her elbows on her knees and her face still in the towel but with enough room for her to stare at the painting in front of her. She had absolutely no idea what her emotions were at that time, but looked at the towel and evaluated how many tears had been soaked up by it, and stood up. She laid the towel over the chair to dry, caught up her purse and smoothed out the front of her dress. She delicately moved the painting onto the chair that she usually sat in behind her desk and went over to the mirror to check that her face did not have tear ruts from her eyes, and without any intent, was able to peer over her shoulder at the painting in the reflection and stared at herself, and then at the painting. She said aloud to herself, 'I remember the last time I truly looked at a reflection of myself, over at Eben's window, and I said that I wasn't sure that I liked you, but that I really wanted to. Do you remember that day, Holly? That was the day you broke up with the only man you ever loved, and probably ever will. I'll fall in love again, and someone will with me. I know that now. Do you know why, Holly? It's because now I truly do like myself, and from this day forward, I always will'.

Holly entered the kitchen, and reached her hand out to YaYa, and said, "Let's go to the police station you Japanese outlaw, so I can spring you out of jail!" she laughed, as did the others.

She held the door open and Elsa called out, '"Good luck you two. Let us know if we have to bail you out!"

"I promise you Elsa, if I ever see the inside of a jail cell, it will only be because I have a fantasy I need to be fulfilled!" as they again all cackled.

"Richardson!" Captain DuValier bellowed. The young corporal had just arrived for work, fifteen minutes before his shift, as per usual. He stepped into the office as the Captain said, "Please close the door and take a seat," which was unusual because the Captain's protocol was to always have his officers stand while in his office. Corporal Dalton Richardson would have preferred to stand, but no one bucked the Captain, even as congenial as he was.

The bespectacled Richardson pulled up a chair and set his husky, muscled twenty-six year old frame into it. He was thankful that went to the barber for a shave and a close-cropped haircut after returning from Ogunquit. That he did so in anticipation of seeing Miss Meadows on this day was not something that he wanted to admit, but it was out of his once a week barber routine.

"It's approaching three years since I hired you, isn't Dalton?" the Captain stated as he dispensed with some papers and leaned back in his chair while folding his hands over his belly.

"I believe it's about that, yes sir," Dalton stated.

"Relax son, we're just going to have an informal chat. I remember that when you interviewed for this job you said you wanted to be a career police officer. Now that you've had a good taste of it, is that still the case, son?"

"Yes sir, without a doubt."

"Fine Dalton, that's just fine. We're happy to have you and you're doing a fine job."

"Thank you, sir," the Corporal replied with a blushed face, though trying to maintain his serious composure. He always projected a serious character, even at church. But he had been known to enjoy a snort or two, but only during hunting trips with his childhood friends. For the most part they had all gotten married and were starting families, so Dalton's circle of friends that he could do 'male' things with was shrinking each year. He had a girlfriend that he had known since school, but it was more of an arranged type of relationship, in which he felt obligated to present small gifts on holidays and the like. Because of his religious beliefs, he had never been intimate with the girl, nor with any other, mostly due to the fact that she was not the most attractive girl nor was she very delightful to be with. She was basically a younger version of his mother. This Miss Meadows on the other hand, was more beautiful than any of the pin-up girls he had ever seen and collected in a satchel in the back of the closet in his apartment. Better yet, she smelled delightful and was funny, bubbly and smiling all the time. He had surprised himself last night when laying in his bed he did not fantasize about her in a sexual way, for that was what he intended to do with the petroleum jelly and a towel, but rather he thought of them taking walks on the beach, camping in the woods together and having dinner with his extended family, as she would be the apple of everyone's eye.

"You know I have been in this chair for quite a few years, and I have learned a few things along the way, as you can imagine. The most important thing I have learned is that to keep my job I must form alliances, do you know what I mean by that, Dalton?"

"Probably not, Sir."

"Good answer, and the correct one, I might add! How did you find Miss Meadows to be yesterday? We don't see the likes of her kind very often in these parts, do we?"

"No Sir, we certainly don't. I was very impressed with her temperament."

"As well as her beauty, no doubt," sniggered the Captain.

"Yes Sir. No doubt about that," Dalton smiled.

"Do you think she will actually show up this morning, Corporal?"

"I don't think a nor'easter could keep her from honoring her word, sir. I just have that feeling about her, sir," Dalton replied.

The captain measured the young man and said, "Instincts young man, instincts is a primary requisite of being a good officer, and I agree with you; she'll show up. When she does, I'll want to talk to this Japanese artist in private for a while, so tell her that I asked you to show her around town for say, a half an hour, understood?"

"Yes Sir, I am curious a bit as to why, if you don't mind me asking."

"Alliances Dalton, alliances. That's a crazy bunch down at Perkins Cove by all accounts. Part of our job is keeping the peace, not just reacting when the peace is disturbed. It's a lot safer for everyone if we manage people as it were, rather than being forced to knock heads together, would you agree?"

Dalton nodded.

"We've got us a very delicate situation down there in the cove. We've got naked women lounging around, and most say they are all prostitutes. We've got bootleggers using that cove for protection, and they don't like the attention those women bring, understandably. There aren't too many hidey-holes for those boys to sneak their booze into the bay between Kennebunk and Portsmouth, so them naked girls laying on the rocks basically reduces that number by one, savvy?"

"Yes Sir, I'm beginning to see where you're going with this," Dalton brightened as the concept of the value of forming alliances was filling his brain.

"I thought you might. Stick your head out the door quiet-like and check to see if Drake is in will you?" the captain directed.

"He doesn't seem to be about yet, Sir," Dalton said as he sat back in the chair.

The captain looked Dalton square in the eye and said, "Thank you Dalton. Now, do you think Miss Meadows is a whore?"

The young man was completely taken aback by the question, but held the captain's eyes while pondering his response in all the seriousness the question warranted. He swallowed hard and said, "Sir, I'd say it is more likely than less in some manner, but frankly I still admire how she handled herself in here yesterday. I have to confess that your walls don't bury the sound in here much if we really want to pay attention out at our desks. And frankly, with a gal like her in here yesterday, we all were listening pretty closely. Sorry Sir."

"That is why I asked you to peek outside to see if Drake was about, but I'll get to that in a minute. I consider it to be in our best interest to have a set of eyes and ears down there in the cove, and Miss Meadows likely thinks that we have done her and her clan quite a favor by demonstrating a bit of kindheartedness for the situation with this Japanese fellow. I want to cultivate that gal's loyalty to us. I want an alliance down in the cove that might balance the 'goings on' down there, rather having to rely on the fishermen. Oh they're trustworthy enough, but that's a tight nit group to be sure. I know who the bootleggers are in that bunch to a certain degree, but we'll leave that up to the federal boys unless they force my hand. That's what I tell the Town Council anyway, and they seem to agree that this is the best approach, at least for now. Have you ever heard of the 'Second Clan', Dalton?" the captain asked.

"No Sir, but I have heard of the Ku Klux Klan," Dalton replied.

"You are a practicing Catholic, are you not?"

"Yes Sir."

"I was raised a Baptist myself, but my church-going days are limited to the times my wife absolutely insists. Not being a married man, yet, you likely won't understand. Anyway, The Second Klan is kind of the second coming of the KKK, though it is not likely that we'll see any hangings of our darker folk, though we might if we let them go unchecked. These fellows don't want anyone other than 'their kind' in our communities, so that means Catholics, either Irish or Canadian, are persona non grata, as they say. Anything other than a white protestant is not welcome. They spout about 'Americanism', but it'll cost you a ten dollar 'klegel' to become a member. Like with all religious organizations, the 'higher ups' end up rich while the members suffer and are squandered. It ain't easy to leave these kinds of organizations either. Have you been approached Dalton?"

The young man's breath halted for a moment, before admitting nervously, "Yes Sir, I have."

"And your response?"

"I told him I would think about it."

"I expect you are taking your time. You know our Sergeant Drake has been on the force for almost twenty years, did you know that?"

Now visibly nervous, Dalton replied, "I did not know that."

"How do you get along with Drake? Do you consider him to be a good officer?" the Captain queried.

"I guess I get along fine with Sergeant Drake. He is my superior officer."

"Good answer, but you didn't answer my question, did you?" the Captain measured, "But no matter, your non-answer was an answer in itself. I recognize your loyalty to a brother officer and commend it…to a point however. So as long as we understand each other now, has Drake been pressuring you to join the Klan recently, and while you're at it, how much money did he offer you to keep silent after your first visit to the Meadows place down in Ogunquit?"

Knowing that the Captain was likely well aware about Drake and his heavy-handed style of law enforcement, Corporal Richardson recognized his opportunity to voice his increasing concerns about Sergeant Drake, who he had continually attempted to distance himself from, but yet remained dutiful to Drake's directives. "May I speak freely, Sir?"

"Please do."

"Drake put fifty bucks in my hand just the other day. He said it was a gift from Mr. Meadows. He wouldn't allow me not to accept it, saying that brother officers have to stick together. That's what he always says by the way, when he shakes down a pub and such, I'm sorry to say. We don't have much choice in the matter, but it makes me feel pretty rotten. He also said that now that I had the money, my ten dollar membership fee shouldn't be a problem. Actually, he gave me until today to pay up."

"What are you decided to do, young man?"

Dalton pulled out an envelope from inside his uniform pocket and handed it to the Captain. Inside the envelope was fifty dollars and a hand written note that read, 'NOT INTERESTED', in capital letters.

The Captain took the note and tore it up and threw it into the waste basket at his side, and placed ten dollars back into the envelope. He opened his desk drawer and put what appeared to be two cloth insignias, as well as a couple of pins into the envelope with the ten dollars. In another envelope he placed the rest of the cash, as well as a piece of paper that he had obviously previously written on.

"Alliances, Inspector Richardson," at which the young man blushed noticeably. "Alliances. With increased rank comes an increased responsibility. In this envelope is forty dollars and a sheet of paper that details your expense record. Use your best judgment as to how you spend it. If Miss Meadows actually appears this morning, I suggest your first expenditure might be a scoop of ice cream over at the apothecary so you can strengthen your, er, alliance with her and her group. Let nature take its course, son, but keep your wits about you. Your first responsibility is always to this desk right here. Clear?"

"Crystal, Sir."

"Second, you will now become a card carrying member of the Ku Klux Klan, but do your best to hide your identity and draw the line if they tell you to do anything illegal, or threatening to others. Clear? And remember, the KKK espouses prohibition, but they make a lot of their money doing just the opposite. I want to know who the big-wigs are in these parts and how they operate. Take it slow, but infiltrate these guys, and once a week, come out to the house and report your progress."

Richardson nodded just as a knock on the door by the desk Lieutenant interrupted their meeting. "Cap, that artist gal and some little oriental fellow are in the office, er, sorry if I'm interruptin'!"

"Please offer them some coffee and tell them that I'll be a few minutes. Thank you."

"In this envelope also are your chevrons to be sewed on your uniform, as well as two pins signifying your new rank, which perhaps Miss Meadows will help put on your lapels. And just so you know, your paycheck that is in your drawer signifies your new pay grade. You see Inspector Richardson, I made this decision about your new position well prior to our conversation this morning. Now regarding Drake, I will inform him that you are on special assignment, reporting to me only. When he pumps you for information, tell him your assignment has to do with the art colony, but that is all. He'll likely let it go at that. Any questions so far?"

"No Sir, I think I understand my orders, and thank you for the promotion and your trust, Sir."

"You'll make mistakes, but we all do. You are no longer required to be in uniform by the way, unless instructed otherwise, by me. But again, use your best judgment. Now, please show this Jap fellow into my office and go take Holly out for a sundae. I should be done with her friend in a half an hour or so. Oh, and make him feel welcome a bit before showing him in. I don't want him peeing his pants on my floor!" he smiled.

Dalton rose, and vigorously shook the Captain's hand with a mutual respectful stare and exited the office.

He passed by the Lieutenant's desk and motioned to Holly to wait another minute or so, and went over to his desk and removed his pistol sling and jacket. He fished the two pins signifying his new rank, and the forty dollars from the envelope and put them in his pants pocket, and placed his holster sling back across his shoulder and went over to the bench where Holly and the Japanese gentleman were sitting.

"Good morning, Miss Meadows!" He shook her delicate hand. "And you, Sir?" he said as he offered his hand to YaYa, who meekly stood up.

"May I present Mr. Yasao Kuniyoshi," Holly said as she also rose, while YaYa earnestly bent forward at the waist, as was his custom, and then gently shook Dalton's hand, which it basically disappeared into. Dalton took a step backward and tried to imitate the Japanese greeting, which greatly impressed both Holly and YaYa.

"Good morning Sir. It is a pleasure to meet you, though I will need some help pronouncing your name," smiled Dalton, just as Drake appeared in the doorway to witness the mutual greeting, which he clearly did not like.

Seeing Drake out of the corner of his eye, Dalton quickly spoke, "I am Inspector Richardson, would you please follow me, Sir, and Miss Meadows, and I'll be right back. The Captain has instructed me to address a couple issues with you while he meets with your friend, please," as he motioned for Holly to sit back down.

He led YaYa to the Captain's door and put his large hand on the slighter man's shoulder and whispered, "Our Captain is very nice, please feel at ease," which greatly relaxed YaYa.

Dalton quickly returned to Holly, hoping that Drake wasn't being his overbearing, threatening self again toward her, which is why he said to Holly that he was under Captain's orders so that Drake might leave her be. As he approached the bench that Holly was just raising from, Drake spoke out from his desk, "Richardson!"

"Yes Sir," Dalton replied as per usual, albeit without the customary salute now voided by his new rank.

"Did I hear your introduction to these folks correctly?"

"Yes Sir, the Captain informed me of my promotion only this morning, Sir," Dalton said earnestly.

Drake moved away from his desk and stared at the younger, yet slightly taller man and asked, "Do you have the chevrons?"

Dalton brought them forth from his pocket and said, "I haven't had the chance to put them on yet, Sir."

Drake measured the man again and put out his upturned palm with the expectation of Dalton handing them over, which Drake did not. Drake looked at Dalton with rare kindness in his eyes, smiled and said, "Inspector Richardson, it would be my honor." Dalton placed the pins in Drakes palm and stood at attention and said, "Thank you, Sir. That means a lot."

Drake applied the pins on Dalton's lapels, patted them down and stood back for an appraisal.

"For old time's sake?" he asked as he came to attention and saluted, to which Dalton responded in kind, as the other officers in the all stood and voiced in unison, "Here, Here!" The salute concluded, Drake said, "Carry on, all!" and turned on his heel back to his desk, completely ignoring Holly.

"Miss Meadows, will you join me for a moment outside?"

"Of course, Inspector Richardson," Holly said, in obvious deference to the scene she had just witnessed.

As they reached the street, Dalton boldly held out his elbow for Holly to grasp, which she did while saying, "That Sir, was quite impressive, and may I offer my sincere congratulations. That is quite a promotion for such a young man, is it not?"

"Thank you ma'am, and please call me Dalton, Holly. It caught me by surprise also. How about some ice cream to celebrate?" he asked with a new swagger of confidence.

The two of them crossed the street to the apothecary where there was a lunch counter. They cut quite a sight for all who saw them, and Dalton was sure the rumors would fly before the day was out, but he did not care one bit. The most beautiful girl in the world was on his arm and that was that.

Holly offered, "Sergeant Drake certainly appeared to be impressed also?"

Just as he reached for the apothecary door, he smilingly whispered to Holly, "Drake is a complete jackass and a discredit to the uniform. If he ever tries to bully you again, I'll wring his ignorant neck myself!"

Holly was shocked by his words but then recovered in a giggle as they entered the shop.

"There is a reason he has never raised past the Sergeant level, as you might imagine, but my feelings about him are our secret, Holly. May I trust in that?"

"You surely may. Your wife will be very proud of your promotion, Dalton. I bet you can't wait to share the good news," she smiled.

He measured the girl's inquisition and motioned for the counter girl so that they could order, which they did.

He smiled at Holly, and said, "You women are always so clever. I live in a small, shabby one room apartment, Holly, and have a relationship with a gal that I don't want to be anything more than an acquaintance. Would you ever consider going on a date with a cop, Holly?" he blurted out without actually realizing what he just said until it was too late.

The counter girl brought their ice cream and Dalton placed a few coins on the counter in payment, and took a spoonful of his ice cream so he could avoid her gaze, and perhaps the letdown of the expected denial.

"Dalton, aren't you supposed to look at girl when you ask her out on a date?" she pleaded a bit.

"You are right, Holly. That wasn't very manly of me was it? It just kind of came out without my realizing it, but yes, ma'am," he said as he looked directly into her eyes this time, "May I have the honor?"

Holly held his gaze for an extended moment and said as she placed her hand on his forearm and said, "As a matter of fact, Sir, I kind of beat you to it!"

She reached into her purse and handed him the envelope she had addressed to Corporal Richardson, and then asked the counter girl if she could borrow a pen. The girl returned with a Waterman ink-filled pen and Holly shook it next to her ear to confirm that it had some ink. She took the envelope back as he read the invitation to the 4th of July extravaganza down at the Sparhawk Hall. She crossed out 'Corporal', blew on the ink for a few seconds so it would dry, and wrote above it, 'Inspector Dalton Richardson', and laid the pen back down on the counter so the waitress could fetch it at her leisure.

"Do I have to get all gussied up, Holly?" he asked.

"No Dalton, just come comfortable. You understand that I am going to be very busy that night and for this next week obviously, with all the arrangements, and you know I, as the hostess, have certain responsibilities to our guests, but I'll be hoping that my last dance of the evening is with you," she said as she held his eyes and she gripped his arm a little tighter.

"I am truly honored, Holly. I will be there for as long as I can be. I don't know when I have to be on duty, but a hurricane couldn't keep me away. Now we must get back to the station, I imagine Mr. YaYa has had a morning of it!"

They arrived at the station to see YaYa sitting outside on the steps with a huge grin on his face. He stood as Dalton and Holly approached and Dalton signaled for a hack, which soon clopped up. Just as Holly was being helped in she exclaimed, "Oops, I forgot something!" and she hopped up the stairs back into the station, soon followed by Dalton. Captain DuValier was standing next to the Lieutenant when Holly said, "Oh excuse me Sir," as she dove into her purse.

"What is it Miss Meadows?" the Captain smiled.

"Oh first, these are my references that I promised, and this is for you. Thank you very much for meeting with Mr. Kuniyoshi. I am sure he is sufficiently informed now, and I will keep a closer eye on our friend. Also, I wanted to tell you that I have accepted your advice and I am going to hire some guards to patrol our grounds when the artists are working with our models. We will be much more discreet than we have been. Thank you again, Sir," she shook his hand and took her leave. "I hope to see you at the 4th of July festivities, Dalton!"

"Thank you Miss Meadows," the Captain called after her as he looked at the two envelopes she had given him. The first was labeled 'References' and the second was addressed to Captain & Mrs. DuValier, which was clearly an invitation. He looked up and said, "Inspector Richardson! Did that young lady just address you by your given name...you rascal!" At which the entire staff chuckled as Dalton turned beet red. All were jovial, except for Drake.

It was getting close to noon when the hack came to a halt outside the Ogunquit Apothecary. As YaYa helped Holly off of the seat she could see Mrs. Spenser staring at her through the glass window, and Holly thought to herself, 'Oh crap, I'll have to deal with this sour old bitty again', but she strolled to the door as YaYa hurried to open it for her. As she entered she turned briefly to YaYa to encourage him to enter with her, for he was also reluctant when Holly had confided that her first reception by the couple was less than friendly. She suddenly heard Mrs. Spenser exclaim, "Good morning Miss Meadows, it is good to see you again," which utterly stunned Holly to the point of almost innocently pointing to herself as if to say, 'Are you sure you are talking to me?' This unexpected gesture of kindness really threw Holly off-kilter a bit, but she was rescued from the awkwardness when Mr. Spenser interceded with a jovial welcome of his own.

Holly recovered from her surprise and replied, "Well yes Ma'am, Sir, it is a fine morning in our beautiful place by the sea; it truly is! May I present our visitor from Japan, Mr. Kuniyoshi, who prefers to be addressed as Ya by his friends, and Ya, please meet Mr. & Mrs. Spenser."

Both Donald and his wife came around the counter with

broad, welcoming smiles and began to extend their hands just before YaYa bent at the hip in a solemn and sincere gesture of welcome, as was typical of his heritage. Taken somewhat off-guard by the moment, both of the Spenser's made a genuine attempt to imitate the gesture and as soon as they both unbent themselves YaYa smiled broadly and grabbed for their hands to heartedly shake them both, which greatly impressed the Spenser's. Holly interjected, "You have made Ya feel most welcome by bowing in his cultural manner, and though he does not speak very much English, you have likely made a friend for life. Thank you both very much," Holly said sincerely, especially to Mrs. Spenser.

"In his country you would be known as 'Chemists', and they are very highly revered," Holly stated.

YaYa and the Spenser's continued to exchange niceties about the weather and his visit for the next few moments as Holly withdrew the list that Byzar provided and compared it to Spenser's pricelist, only to find that most of the items from Spenser's were priced only slightly higher than what could be procured out at the rum-line, so she filled out her order for Mr. Spenser and handed it to him while he was still engaged with YaYa. He had noticed Holly comparing two pieces of paper and whispered to Holly as they excused themselves toward his counter and said, "I see you are comparison shopping, young lady! That is very wise of you. How do my prices compare?" he asked.

"Honestly your prices are only a little higher than others, but we prefer to support our local businesses. Your opium and laudanum are a bit higher but I prefer to purchase quality rather than taking a chance on medicines from unknown sources," she said.

As he fumbled with jars and bottles, Spenser asked

hopefully, "Might I inquire as to which of my competitors you have visited?"

Holly thought it a bit forward for him to ask, but decided that such a question was in character for such a gent and replied, "Of course you may, I don't find that inappropriate at all. I have quotes from Wells and Portsmouth, as well as the ships out there on the rum-line; never hurts to explore all the available options. Your hometown service is highly valued by my circle, Sir."

"My wife and I greatly appreciate your loyalty, and by the way, Miss Meadows," Spenser said as he leaned slightly toward her and lowered his voice and whispered. "Both I and my wife feel that we mistreated you on your first visit, and feel poorly for it. We feel victim to that we preach about on Sundays, being that we succumbed to rumors. I hope you will forgive us?"

"I appreciate that, Sir. I am not my uncle, and I certainly recognize the uniqueness of our art school and the commotion it has presented. Along with the police department, I am initiating some modifications to our operations designed to minimize our impact in the community while maintaining our rights to conduct our business. I am charged with the task, and I know that all agendas cannot be completely satisfied, but I am going to try to assure that we will be good neighbors."

"That is very well said, young lady. You continue to be quite impressive. May I carry you packages to your taxi?"

"Ya, if you please," Holly said as she caught YaYa's eye and motioned for him to get the packages from Spenser, while she dug into her purse for the required cash.

"Please pay my wife at the register, Miss Meadows, and thank you very much for you patronage," Spenser said as he motioned for Holly to proceed to the register where Mrs. Spenser had stationed herself.

"Hi Mrs. Spenser," Holly smiled as she dug into her purse for the requisite amount of cash. "Oh by the way, Sir, Ma'am, this invitation is for you in the hopes you will be our guests for the 4th of July festivities at the Sparhawk Hall. It is my understanding that Senator Fernald, Judge Johnson and many State Representatives are planning to attend to receive the princess that we have been hiding for the Government. Oops, I guess I just spilled the beans, haven't I!" Holly declared while feigning surprise.

"Ah, so that is what you spoke of yesterday. We will keep it close to the vest. That is indeed exciting for our little town. I, for one will not get any sleep if you don't continue spilling the beans, young lady!" Spenser smiled in anticipation of hearing all the details. "Oh please do," Mrs. Spenser chimed in, almost embarrassingly so.

"No sense in trying to put the beans back in the can!" Holly laughed along with the Spenser's, who were now unabashedly engaged in the conversation. "The royal is a young lady we were hiding from those who wished her harm back in her home country as a result of the war. She still doesn't know about the welfare of some of her family back in her home, for she was spirited out of the country for her own safety and the US government secretly placed her in our art school so that rivals couldn't find her. Evidently the rivals have been dealt with and she can now reveal her identity and live without worry for her personal safety. She is a very sweet girl," Holly informed them, all the while knowing that the entire story was a fabrication.

"Oh my, how sad, and yet exciting. Will she be in your school for long? Have we seen her around town?" asked Mrs.

Spenser, who was obviously immediately intrigued with the entire fairy-tale.

"You may have, Ma'am. She looks like a gypsy and always walks with the models from the school. You may have heard of the girl who dances on the beach that causes quite a stir? Well, that young woman of supposed loose morals is none other than the Sultana of Crisana! Crisana is a country somewhere in the middle Europe. She is like the queen of England, in her country. Can you imagine? I heard that some of the guests at the Sparhawk were complaining that the dancer on the beach was a trollop, and yet they were talking about a queen! People assume too much without the facts sometimes," Holly concluded, letting her final statement linger.

"Anyway, we have to go. I hope to see you at the event and I will be sure to introduce you to her. She is quite friendly and enjoys talking to the local people and learning about their lives and customs. She will likely join me at Vassar in the fall to begin her studies."

"I didn't know you were a college girl! What do you study?" Mrs. Spenser stated in a bit of surprise.

"Yes. I begin my second year in the fall, and my major is mathematics, with a minor in art history. I hope to graduate a year early," she admitted.

"Oh my, that sounds impressive. It's no wonder your uncle chose you to help him manage his affairs," Mrs. Spenser continued.

"I try to keep on top of things so my uncle can concentrate on his art and writing. It has been quite an education so far, as you may imagine. I really must get Ya home. We have a great deal of planning for the upcoming festivities, and I do hope to see you there. Remember: let's keep the beans to ourselves, if you please?" Holly asked as she stepped gaily through the door, knowing that the entire town would likely know about the Sultana by the time the sun retired for the day, and that was just what Holly intended to happen.

"How on earth can you sit still in the sun for so long, Captain Sunker?" one of the models asked as she watched the eight artists paint the posing Captain. He sat wide-legged on a sweat-soaked pillow on top of an overturned pail. He wore only his hat and his boots with a towel flung over one thigh conveniently hiding his genitals that seemingly hung almost to the ground. The towel was held in place by the weight of his belly roll on top of his upper thighs. His ever-present, unlit pipe was clenched between his teeth to the left. Behind his makeshift seat a pitcher of ice cold alcohol-laced lemonade balanced on the rocks within easy reach.

"It's not uncomfortable at all, lass, even when the sweat rolls down the crack o' my ass," he guffawed, which drew similar hoots from the rest of the gathering. Sunker had yet to leave since arriving at dinner the night previous, and still was the star of the show, as it were. He was awakened in the late morning by breakfast in bed from Lesley, and a blowjob from Lauren. The breakfast was good also, he thought. He figured that sitting out and getting sunburned was a small price to pay for the services received, and he was really looking forward to a healthy dose of beer as soon as he felt it was proper to take his leave politely. He made sure to tell the gathered artists that he would be happy to return in a few days so they could finish their paintings of him, thereby hopefully assuring another go-around with the two models once he recovered from the first, and quite extended session.

"Elsa, it seems like I haven't seen you for ages, you too Byzar, I miss you guys!" Holly said as she joined the two, and Meadows, in his lair for a meeting.

"You have been very busy my dear, we all know," Elsa smiled. "Let's all have a cookout when we're done here. A nice relaxing evening is in order, don't you all think?"

"A banner idea! A nice evening to watch the stars arise amidst the ocean waves," Meadows whispered poetically. "Let's begin. How are we doing with the invitations, ladies?"

Elsa nodded to Byzar and the girl took her cue. "The invitations have gone out and Mr. Jacobs sent word that all is arranged on his end. Dinny has provided more than enough liquor and has agreed to allow us to pay after the proceeds are received, as well as allowing us to return any that is not used."

"That is really nice of him, Byzar," Holly said with mirth. "How on earth did you convince him to agree to such terms, I wonder?"

"I simply asked him, that's all," Byzar replied in mocked offense.

"Is that some 'gypsy spell' you have over that innocent boy," Holly chided, while all giggled.

"Once the festivities are concluded, I intend to let Dinny teach me how to sail, and I will teach him how to properly eat a clam; draw your own conclusions!" Byzar snickered and continued. "The latest politician to be invited is some gent named McIntire, who lost the last election for Governor. Even if the politicians don't show up, they'll likely send their underlings in some form. Oh, and Judge Johnson replied that he will attend.

"Did we send an invitation to Governor Milliken? I understand he is a staunch prohibitionist while never refusing a drink himself. Typical of the 'do-gooder' ilk, is it not?" Meadows commented.

"Ya, he probably is faithful to his wife too!" Elsa commented while they all chuckled in agreement.

"I understand he has quite an interest in the motion picture industry, which likely means he supports the arts also. It would be a real boon if we could ever get someone in his position to visit us. Even if he doesn't show up or reply, let's make a point of introducing ourselves in some fashion after the festivities," Meadows concluded to the nods of all around.

"How are our accounts, Holly?" Meadows asked.

"All square and healthy, and the models all have a small stipend for their personal needs and whatnots. I propose that we all take a break before the weekend if we can. I know the girls want to get all gussied up and do each other's hair and such, and frankly, I would enjoy a little sisterhood time myself. How 'bout you Byzar…Elsa?"

"I think a break from the rocks and easels would do us all some good," Meadows interjected. "Let's let everyone know that after tomorrow, all are responsible for their own meals and that the kitchen will be open and stocked. Holly, why don't you give Mrs. Parent a hundred bucks and tell her that her family won't be expected back at work until Tuesday. Agreed everyone?"

"Done," said Holly. "I have a few more hours of desk time

to finish but then a relaxing cookout and a couple days of lounging around are in order. I think I'm going to curl up in my blankie for quite a little while. If some hunky chap happens to wander by, send him up to my blankie, won't you?" she chortled.

"Well if a hunk does show up, I doubt our girls would let him get that far, and even if they did, I doubt there'd be much left of the poor bastard!" Byzar chuckled.

"You're probably right, Sultana of Crisana! I might have to make do with just watching and a vegetable of my choice!" Holly responded to the laughter of all.

The evening was proceeding as perfectly as Meadows and his crew could have imagined. Jacobs and the Sparhawk received all the profits from the food service, while Meadows Art School furnished the bar and other sundries. Elsa managed the two rooms that Jacobs provided at no cost, so that the models could be rotated comfortably through them at an efficient pace. Leslie was in most demand, for she was insatiable in her acquisition of short-time clients. As the festivities approached midnight, she had averaged three clients per hour, and the party had started almost seven hours earlier. Elsa handled the money, and Leslie pocketed a healthy ration of tips. The other models were active but a bit more modest in their conquests. All in all, Elsa was seemingly relieved of her tasks as resident *mama-san*, as by this time discreet word of the models indiscretions had been effectively passed around the male clientele of the party. Holly was kept 'off-the-market' for the time being, as it was decided that it would be more productive for the school if she would be able to nurture her relationship with the newly promoted police officer from the town of Wells. So far Inspector Richardson had failed to show, but Holly was confident that he would. What she didn't know was that Richardson had been present all along, but had effectively hid himself among the throngs of guests so he could observe from afar. Elsa had a list of suitors for both Holly and the star of the evening, the radiant Sultana of Crisana. These two girls would be entertaining their clients for thirty minutes at a time at a small cottage that Meadows had secured earlier in the summer on Obed's Lane, a healthy stone's throw away from the Spar. Both girls commanded a healthy price, with Byzar's charms worth almost twice that of Holly, and as soon as the evening winded down, they would commence their schedule. Holly and Byzar had been the most sought after dancing partners of the evening, and both had grown quite weary by this time of the night. They caught each other's eyes and enjoined for a trip to the ladies comfort room for a well-deserved breather. Elsa followed and the three discussed their impending carnal schedules, as well as a brief accounting of the evening's proceeds from the efforts of the models. Elsa estimated that before the holiday weekend was concluded the school would likely net over twenty thousand dollars from all the girls' activities alone, not including alcohol sales and such. Meadows would be entirely content with the outcome of the weekend, and all concerned would enjoy healthy bonuses they concluded.

As they emerged from the comfort room for a final hour of dancing and entertaining, a handsome young man dressed in a casual brown suit stepped into their path in a seemingly invisible manner and spoke with his blue eyes affixed directly at Holly, "I wondered when the prettiest girl at the ball would reappear?"

Both Byzar and Elsa immediately withdrew with startled and appraising glances, as Holly blushed and eventually found her voice.

"Why Inspector Richardson, you seem to have appeared out of thin air, Sir. Where did you come from?" Holly asked.

Byzar couldn't help herself and spoke without reserve: "Heaven, obviously," while Elsa nodded in agreement.

All eyes held for a moment before Holly found her composure by making the requisite introductions. As Dalton shook each woman's hand, they melted like butter with his touch and one could almost feel their knees quiver through the floor. Byzar quietly spoke after the introductions concluded by commenting, "Well Sir, it is quite a pleasure to meet such a fine representative of your country's government. If all of your officials are like you, then your country is obviously in fine shape. If you care to dance before the evening is out, it would be my honor, Sir?" she asked boldly.

"Miss Sultana of Crisana, you favor me with such kind words, and I in turn would be wholly honored to be fortunate to share a dance with you, but alas, I must confess that I am at the mercy of my heart, and it longs for the touch of only one. Holly would you do me the distinct honor?" he said as he held out his arm toward Holly.

Holly, as hardened as she was, was completely flustered at the surprisingly confident manner of Inspector Dalton Richardson, and placed her hand on his arm without realizing it, and floated along at his side as he angled for the dance floor. The entire room seemed to be held hostage by the sight of the two of them approaching the floor, for any soul could recognize the magnetic connection between them. As he held out his arms to begin their waltz, he drew her closer than he should have, and bent down to whisper in her ear, "You'll have to lead, because I have no idea what to do now!"

Holly leaned back and laughed with a delicate, animated giggle.

"Follow me kiddo," she chuckled as she began to subtlety direct him with her eyes and manner to enjoin with the music. Three dances had been concluded before they realized that they had not taken their eyes off one another. Holly imperceptibly shook herself to her senses and realized that her plans of taking this man to her blankets on the beach would have to be postponed due to her obligations for the balance of the evening over at the little cottage, and it immediately depressed her.

"Dalton, er' Inspector Richardson, your appearance has made my night, and may I be so bold as to say that I am as attracted to you as you are to me. Am I correct in my assumption, Sir?" she said as they strolled out onto the veranda. Holly caught Meadows eyes at the bar for a moment and he nodded his approval and appreciation of the enjoined couple.

"Holly, you couldn't be more correct. You are simply lovely," he said as he swept his hand behind her head and swooped in for a quite unexpected kiss.

Holly melted in his arms, and after their lips separated, she placed her forehead on his chest and said, "Please don't do that again, for if you do, I will fall more helplessly in love with you than I already am, and that simply cannot be right now."

She gently released herself from his grasp and headed directly back to the ladies comfort room, hurrying her pace through the crowd as the tears began to flow. She reached the comfort room and dove for a cushioned stool in front of one of the large gold leafed framed mirrors, and sobbed.

"Crap!" she said aloud.

From behind her a strange woman's voice announced, "Even whore's fall in love, my dear."

Holly turned in anger and was gritting her teeth as she was about to pounce, when the dignified older woman fixing her hair in front of another mirror interrupted, "Just calm yourself young lady. You don't seriously think you and your models are the only whores in the room do you? Most of us high society gals are just the same but in a different way. It is one of God's cruel tricks on us women. He gives us a vagina to play with, but encumbers it with pregnancy. He gives us a brain, equal or better than that of a man's, but places us in a society where we are not permitted to use it to support ourselves. What is left for us, I ask you? Listen honey, if you figure out a way to use your charms to your best advantage, then do so, by all means, and I mean all means. The other trick God plays on us is that just as soon as we figure out a method of supporting ourselves with our charms, he sends some irresistible man creature down to us, and we fall hopelessly in love with the bloke. Every person in the room knew you were a goner the minute we saw you hook arms with that delightful piece of beefcake you were dancing with. But it could be worse you know. You could be me. I'm married to a slob that is thirty years older than me. He is a politician of some note, so we are wealthy and enjoy the fruits of society. I fell in love with a seaman a few years ago, but it will never be unless my old bastard kicks the bucket. Maybe his heart will blow up while he is pumping one of your models tonight. I sure hope so, dear God I do. Hell, he might even be humping you when it happens. Oh, and don't think you gals are so clever, every woman in the place knows about your 'art school'. We're mostly irritated that we can't join in the fun!"

The woman stood and brushed the front of her obviously expensive gown and turned for the door, never once glancing at Holly, who was still befuddled by the honesty and accuracy of the lecture she just received.

"I hope Dalton leaves," she said aloud to the mirror in front of her.

"He's having a chat with Valentine," Elsa quietly said as she slid over to massage Holly's shoulders. "I heard that woman's words also, and there is nothing she said to disagree with. I know what you are going through right now, but get through the night, and finish your tasks. Go on a date with your beau later in the week. But now, we must finish our jobs here, yes?"

"Yes Ma'am. I know. It just hurts. I'll be worth every penny tonight, trust in that. I just wish I was loving that man right now, rather than being a righteous whore tonight, but that is what I am, isn't it?"

"We all are, Holly, just as that woman said. She just does it in a different manner than we do. Now clean yourself up and let's see if we can get you and Byzar over to the cottage without anyone being the wiser, and I'll start bringing over our customers. You have five and Byzar has eight, and they have paid very well. I also have a full schedule for the both of you for tomorrow, and then we'll see what the new week brings. Good to go?" Elsa asked.

"Yup. The sooner we start, the sooner it will be over. I hope Valentine doesn't hurt Dalton's feelings or tells him how I am spending the night" Holly wondered aloud.

"You know better, Holly. Meadows has a lot of maliciousness in his soul, but he respects you very much. Trust him. If anything, he is probably creating a scenario for the young man to be available for you after the festivities are over and your duties to the house are concluded. Keep your head about you, girl, he butters our bread very well, as you know."

"Thank you Elsa. I needed the pep talk and to refocus. I know my tasks, let's get with it shall we?"

"Inspector Richardson, are you not?" Meadows whispered as he sidled up next to the hulking young man leaning on the railing, who was trying to disguise his tears in the foggy ocean air that wafted in from the salt-water infused Ogunquit River only a stone's throw below the deck where he stood.

Dalton turned toward the whispered voice and initially saw nothing, then lowered his eyes onto a very slightly built middle aged man with a hint of a moustache and the most ghostly set of eyes he had ever seen. Immediately he knew that he was in the company of Valentine Meadows, the object of as much curiosity as had any single individual been during his time as a peace officer, and not much of it favorable. The eyes, those menacing vacant set of eyes he had always been told of now were boring into his soul as if his every fiber was immediately available for manipulation by this diminutive fiend. Dalton caught his breath both from the astonishment of Meadows presence as well as the raw fissure that had been carved into his marrow by Holly's abrupt parting and confusing words. She implied that she loved him, but what exactly did that mean? Was she really a courtesan, as his Captain had implied, or was she really just an innocent niece of a devious man?

He shook himself out of his fog and rasped a delayed reply to the man standing at his side.

"Yes Sir, I am Richardson. My apologies. My head was elsewhere."

"The affairs of the heart take precedence in most cases, young man, especially when they are not entirely expected. My niece is a fetching creature to be sure, is she not?"

Dalton again did not immediately reply, nor did he hold his gaze with Meadows, for he returned his moistening eyes back to where the stars met the ocean off in the wandering distance.

Meadows continued, "Forgive me, Sir. I am Valentine Meadows, Holly's uncle, and I, like the rest of our little fraction of the world here at the Sparhawk just witnessed the obvious emotional electricity you and she just shared, and perhaps long for, and remember those rare occasions that we humans are fortunate enough to experience, outcomes notwithstanding. Love can climb mountains we are always told, but most times the task at hand is simply too daunting to even attempt, as I fear it might be for the two of you."

By this time Meadows had tactfully withdrawn his offered handshake and turned to lean onto the railing, realizing that the Inspector had no intention of shaking his hand, for the young man was aware of his proclivities, and likely was abhorred by them. Still, the young man was recently wounded in the heart, and Meadows recognizing the vulnerability, swooped in to seize the opportunity to attempt to create a personal connection from which he could call upon if ever he needed a favor or a request fulfilled. To Meadows it was all a continual game, this manipulation of lesser intellectual beings for his advantage, and it was so very rare to be challenged by worthy adversaries, but the perpetual hunt for foes of every kind made life worth continuance. He enjoyed tearing down the righteous and exposing their perpetual hypocrisies and he nominated Inspector Dalton Richardson as his new conquest. With the exploitation of Holly's charms, deflowering this young man would almost be too easy, but an enjoyable diversion nonetheless.

Dalton cleared his head with a quick shake and turned toward Meadows and offered his hand, "I am sorry Sir for my rudeness, my mind was elsewhere. You are Mr. Valentine Meadows, yes, yes, I am remembering now. You are one of the artists down here in Ogunquit, and Holly's uncle, she tells us. I am pleased to finally make your personal acquaintance. You mentioned a mountain to climb I think. Again, my apologies, my thoughts were elsewhere."

Meadows shook hands and wondered if his hand was just enveloped by a bear paw, and replied, "I certainly understand Dalton, Holly has that effect on people, losing their trains of thought as it were. May I call you Dalton?"

"Yes Mr. Meadows. You mentioned mountains?"

"An age old conundrum, young man. A man and woman fall in love and love knows no circumstances. Circumstances can seem like un-climbable mountains but in most cases the mountains are nothing more than molehills where love is concerned. The question is whether the love in its essence has the temerity to see mountains as such, would you agree?"

"I am afraid you are speaking in terms above my pay grade, Mr. Meadows, but I think I understand your intent," Dalton said as he turned to measure the man by boring his own stare into the set of eyes that wilted most, if not all others. Emboldened by Holly's admission of affection for him, and also by his charged task from Captain DuValier, Dalton cut to the point, "Mr. Meadows, is Holly your niece...legally, I mean? If she is not, you'd be saving me a great deal of time and paperwork, for I will find out the truth anyway, as you know. So is she or not?" he said as he towered a little closer than appropriate; a trick he had learned from his former mentor, Sergeant Drake.

Meadows immediately sobered a bit as the young Inspector seemingly grasped the conversation abruptly away from the heretofore confident and smarmy Meadows.

"Uh, no she is not my niece, Dalton. Not legally I mean," Meadows struggled to blurt out as he took a subconscious step back to create a little more space between the two. Meadows fell back to his childhood in his mind very quickly, remembering himself to be the coward at every turn. Those of brave and strong bent naturally held their ground at the least when bullied in such a manner, and it wasn't until Meadows had learned that his intellect could be a very effective bullying tool, did he ever embolden himself to face aggression such as Dalton's unexpected boldness.

Dalton pressed on.

"Word on the street is that your art school is really a front for drug dealing and prostitution, high priced for sure, but prostitution nonetheless. Is there any merit to these rumors, Mr. Meadows? Frankly I could care less, Mr. Meadows, even if I were on duty, which I am not. Regardless, I could never afford the prices either, so Mr. Meadows you see, I could give a shit either way. So why don't you help me out here a little, Bub? Is Holly a whore? It would save me a good deal of anguish, 'cuz obviously I could fall for her hard. Knowing she's really a whore, regardless of price, sure would save me

203

the effort of having to find out the truth, while I am on duty. If I find out while on duty, then I'd have to do as I am charged, and that would be bad for you, Meadows. You get my drift, Bub?"

Meadows smiled, which surprised Dalton a little, and turned back to the railing before speaking. "Holly is everything she says she is, Dalton. She is in college and acing all her courses, as I understand from her professors. She is the only daughter of a now deceased attorney in New York, of some repute I might add, and she is now the manager of the affairs of the art school. It is an art school to be sure young man, quite renowned also. However, you are perceptive and I can certainly understand how rumors come about, given the style of art we favor. How people associated with the school conduct their personal lives is not my business, nor is it that of Holly's, Lord knows she has enough on her plate just with the business of operating the school. She has proved to be indispensible, really, and quite a pleasant surprise as to her astuteness, as you have turned out to be, young man."

"Good answer, a wise man once said to me," Dalton said, thinking of his recent conversation, verbatim, with his Captain, "but you did not answer my question, did you?"

Meadows thought for a moment while considering how to respond. He spoke his private thoughts aloud unintended, "Well you are certainly a greater challenge than I would have thought, Inspector Richardson, and you are correct in that I did not answer your question, nor any of them, did I? As to the question that really concerns you at this moment, I think that is more appropriately addressed to the object of your affections. A gentleman does not speak of these things, nor of the conduct of a lady, and Holly is, by all means, a lady. However I doubt if my opinion is of much use to you, and truth be told I doubt if my opinions mean much to anyone anymore." Meadows directed his attentions solely to the expanse of the ocean before him and continued, "You know young man, I am highly sought after for my opinions in the art world. That is how I make my living, and I have done very well in that regard. Everyone values my opinions of art, its trends, and particular economic values for specific works." Meadows went on a bit longer before turning toward Dalton with a question, only to find that the young man was no longer there, nor likely had been for quite some time, for he was nowhere in sight. Meadows sighed and thought, 'He probably got all the information he needed in the first minute of our conversation anyway. Crafty young man, he. I haven't been played like that in say, forever. Kudos to him, the bastard.'

"You are becoming quite the sailor, I hear," Meadows whispered to Byzar as they sat on the front porch on wicker rocking chairs, gazing out at the early morning sunrise.

"I really like being out on the water, and Dinny is really a patient instructor. Elsa, you should come out with us, you too, sometime, Valentine!"

"I am afraid I have had my fill of the ocean, my dear. Every time I travel to Europe and back I eventually get seasick. When I travel across the ocean now, I basically crawl into my bunk and pop as many pills as I can so I can pass out through the entire ordeal. Waves and I do not get along," Elsa said.

"Maybe next summer I'll have your Mr. Dinny provide us

with a sailing dory, so you can take out our guests as well, young lady. That is if you are not sequestered in some regal castle somewhere in the world by then, Madame Sultana!" Meadows chimed in. "However the way things are going, you might be barefoot and pregnant with a brood of little Dinny's by then, from what I see," he smirked.

"I'll have you know Sir, *my* Mr. Dinny has been very well trained in the past month, if I may say so myself. The odds of me being impregnated by that wonderfully simple man are very slim, for I know his every twitch, and at the exact time. My little eggs and his little swimmers, well, from nary 'tween shall they meet, or something like that!" Byzar giggled.

"He is a very easy guy to like however, and I do like him very much. But anything more than that is simply not on the menu, I can assure you. I do enjoy pumping the bloke...for information also!"

"How is our Holly doing?" Meadows asked. "She stays at her desk much too long these days, and from what you say Elsa, she is not as enthusiastic about entertaining our gentlemen clients as she was earlier in the summer. Do we have a problem with her?"

"I don't think so Valentine. She certainly doesn't receive any complaints that I know of, but I also miss her funny-bone personality that we have become accustomed to. She used to be a much more social gal, and I miss that Holly also. Byzar, what do you think?" Elsa asked.

"I think she has fallen in love with that cop, and has perhaps realized that she can never be in love with anyone, because of her job. Silly girl. I'd almost say stupid girl, but we all know she is anything but that, don't we?" Byzar said. "She and I need to have some girl talk so I can remind her how her bread is buttered and that being a small town cop's wife would be an exceedingly dreary life. She needs to use her connection with that hunk to our best advantage and protection. Screwing a cop is the perfect setup — she just needs to be reminded to keep her heart out of the equation, and remain the sultry slut she truly is!"

"Well said princess, and please let me know if we have anything to worry about after your girl chat, eh?" Meadows appealed.

"I think I'll wander around and find her. Now is as good a time as any," Byzar said as she took her coffee mug to the sink and rinsed it out, and hung it on the hook on the wall bearing her name, right along with all the others.

"Elsa, we seem to have hit the jackpot with Byzar and Holly, haven't we?" Meadows commented. "How did we get so lucky?"

"Oh Val, I don't know how we could have gotten any luckier. I do feel a bit uneasy about losing control of our operation however. I mean I feel almost useless because of how well they do their jobs and the responsibilities both have naturally assumed. Holly practically runs the place now and Byzar keeps the other models in line like a mother hen. She quiets any drama from the girls and handles all the client issues before I am ever called. I have so much free time these days it seems," Elsa wondered.

"Nonsense Elsa. From my perspective you are simply reaping the benefits of your expert training. They admire and adore you, as do I, of course. You and I continue to attract new faces to our little cove, and our Holly and Byzar take it from there. I'll tell you this Baroness," Meadows whispered on, "having Holly run the operation means the world to me, and the deft manner that she has dealt with the police and our suppliers have me in awe of the young lady. I think there is a bit of genius in that pretty little noggin' of hers, and I am truly glad that she is on our side. My biggest fear now is losing her to some man or other business. I know Jacobs would hire her in a heartbeat to manage his hotel, and not just because he wants to bend her over."

"You are, as always, very kind Valentine, and you are my dearest friend," Elsa said as she grasped the frail man's hand. "What do you intend to do with the girls at the end of the summer season?"

"I hope to keep Holly at my side at this point. Sometimes I think that I cannot function without her. I have grown so accustomed to having tasks already completed almost before I even think of them. She may want to go back to school however, but isn't the point of schooling to make one more marketable? I doubt she could find suitable employment even after she graduates that would compare to the compensation she receives from me, so it will be a bother for us both. Byzar I haven't thought of yet, but she has proven herself to be quite an asset also. I just don't know whether I have a place for her at this point. Certainly the Sultana of Crisana cannot come to New York City, for she'd be exposed in a heartbeat and that would not play well for my reputation at this juncture. I am not even sure that we can bring her back next summer, and I still worry that our little charade will be exposed before the summer season is over even here in our little hamlet. Do you have any ideas Elsa?" Meadows inquired earnestly.

"Actually Val, I do. What would you think of sponsoring Byzar to come to Europe with me? She would function for me in much the same manner as Holly does for you. It would allow me to funnel future and foreign clients your way in a much more efficient manner, I believe, as well as expanding your influence into Europe within the art appraisal world.

What do you think?"

"I think it is a banner idea Elsa, even without calculating any of the angles! The art world on the other side of the pond remains haughty and persnickety, but having a direct access to the New York City market is certainly nothing to sniff at, at least for those who utilize the investment options that art provides. I've spent enough time over there, and have enough contacts to get you both started in increasing our client base for appraisals. We can even expand my magazine articles to include a European edition. This is positively inspiring, Elsa, what a grand idea, darling! Work out the details as we only have another month here in the cove, and I am ready to return to the land of the living back in New York! Elsa, you never fail, do you?"

"It gives me something to look forward to also Val, and, oh dear I think Byzar and Holly are having quite a girl talk in Holly's office, did you hear that loud bang Val?"

"How could one miss it? Do you think we should intervene or let them figure it out?" Meadows asked with sincere concern.

Both Elsa and Meadows held still at the table to see if there was to be any more banging coming from Holly's office. The loud noise sounded like a thrown book hitting a wall, followed by a short burst of a non-descript emotional shout. Listening closely, they both could hear some muffled chattering coming from the office. Elsa spoke up, "Well, there doesn't seem to be any bloodcurdling screaming forthcoming, so maybe you and I should stroll over to the school and calm the natives, as it were, for they for sure must have heard also. Girl talk can sometimes be quite emotional, darling Val. Take my arm and let's go for a stroll."

The two left the kitchen and headed out into the bright

sunny morning while still within earshot of the chattering 'girl talk'.

"It just hurts sometimes, you know Byzar?" Holly cried. "Sometimes it really gets to me. I like romance and all the drama that goes with it. It makes me feel alive and wanted, for me, for me!" as she gestured toward her heart with her left hand, as she bent to pick up the ledger book she had just violently thrown against the wall in anguish.

"Have you ever been in love Byzar, I mean bone-numbing, breathless love?" Holly pleaded.

Byzar replied, "I won't permit it. My love is my commodity, and I sell it to survive, it is as simple as that. Girls like you and me do not have the luxury, nor the time for such a trivial thing, at least not at our age. I thought you already had figured that out?"

"That is sad, Byzar, that is truly a sad way to live," Holly said as she cast her swollen, teary eyes on the seemingly innocent girl leaning against the wall.

"Holly, sit down for a moment and listen to one of the few people in this world who understands what it was like to live your childhood. You know mine well enough to know that neither of our pasts are very pleasant, right?"

Holly imperceptibly nodded as she returned to her desk chair.

"Look at us now. Look at our future now. Men will come and go. In a few years our youthful appearance will be lost, and we'll be replaced with younger and prettier girls — perhaps none prettier than you, but younger, fresher versions to be sure, correct? You and I are a pissed-off, or a jailed Valentine Meadows away, or a dead Valentine Meadows away from working the corners every time the sailors have shore leave. Look at Elsa, she is insane, I mean truly insane, beautifully I know, but insane nonetheless.

"Why? Because she has lived her entire life living on the edge of hunger. Her extravagance is her only meal ticket, and that is only fed at the whims of wealthy haughty women, for she is too old and worn out to be an attractive fuck anymore. I'm not going to be her in twenty years. I'm going to save every coin I can, and exploit every deep pocket I possibly can, and I have the sensuality to do it. When I'm Elsa's age, I'll have a well-stocked bank account or a teetering aged husband, or be a wealthy widow. When that is accomplished, then I will consider love, and I will tell you that when I finally permit love to enter my heart, I will fall as hard as a woman can fall, and why is that? It's because all of the denying I will have done, and all the abuse I have taken will be worthy of finding true love. I will not allow myself to be Baroness Elsa at forty five years old. My body now is my tool to be sure I will never, ever go hungry again. When I am no longer desirable and am too old to trade money for my sex, I will not be hungry. Why do I not permit love you ask? That is the answer, and you, you delightful, smart, funny and drop-dead beautiful young lady — and a lady you truly are — better take a good long look in the mirror and chart your course, and realize what ocean you are sailing on. Our options are few, Holly, and you better get a grip pretty quick. I worry about the end of the summer and what Mr. Meadows intends to do with me, if anything. I don't have any prospects right now and I am getting a bit nervous, even though something might turn up with this Sultana malarkey. You, on the other hand are likely going to be going to New York and continue on as Mr. Meadows aide-de-camp, unless you let your emotions get ahead of your judgment. I mean, Holly, that cop is a hunk to be sure, but what the fuck are you thinking? Do you think you can be a cop's wife? Do you think you can live in this town after being a model here? You think you can take your children to school in this town? Your job is to cultivate that uniformed ape for the best advantage of this operation. I'm not going to stand by and let you screw things up here, and threaten the best shot in life I've ever had," Byzar scolded as she walked over and firmly grabbed Holly's face in both her hands. "Know this sister, and I love you like a sister, but if you start screwing this little arrangement up because of your flighty little heart, I'll, well I won't permit it. Remember, I am a gypsy at heart, and I will personally slit your pretty little throat." She stared into Holly's teary eyes and squeezed her head in her hands just a little tighter. Holly was about to take a swing at Byzar as anger boiled in her, but just then Byzar emphatically released her hands and stepped back with all the sweetness her eyes could conjure and said, "Holly, the problem with being actresses, and whores like us are the best in the business, is that it is often difficult to tell when one is acting, and when one is not."

"Come on outside and mingle, and maybe drop your robe and pose for a while. Lying around naked on the rocks amongst all the roving eyes and the salt breeze might free your mind of silly notions, my friend!" She lightly skipped out the door, seemingly transformed into a little girl without a care in the world.

Holly was befuddled and completely dazed by what had just transpired. She also felt a twinge of fright, not so much by the direct threat to her life from the sweet little gypsy, for such violence was a fairly well known trait of the travelling bands, but her uneasiness was borne of how quickly Byzar was able to transform from a threatening murderess into a seemingly carefree little girl in an instance. Holly knew she would never feel safe sleeping near Byzar ever again. She was truly spooked.

The delivered message resonated however, and everything Byzar said was, in the truest sense, her reality. Holly's rather comfortable upbringing could not match the streetwise little gypsy's tainted and hard outlook on life. Oh Holly was wily enough as well as savvy, but Byzar had completely exposed Holly's inherent naïveté. She considered Byzar's speech again and again, and evaluated each point on its merits, and began to formulate conclusions with a few disagreements. Holly knew that she could never survive without the potential possibility of being in love. She concluded that she just couldn't consider it anywhere near where she worked. Dalton was as fine a man as she might ever find, but she had to shut her heart to him immediately, and proceed in a charade designed to have the big galoot fall for her. He was a tool to be used, and necessary for the safe operations at the art school, which she was responsible for. Placing her livelihood, as well as that of the others who depended on the school operations for their livelihoods, above her heartstrings was an immediate and easy decision to make. Once she had this decided, it felt like a huge weight was released from her shoulders. She only worried a bit about the next time she would see Dalton, because of the chat he had had with Meadows, but also whether she was cruel hearted enough to pull it off.

She sat in her chair and gazed out toward the rocks where three models were posing in various stages of undress while a dozen easels were attended by guest artists. She wondered aloud, "Aw hell, he probably knows I'm a whore anyway, so what the hell was I thinking? I'm gonna go out and find that little bitch and thank her and give her a hug. But I think I'll also tell her that I'm bigger and stronger so if she ever intends to cut my throat, she better make sure I'm unconscious, because if not, I'll kick the shit out of her.

"Then I'll tell her that I love her like a sister also!"

"Hey Din, did you hear that a whole passel of revenue agents arrived in Portsmouth?" Eben asked as he untied his nail pouch. His cabin shell was almost finished and he could slow down on the construction process now that he had a roof over his head. He would have plenty of time to finish the inside in the fall, when the liquor business slowed down after the tourists disappeared.

"I hear that Portland has a passel of them also all of the sudden," Dinny replied. "Ya know what else? I hear that the outfit that built the Dixie III is building four more boats for the government that are faster than the Dixie. Probably lighter too, since they won't have to fill the cabin walls with sand to stop the bullets, I'm guessin!"

"Don't you think the rumrunners will shoot back, Din?" Eben wondered.

"Oh I expect they will, but the runners ain't doin' the chasin', they're doin' the runnin', so if'n they're shootin', the new boats only gotta be protected at the front, not all the way around like the Dixie, so I expect the new boats will be lighter anyways, don't ya think?"

"That's some good thinkin' Din. I'm also thinkin' that the Dixie and them boys might attract most or all of the attention of them agents so all this new activity might be a good thing for us all the same. Keep the pressure off of us, ya know? Nonetheless, why don't we change our deliveries up for a spell, just in case we're getting too predictable?" Eben suggested.

"Im with ya pard! I'm a little leery of that cop who comes down to visit Holly and ask bunches of questions though. I've heard he's been around out of uniform also. I think we ought to keep an eye at for that gent and avoid him like the plague."

"Yea, I doubt we're big enough fish to worry about compared to the Dixie III outfit, and I'm guessin' that he's really tryin' to dig up more dirt about what that art school is really doin' but we really need to keep an eye out for him for sure," Eben offered. "See if Holly will let you deliver a big enough load to last them through the summa, would ya? Offer a discount if she won't do it. We got no moon in a few days and I expect all eyes will be on the water, and we'll be deliverin' from Pa's barn. Maybe that's the best way. Either that, or maybe we can wheel it over on a wagon in the middle of the day; hide it in plain sight kind of deal? If Holly's so all freekin' smart, let her figure somethin' out, heck, I don't know. What ya think?"

"I think I'll wander by in the mornin' and visit that crew when they're wakin' up. Them gals like to sit on the rocks in the mornin'. That way I likely won't have to visit with that evil sonofabitch, Meadows, and maybe the Sultana will want to go for a sail," Dinny offered.

"You sweet on that gal, Din?" Eben asked.

"Tough not to be, Eben, but I know anything beyond an occasional sail and skrewin' ain't in the cards. I sure ain't gonna fall like you fell for Holly, even if you won't admit it," Dinny chided.

"Inspector Richardson!" Capt. DuValier chided, "So good of you to grace us with your presence. I see that you have been cashing your paychecks so I know you are still among the living. Would you care to have a chat in my office?"

Inspector Richardson was obviously a bit embarrassed to be called out in front of all of his cohorts, but then figured that the normally reserved Captain likely had a reason for doing so, and he let the slight pass as he entered DuValier's office, and closed the door behind him.

"What have you learned Inspector?" DuValier asked as he leaned back in his worn-out brown padded chair.

Dalton brought out his notebook and said, "I have a checklist. I've divided my report into two parts, the first being things I can prove and second, things that I cannot yet prove but are confident are true. I decided that I would not make any arrests unless citizens are in imminent danger or illegal activities are being flaunted in public. I hope you find this approach to be acceptable."

"I have every confidence that you have a good grasp on the purpose of your assignment, please proceed. I think I am going to enjoy this!" DuValier said with a smirk.

"Alright, here goes: Mr. Jacobs at the Sparhawk is a thief, and not a very good one at that. I don't think he can help himself. I've watched him enter rooms countless times and guests later report thefts to the front desk. He thinks he is clever by robbing guests usually just before they are scheduled to check out. Typically the guests go for breakfast on the day they check out, and he waits until they are all eating and he slips into their rooms, usually in and out within ten minutes. When and if the guest discovers the theft, they usually don't have the time of inclination to wait for the police to arrive to make a report, so they make a claim at the front desk and then hurry off to catch the train or whatever. All soon forgotten once home. We can easily set a trap and catch him in the act if you choose," Dalton concluded.

"A good ace to have in case we ever see the need to play the hand, what's next?" DuValier asked.

"The bootlegging crowd is mostly made up of small timers around Ogunquit. I have names. The most prolific outfit is the three gents that own the Dixie III speedboat, which I know you are aware of. They are a crafty bunch. They make fake runs into Perkins Cove for the purpose of making the revenue gents continue to think that the Cove is their favorite place of business, but it's not. It's just a ruse they use to keep the government boys busy, and it appears to be very effective," Dalton said while obviously hoping his Captain would ask for further information, which both Dalton and DuValier knew he would.

"You are grinning like a Cheshire cat young man, so go ahead and impress me!" the older man sighed. "I can see that you can hardly contain yourself so consider yourself commended on your investigative prowess. Police work can be fun, can't it?"

"Yes sir, I did enjoy figuring their methods out, though I'm sure there are more to discover. When I first started to investigate the flow of booze, I quickly concluded that chasing these guys around was a waste of effort, so I decided to try to bite the apple from the other side, and stake out their delivery points and then retrace their steps by eliminating their 'obvious' recent behaviors and then learning what they weren't doing, if that makes any sense?"

"Well it does and it doesn't young man. Why don't you blow a little more wind up my arse and maybe I'll catch your drift before it turns into a squall?"

Dalton was a little taken aback, but smiled as he realized DuValier was enjoying the discussion more than Dalton could have hoped for and said, "Yes...well sir...that was truly eloquent! Anyway, it turns out that these guys really use the fastest boat in the region for fodder with their pals down at the cove at their drinking sessions. Here's how it works: they load the three gallon tins of booze into a weighted fishing net that they tow towards shore very quietly and when they get into the lobster fishing grounds, they add a little more weight and affix lobster buoys to it and let it go. Then they idle over to where they know the revenuers are on surveillance, and then speed by toward the cove. The revenuers can't keep up and the Dixie III gents get into the cove, make like they are offloading contraband, and speed away just in the nick of time. Should they ever get caught, all they were off loading was fishing gear. Meanwhile the next day, the sputtering lobster boat makes its rounds and tows the stash into the harbor in broad daylight with no one the wiser, and the stash appears to be like any other delivery. Pretty clever, don't you think?"

"I won't ask how but you say you can prove this, in a prosecutable manner I mean?" DuValier inquired.

"Not a doubt in the world, Sir. We just nab the lobsterman with the stash attached to his boat, and I expect he'd start singin' when faced with losing his livelihood if we impounded his lobster boat!" Dalton replied.

"That's a fine piece of detective work, Richardson, and let's keep this little tidbit in this room. Yet another card in our deck! Is there more?"

"A few more items, Sir. The local KKK is basically all bluster and little action. Our Sergeant Drake is their bullyboy for sure. I think, rather I know, that he enjoys it. The KKK big shots walk a tightrope with him, because they need him in their corner, but he knocks heads without their authorization and is creating more problems than they appear to be having a tolerance for. I think the KKK boys will take care of Drake in-house, if you get my meaning. Drake is frustrated that he isn't ordered to do more head busting so I don't know if Drake will disappear of his own accord, or the local guys will make him disappear. Whichever way it goes down, I think Drake is going to disappear one way or another. I think it is a serious reality, sorry to say, Sir."

DuValier sat for a moment, looked at Dalton, and then sighed. "I'll have to ponder on this one a bit. Having a chat with Drake is likely useless at this point, because he is in too deep. I wonder if a transfer might be a good solution, but I doubt if I can get him far enough away to save his hide and I'm not sure I want to dump a guy like him on a fellow administrator. It certainly is a ponder. How much time do you think we've got before things blow up one way or another for our dear Sergeant?"

"I think something is imminent, or at least by the end of summer, Sir," Dalton replied.

"I was afraid of that, because summer is over in a couple of weeks. I have other sources saying the same thing, so again, good detective work young man. Is there more?" DuValier asked.

"The last bit of news falls into the second category: that

being things I can't prove, yet, but I am confident are true," Dalton said with a bit of discomfort. "At least some of the models down at Valentine Meadows' art school are, in fact, high priced prostitutes. I haven't spent much time investigating this but have eavesdropped on a number of liquored-up gentlemen whose boastings are quite informative as to costs and the prowess of some of the gals. Seems that foreign royalty gal is particularly popular, and yes, sadly, the niece, Holly is quite sought after, if these, uh-hum, gentlemen are to be believed. And no, Holly is not truly Valentine Meadow's niece, he just calls her that. Frankly, I don't think Meadows is interested in females or adults if you catch my drift," Dalton said summing things up.

"I am truly sorry to learn about Miss Meadows, Dalton. I hope you are okay with the knowledge and can separate any feelings you have for the girl. Sometimes life is cruel. I'll tell you this though, in my experience gals that turn tricks generally don't have comfortable stories to tell about their childhood. Setting the religious babble aside, sometimes people do what they have to just to survive," DuValier stated with great concern for Dalton.

"I understand Sir, and appreciate your thoughts. I still admire her attributes and she truly is a beautiful woman. She's not a small town girl by any stretch. My intention is to string her along for information, nothing more, but thanks again for your concern," Dalton replied.

"Good job Inspector. I'm glad you've got any affairs of the heart squared away. Now where do we go from here, is the question. Why don't we visit again in a couple days and we'll plot a course. Go about your business but take a little step back. Why don't you take a couple days off and put your badge in your back pocket, so to speak. You've accomplished the tasks we set a few weeks ago, in fine fashion I might add, and now I need to gather all this information in and make some decisions," DuValier said.

"I'd really like to keep going, Captain," Dalton said before DuValier interrupted him.

"No Dalton, get away for a couple days, and I'll make that an order. I've got other irons in the fire and I need you to disappear. I appreciate your position, because I know how immersed an undercover guy can get, but I know you trust my judgment, and I trust you to follow my orders. I've got my reasons, young man," DuValier said in a gentle, yet stern manner.

"Yes Sir. I'm sorry Sir, I didn't mean to...,"

Again DuValier interrupted, with a wave of his hand and said, "I know Dalton, I know. You've done a better job than I could have hoped for, now get out of here and get away from your work for a couple days. Leave the door open when you leave, please."

"Thank you Sir, for everything," Dalton said as he stood up and opened the office door. As he walked out of the building, he looked at his colleagues all sitting at their desks, including Sergeant Drake, and recognized their appearance of being immersed in their work, just like he used to do, and wondered how much of the conversation they had all heard. As he stepped down the police station steps out into the mid-morning crispness that only a Maine summer can provide, he felt some relief that Drake's desk is the farthest away from DuValier's office.

"It's like this every year at about this time, Byzar," offered Dinny as he settled his back against the transom while nestling the tiller under his armpit. Byzar settled onto her pillow on the port side of the dory just aft of the centerboard after hoisting the sail. "Toward the end of every summer, one day the water seems to turn a deeper shade of blue, the water temperature drops about ten degrees, the morning air has a palpable crispness and little white caps begin to appear. It's Maine's way of telling us all that summer is going to be over very soon, and each morning is like the summer folks being encouraged to find their suitcases. Up until the last couple of years, our little town would revert to its normal shuttered settlement, but now the construction of summer places and hotels keeps our little village humming right along. Have you decided what you are doing after the summer?" Dinny blurted out without the awkwardness one might expect in being so innocently forward with a beauty of Byzar's societal station—real or contrived.

Byzar and Dinny had reached the proverbial silent understanding that while they enjoyed each other's company on these sailing excursions and their playful dalliances, both knew that this was the extent of the relationship. Byzar was of course well versed in separating herself from any emotional attachments, while Dinny was quite proud of himself for maintaining emotional distance also.

"I confess to you, Dinny, I'm going to miss you, truly, but the world calls as you know. This will be our last sail so let's really enjoy ourselves; what do you say?" Byzar announced while revealing nothing about her future plans, other than implying that she was departing Maine in the very near future.

Dinny again blurted out his somewhat emotional reply,

222

"Gosh Byzar, do you think you will be back next summer?"

"All I can tell you Dinny is that I'm leaving the country. Would you write to me if I sent you're a letter?" she asked.

"I surely would, though I'm not much with writin' and such. I've never gotten a letter, much less one from another country! Wouldn't that be somethin', me gettin' a letter from another world?" he wondered excitedly.

"Well that settles it, Dinny, my very good friend. Once I am settled in my new country, you'll be the first person I write," she said as she readjusted her seat so she could snuggle in next to Dinny's other arm.

Dinny couldn't help but wondering aloud as the dory plied through the gentle ocean, "Who'd a thunk that a feller like me, would be sailin' along on a beautiful Maine mornin' with a more beautiful foreigner Queen or some such!"

The Sultana blushed and reached up and pecked him on the cheek and said, "Oh Dinny, you are the sweetest guy — you really are."

Dinny buried his nose in Byzar's hair and took a deep breath as he pressed a bit harder. Both could feel their mutual comfort in the others bones, but knew the impossibility in the marrow. Dinny whispered, "Can you smell the storm M'Lady?"

"I actually think I can smell and feel something in the air; it is almost a foreboding, spooky feeling. Could my instincts really be true?" Byzar wondered.

"That's what all our sailing time has given you, or inspired an ability you never knew you had. Some fishermen never have it, some are born with it, and some get it through experience. Once you have it, you'll never lose it....just like you'll never forget the smell of this part of the ocean. A nasty storm is a-brewin' for sure, and the first storm of the winter always claims someone. When we get back, you'll see a lot of the boats will be tied higher and fast with more than one line. We fishermen are known to be a spooky bunch about such things!" Dinny explained.

"We'll set an easterly course against the waves so if the conditions kick up, we'll be able to come back in a following wind. I got a feeling it's goin' to get snotty before we know it."

Two hours later the wind had indeed picked up and Valentine, Holly and Elsa were sitting on the porch gazing out at the bobbing dory as it made its way back toward the cove.

"It's getting to look stormy out there all of the sudden," Holly announced. Meadows just nodded as Elsa remarked, "Do you think they are in trouble out there?"

"They seem to be heading in the right direction but they might have a little trouble turning into the cove with the waves getting larger by the minute. I'd sure hate to be on one of those schooners out on that rum line tonight, that's for sure," Holly commented.

"I am sure that those scalawags out there have seen a lot worse, but I share your sentiments my dear," Meadows whispered, "but I'll tell you who I do worry about, and that's the bootleggers. Greed will inspire them to make their runs tonight because they figure that the Feds won't test the fates in such weather. Ah…the risks of the heartier breed! Me, well I think I'll go upstairs and open the window and enjoy some of our happy juice and float on the winds. Perhaps one of you ladies will visit me later tonight and warm my blankets and soothe my weary soul. I'll be too tired for any strenuous conquests, I'm sure, but I would greatly appreciate any attentions you may provide, as well as making sure that when

I am off in dreamland, I have enough blankets so I don't catch my death of pneumonia!"

Holly chimed in before Elsa could comment, putting her loving arms around Meadows neck from behind as he was still seated in his porch chair, "I'll make sure you are taken care of after you reach la-la land later on tonight, as I can feel the temperature dropping every minute. Are you getting a little chilled also, Elsa?"

"It is getting a bit brisk, though it still seems that we should have summer, doesn't it? Yesterday it was summer, and today it feels like winter is just around the corner. Maine weather is quite fickle, it seems."

"Before you retire Valentine, shall we discuss how we will purchase passage for Byzar and Elsa back to Europe, and provide for their needs for the winter?" Holly asked.

"Are there sufficient funds in the summer account to accommodate their requirements?" Meadows asked Holly.

"More than sufficient, Valentine. July and August have been very profitable; well beyond your initial projections."

"Then you gals work out the details, and Holly will visit the bank and withdraw the necessary funds. Now I think it is time for me to adjourn to my room, ladies," Meadows whispered as he gathered his lap blanket and shuffled off to the stairway without a backward glance. When Holly and Elsa heard the last footsteps at the top of the stairs, they looked at each other in an awkward silence. Holly finally broke the silence, smiled and asked, "Elsa, I need your help with this. Please tell me how much money I should withdraw for you and Byzar, I wouldn't have a clue."

"This is a bit awkward to be sure. We will be in Europe for at least nine months before returning here for next summer, so two round trip tickets and, say two thousand per month for our needs — what do you think dear?" Elsa offered.

"How about twenty-five thousand dollars, some in cash, some in the form of bank drafts, or whatever the bank suggests, for each of you? Then each of you can sort out the details of passage and living arrangements once you arrive. How does that sound?" Holly asked.

"Oh dear, Holly, does Val have that much in the bank? That is quite a sum!"

"He does, and much more. I think Byzar is going to be quite astonished, but after we visit the bank, my task is done and I can turn my attention to closing up shop for the winter and making the arrangements for Valentine and I to move to New York City. I am really excited to experience the city, I've never been!"

"You will find the city to be very exciting, especially in your new station as Val's personal assistant. Lots of well-heeled gents in Val's circle, and I am sure they will all be vying for your attention. I doubt you'll ever have to hook ever again, unless you want to, of course! You might even fall in love, you fickle child!" Elsa chided good-naturedly.

"I hadn't considered any of that Elsa, but now that you mention it, you are likely right. Now my mind will start to wander. I really haven't had any time to think about my new life in New York. I am a bit concerned about Valentine. He is awful forgetful these days, have you noticed?" Holly asked.

"He is medicating himself much too much these days, that is quite evident. And yes, I also have noticed a decline; he's not as sharp as he was earlier this summer. Maybe when he gets back to the city he will become inspired again and begin writing critiques again. His opinions are still the most sought after among those in the arts. With you at his side, my guess is that this will be a banner year all around!" Elsa offered.

"I like your optimism, Elsa, and I truly hope that Valentine gets his head back on his shoulders once we leave here. I am dependent upon him solely for my welfare, and depending on a drug addict is not wise, but I think I can manage him. I just need to get him back to New York sooner than later, I think."

"I think that would be wise Holly," Elsa offered, "and take care of yourself in the process, just in case Val teeters off the edge more than he has. You keep him out of the gutter over here, and Byzar and I will do our part in Europe to extend his influence and by the time next summer rolls around, we'll all enjoy the fruits of our labors back here in this intoxicating place, yah?" Elsa giggled.

"I better go upstairs and check in on Valentine, you know the other night he got so stoned that he crapped a little in his bed. That's what made me very worried more than anything. I think that when we go to town tomorrow, I'll book passage for all four of us on the same train down to New York. That way you and Byzar can crash at Valentine's place until your boat leaves, and perhaps the transition back to the real world will be easier for Valentine. Maybe we can encourage him to clean out his system at the same time. He has become somewhat belligerent during his decline, and maybe all four of us travelling together will force him to mind his p's and q's," Holly said hopefully as she stood and headed for the stairs.

"Tuck in our friend up there, Holly. Even a limp, passed out addict appreciates a little fondling before slipping off to La-La land, my dear. Not that you need to, but it's a great way to keep yourself in a gent's good graces, yah?" Elsa advised.

"Yah, mine Baroness" Holly chuckled in her best attempt

at Elsa's contrived accent, as she ascended the stairs for the evening.

It was close to midnight when Holly descended the stairs into the kitchen. Byzar and Elsa were enjoying an evening chatting about all their plans for a sponsored year in Europe, fueled by warm tea infused by the wonderful liquor that Dinny supplied.

"Is this a private party, ladies?" Holly mused.

"Only if you don't enjoy our little concoction, sweetie," Byzar snickered. "You look like our little recipe might cheer you up, 'cuz you look a little out of sorts, dearie."

"No, I'm fine, just a little concerned about Valentine. When I went to his room earlier tonight to tuck him in, he was passed out and really chilled. His windows were open and he had fallen out of his bed. I managed to get him into bed and he pissed on himself and didn't even know it. He was really out of it, and his whole body was really cold. I cleaned him up and lay with him for a while to warm him up, and when he eventually became somewhat coherent, he started coughing a lot. He is not a healthy man these days. We need to get him out of here soon, because if he is trying to drug himself to death, he is doing a good job of it," Holly stated matter-of-factly. "To be blunt, we need him alive for our own sakes."

"He doesn't look good these days either, I've noticed, and he's just not the same old Val," Byzar chimed in. "I don't spend as much time with him as you both do, but he also seems to be losing weight, and he really hasn't got it to lose.

He barely weighs more than a scarecrow as it is."

"Listen to the wind; it is really a raw, dark night tonight. I get the chills just looking out at the waves crashing on the rocks. I can't imagine being out on the water on a night like tonight; so dark and gloomy," Holly offered. "I'm so glad to be snuggled up in our little kitchen, with our little friends," she said as she raised her mug to her two tablemates and took another sip, all in unison.

It was midnight and the gals were winding down their evening. From the nearby fishing village they heard a sudden flair of activity. Byzar stood up and wandered over to the window to investigate and said, "Something must be wrong, all the fishermen are lighting torches and heading for the shore and their skiffs!" She grabbed a blanket and threw it around her shoulders and opened the door and stood against the rail on the small landing and peered into the darkness as fishermen came closer to the inlet. "What's going on?" she yelled to no one in particular, hoping that the news wasn't bad, and somewhere in her heart pleading that the news didn't involve Dinny. Out of the darkness a voice called back shouting, "The Dixie III has blasted the rocks and she's gone under, we hear. All her cargo is floating in the brine!"

"What of the crew?" Byzar called out, relieved at least that Dinny was not involved. "They all made it ashore," the voice called out. By this time Elsa and Holly had joined Byzar on the landing and all watched men seemingly springing up from the ground to venture out into the waves in search of the floating cargo, likely to be the 180 proof Belgian booze in three gallon tin cans that the Dixie III was noted for supplying.

"If I weren't so looped I'd join in the fun!" Holly said as she turned back into the kitchen,"and if it weren't so fucking cold out there."

"They'll all have their fun tonight," Elsa said. "I bet the entire town will be catatonic by lunch tomorrow. I know I will be if I don't go to bed! Goodnight girls, we have a busy day tomorrow. I hope the banker is sober tomorrow so we can make our arrangements and purchase our tickets down to New York. Ogunquit was fun while it lasted, but now I think Mother Ocean is telling us to go away while we can. The thought of being outside on a night like tonight just gives me the creeps!"

The three women staggered up the stairs and fell into their beds amidst the muffled shouting and activity all around the house. Holly curled up in her blankets and debated whether to look in on Valentine again, and finally decided that she should. She grabbed her candle in its tin holder and tip-toed to his bedroom door. She always preferred the feel and fragrance of a candle over the musty burn smell of electric light bulbs. She could smell the vomit as soon as she opened his door and found Valentine lying diagonally face down on the bed with his head hanging off the corner where he had vomited onto the floor. He had kicked off his covers and when Holly put the back of her hand on his forehead, she found him moist and feverish. "Oh Valentine," she whispered, and still he did not stir. She grabbed a small towel next to the wash bowl on his dresser and after dousing it in the water, squeezed it out and washed his moustache, mouth and chin, and then grabbed the wastebasket and cleaned up the dried vomit off the side of the bed and the floor. There wasn't enough to even give her the heaves but she put the towel in the wastebasket and placed it out on the roof after opening the window to let in some fresh air. She kneeled on the bed and put her arms around his torso and dragged him toward the center of the bed, and then straightened his legs and pulled the covers back over him. After closing the window she went back to her room and stripped her blanket off her bed, grabbed a couple towels from her bureau and went back to Valentine's room and closed the door behind her. The flickering candle settled into a calm flame and the wooden ceiling no longer undulated like the waves she had become so accustomed to rocking her to sleep. She moistened one of the towels after managing to roll him over on his back, and began to dab his forehead, face and neck. After a few moments, he opened his eyes as a tear began to form in the eye closest to her, and was about to speak when Holly placed a finger on his lips and cooed, "Hush now, darling, you just close your eyes and rest," which he acquiesced to do. After he was snoring peacefully, Holly went back to the window and fetched the wastebasket, which the wind had yet to dispense of and put some water from the washbasin in it, swished it around and dumped it out onto the roof, towel and all. She figured that she would be prepared for more bile, should Valentine need to dispense of it. After closing the window, Holly pulled up the only upholstered chair in the room next to the bed, wrapped her blanket around herself, curled up and quickly fell into a deep sleep, synchronizing her breathing with the tormenting waves roaring on the rocks just a stone's throw away.

Elsa and Byzar had both finished breakfast and were dressed for town by mid-morning and most of the school's residents had already ventured into town as the day was too overcast and blustery to lend itself to any outside activity involving easels, and none of the models had returned from their various accommodations at the local Inn's and rented abodes. The 'kept' women were often ensconced in temporary quarters around town that their 'gentlemen' had rented for their purposes. There had been no sign of either Holly or Valentine and Byzar, knowing that a payday of some sort was in the offing after listening to Elsa's hints, could not stand waiting any longer, so she quietly stole into Valentine's room. Holly was still curled up in the chair while Meadows was snoring though he had again kicked off his covers during the night. Byzar touched Holly on the shoulder to wake her up and whispered her name. Both Holly and Meadows opened their eyes at the same time, and it was clear to Meadows that Holly had spent the night in the chair and had also nursed him, as evidenced by the towels, washbowl and displaced wastebasket.

"How are you feeling, Valentine?" Holly softly asked as she leaned over the bed and stroked his cheek. Valentine pondered for a moment, closed his eyes and whispered in a somewhat raspy voice, "Not too well, I think. You stayed with me, I see. Did I have another accident my dear?" he said recalling his loss of body functions on the recent night.

"You were only sick Valentine, and you have the sweats," Holly said. "I will make you some soup?"

"You are very kind, but Robare's mother can do so. I expect you have other tasks than taking care of such a woeful soul as I?"

"Actually I think Byzar and Elsa are waiting for me to go to the bank and depot to make travel arrangements, and I think all four of us should travel to New York together so you can get healthy back at home, if that is acceptable?" Holly asked.

"I am really not feeling well. Do what your think is best my dear, and shut the door when you leave if you please. I just need to rest," he moaned as he quietly dismissed the girls. "And Holly, thank you for attending to me; you continue to be very kind."

Holly smiled a bit, nodded and shut the door as she backed out of the room.

"It will take me only a few moments to dress Byzar, we have a lot to do and half the day is already gone. Tell Elsa I will be right down," Holly said.

It took the three women less than an hour to complete their banking business, much to the consternation of the other patrons who had already been waiting before the trio arrived. Details were handled personally by the bank president, if for no other reason than to preserve his societal standing in the face of the knowledge the three women had of his proclivities. Once informed that they were making arrangements to depart the area, he was all too happy to assist. The big Labor Day weekend was just around the corner and the models, as well as the house, were already fully booked, stocked to the brim with food and drink. There was nothing much more to do other than hurry up and wait for the endless party and the cleanup thereafter. The three women were now just anxious to depart Ogunquit and begin a new chapter; the trip to New York being the first step. Byzar, in particular, was still reeling with the fact that she had more money at her fingertips than she ever thought possible. It was nowhere near enough however, for her to alter her stated life plan, but it was a very healthy start. She was basically in a haze, with her brain off in varied tangents about what she could do with access to such a sum. At the train station she just sat on a wooden bench while Holly and Elsa purchased the required tickets. In the short term Byzar decided to go about her work through the weekend with a renewed vigor, and forestall any decisions until she actually boarded the train for the big city. In actuality, the thought of having so much money at her fingertips almost made her physically ill. Such splendid turmoil, she thought with a smile.

The weekend went off without a hitch, though Meadows saw none of it. At times he found that his legs would not function, and he had trouble controlling his bladder. Holly attended to him as much as she could while overseeing the operations in the house. She barely slept, and the men that she did entertain were shuffled out of her lair in a polite, yet hurried fashion. At one point in Meadow's delirium, he had asked Holly for an attorney, so he could draft his last will, and Holly suggested she find a doctor first. Holly also cautioned about retaining a local, small town attorney, for fear of word of the extent of his estate becoming the source of local scuttlebutt, and the likely attendant problems such knowledge might inspire. Meadows barely knew when it was day or night, as he insisted on his shades being continually drawn. Only the cool, crisp autumn air off the night time ocean gave Meadows an inkling of the time of day.

The weekend's patrons expressed dutiful concern about the absence of Meadows, but were not only far too involved with the festivities and their personal sexual proclivities to give much thought to the diminutive benefactor that if truth be told, wasn't held in high regard by most, and most certainly despised by those who were aware of Meadows reputation with little boys. To a man, they were dutifully impressed at how this buggering evil genius was able to provide this playground of the finest cigars, booze and women, without anyone being the wiser. They figured that by the time all the rumors required investigation, the tourist season would be over and all would be forgotten until the next year. Holly could only continue to hope that this sentiment was correct. Her entire focus was to get through the weekend and get Valentine Meadows, Elsa and Byzar on a train back to New York without incident.

Mrs Parent, Robare's mother, kept a pot of vegetable soup warming on the stove exclusively for Meadows, and restocked it often. She kept a little schoolchildren's slate next to it that said, 'Private Stock-Medicine'.

Early Labor Day morning, just as dawn approached, Holly tip-toed into the kitchen so as not to wake any of the souls passed out on the chairs and couches in various stages of slumber. Robare's mother was already at the stove adding ingredients to Meadow's soup and Holly obviously startled the older woman when she whispered a 'Good Morning' and hugged her from behind, just as the woman was apparently spooning in some sugar to the concoction. Robare's mother quickly recovered and returned the sentiment, and quickly turned away and put the small bottle of sugar onto the spice rack. Holly grabbed the ever full coffee pot and poured herself a mug while taking a seat at the table.

"You are such a fantastic cook, Madame!" Holly admired. "Everyone always comments on how wonderful your meals are. I hope to learn how to cook someday, but I doubt that I have the patience for it, let alone your incredible imagination. I never heard of anyone putting sugar in soup, for example."

Mrs Parent stoically smiled and quietly replied as she was leaving the kitchen, "You are always so kind, young lady, though I pray that someday you won't have to be here."

The comment startled Holly to a groggy alertness and she chuckled to herself, "Wow, that's an eye-opener," and thought no more about it. She had much too much on her plate to worry about opinions on this day. She went to the stove to freshen up her coffee and reached for the ever present sugar bowl on the kitchen table, only to find it was empty. She got up and went to the pantry to refill the bowl from the wax-sealed wooden keg of sugar and after replacing the lid, she returned to the kitchen table and sat down. As she took her first sip of her refreshed cup, her eyes innocently drifted to the small bottle of sugar Robare's mother had used in Meadow's soup, and stared at it for a few seconds.

"What is so special about that sugar?" she thought. "I wonder if it a special kind of sugar just for soup?"

She got up and ambled over to the spice rack and retrieved the bottle and took it back to the table to examine it. She pulled out the cork and immediately knew that the bottle did not contain sugar of any kind. The white substance was fine, not coarse like sugar. It didn't smell like sugar either. She wetted her finger and touched the powder, and then lightly to her tongue. She withdrew and crunched her face as if she had just tasted sour milk, only this powder was bitter. She put the cork back in the bottle and examined it for markings. She could see where a label had been washed off the side, and when she looked on the bottom, there was a faint marking. Holly held it to the light and could barely make out the letters, 'XXX'.

"Holy shit!" Holly blurted out loud when she came to realize that Mrs Parent was slowly killing Valentine Meadows.

She pondered and put the bottle in her robe pocket. Her head swam with thoughts and different realizations with each breath. The why was easy to figure, given Valentine's history with the boy. It wasn't as if Robare's parents hadn't sold their souls and traded their only son's little ass to the diminutive demon that Meadows was. An exchange for an escape from Europe, gainful employment and a better life was the implied and unspoken trade. Holly knew that Valentine Meadows was an expert at purchasing people's sensibilities in order to avoid harassment resulting from his various proclivities. All anyone had to do was actually look at the entire Perkins Cove community to see how he had systematically gutted their souls, via their children, by acting as the apparent community patron saint funding the varied projects. Holly sat back, smiled and said to the still empty kitchen, 'He is a crafty bastard at that'.

But Holly had learned from the master, and began to consider how to proceed. Her first question was whether to confront Mrs Parent, or turn her in to Inspector Richardson.

To what end?

Whether by design or not, Robare's mother had concocted a brilliant plan. Who could discern the source of Valentine's poor health, what with his extended drug use and alcohol intake? She wondered if whether the steady poisoning regime had gone on too long for any expectation of recovery, and if he recovered, what would be his condition?

Then Holly's mind took a stunningly evil turn. What if Valentine did die? What would happen to her without her sugar daddy? Valentine did ask for a lawyer so he could draft a last will. What would his will contain? Would she be taken care of? How long would it take for his estate to be settled? Maybe Valentine felt in his bones that he was actually dying, and probably assumed it was due to his lifestyle and even perhaps his comeuppance for all of his dastardly deeds. Valentine likely did not have an inkling that he, in fact, was being slowly murdered.

Holly again pondered how to proceed, but decided to put off any decisions until the day's festivities were concluded. She still had a house to run. The one decision she did firmly make was that she would keep the bottle of poison. She knew that Mrs Parent would notice that it was missing, and would be greatly troubled by its disappearance; obviously suspecting that Holly would be the culprit. Holly realized this, and knew that this would be to her advantage, for the older woman would be worried that her secret had been discovered and that Holly might contact that inspector friend of hers, and her vengeance on Valentine Meadows might result in her arrest. Mrs Parent would be sick from worry, and Holly decided to let that worry fester, and then confront the woman.

If Holly could convince the woman to write a confession, and telling the woman that she would keep the document private, Holly could continue the poisoning regimen, and if ever discovered, would have the confession to absolve her of any guilt. Yes, Holly thought, this could work out very nicely. She could convince Mrs Parent to provide Holly with all the information she needed, relative to dosage and the identity of the poison. She could convince the older woman to purchase more of it, and even sign a receipt. She might even convince Robare's mother that when Meadows passed, her son would be left a tidy sum of money in reparations for the evil that Meadow's had perpetrated on the lad.

She decided to leave a note for Mrs Parent to meet early the next day, and go from there.

Holly decided that her next task was to convince Meadows to draft his last will in his own handwriting, with her assistance. She would remind Meadows that she was the daughter of a prominent, though deceased attorney, and that she was well versed in the structure and legalities of such a document. In her mind, she knew that it would not matter what his last written wishes were, for she would make sure the document would never see the light of day. Above all, she had to insure that a real attorney was never involved. She would take the document, copy the handwriting, forge the signature and apply the wax seal to the envelope, and see that the envelope was placed in the safe at the bank. Meadows health was failing, so his handwriting would be shaky anyway, so her forgery would not have to be all that exact. Once Meadows completed this task, Holly would continually divert his attention to other matters and continue to remind him that his last will was sequestered in a safe in a small town bank in Maine.

Who could contest?

As Holly rose from the table she felt flush with excitement and accomplishment. She said to herself that Meadows was so far gone, that by the time they reached New York City, all would be convinced that Meadows was suffering from the ague, or perhaps pneumonia. Both would be a readily accepted cause of death.

She tightened the belt around her terry cloth robe, got a clean mug off a hook, lifted the cast iron lid off the soup pot, stirred a bit, and ladled out a healthy portion of soup for Valentine Meadows.

If Mrs Parent was scared, she certainly hid it well.

Holly had called the woman into her office and purposefully did not offer her a seat as Holly went around her desk. On the desk Holly had placed the bottle of poison, a pen and a piece of paper. Holly, ever the actress, stared into the woman's eyes for more than a breath, and then asked,

"Madame, do you have anything you'd like to say?"

The older woman's bottom lip began to quiver, but she forced out a quiet, 'non'. Holly rose from her chair, walked around the desk and picked up a simple wooden chair and sat it next to the desk and said, 'please sit'.

Again Mrs Parent whispered, 'non'.

"Okay, let's try it like this madame. Sit down!" Holly ordered with fire in her eyes. It was an act to be sure, but it accomplished the desired result, as Robare's mother fell into the chair. The older woman's resolve was quickly waning.

"Madame," Holly began, "Our business here can be concluded in all but a few minutes, and our conversation will remain private. On the paper in front of you, please write your full name and today's date and the town you reside in. Next you will write the name of the poison contained in this bottle, and state where you obtained it. Then you will write down the doses you use and identify the day that you began the process of murdering Valentine Meadows. You will then sign the document and leave this room to return to your duties as if nothing happened. If you don't do as I say, I will have you jailed before lunch. As you have seen, I have disposed of the poisoned soup, and there will be no more special meals made just for Mr. Meadows. Any further attempt to do him harm will be met in the most severe manner. Any questions?"

Mrs Parent was sobbing quietly when she asked, "What will happen to me...us, if I write this thing? Does Mr. Meadows know?"

"Madame, you will write as I have instructed and nothing more will be said of it to anyone. It is our secret unless you do not start writing," Holly stated in such a determined manner that the woman could not tell if Holly was angry, disappointed or what.

The older woman then spoke defiantly, "You know what that bastard did to my son…" at which Holly raised her hand to halt even another syllable and again firmly stated, "Enough!

"Our business is this document, and nothing more. Write, and be done with this business Madame!" Holly commanded.

The older woman started to write under Holly's gaze, and Holly coached her so no details were missed. When the woman set down the pen, she slid the paper across the desk to Holly and Holly gently slid the document aside and said, "Now Madame, think no more of this thing…ever," as she waved a dismissive hand directing the woman to leave her office. Just as Robare's mother reached the office door Holly called for her to stop and said, "Madame, perhaps no other mother in this world could have a better reason to cause the slow and painful death of an asshole like that little turd of a man upstairs, but I cannot allow it on my watch. I just wanted you to know that."

The older woman offered a slight smile as if the weight of the world had fallen off her shoulders and nodded toward Holly in appreciation.

"And another thing Madame, I want you to know that I will see to it that your son and your family will be taken care of, should Mr. Meadows pass on sooner than expected."

"Miss Holly, you are one of God's true angels," Mrs Parent said with eyes welling, and then left the room.

Holly waited until she knew that the woman was back in the kitchen and lifted the document to read, making sure she knew the type of poison, how to get more and the dosage.

She folded the document and sealed it in an envelope similar to the envelope labeled Last Will & Testament of

Valentine Meadows that she had forged the previous evening after Meadows had scribbled his wishes in a drunken stupor. Holly had convinced a distinguished looking ship captain to present himself as an attorney to provide witness and Meadows seemed not only satisfied but thankful that Holly had made arrangements to relieve him of this task. All it had cost Holly was a rare blowjob on her knees and letting a man put his hands on the back of her head, as if she liked it.

In the early morning quiet of her bedroom, Holly opened the genuine document and read that Meadows had bequeathed his entire estate to Robare, with no mention of her, Elsa, or anyone else.

"What a complete prick you are Valentine Meadows," Holly whispered to herself as she began to forge a new will, and chuckled in a manner equally as evil as she had heard Meadows himself chuckle many a time when duping yet another unsuspecting soul.

"The old lady was right about one thing," Holly said to the ocean waves only, "I am one of God's angels all right...the fucking angel of death'.

The café remained silent, as Richard Day took a belabored breath. His story had been going on for the better part of two hours and not a soul had moved or spoken. Even Jessie held her tongue amidst occasional sniffles and tears.

"The oddest part of that entire time back then was that when that artist fella that brought all the naked women finally died soon after, hardly a word was spoken 'round heah. Hell, he was prob'ly the most famous art critic in the world just a few years previous, and when he died, there was only a single paragraph funeral announcement in some New York newspaper. No funeral, no celebrations of life; none of that. Heck, no one ever wrote a book about the fella near as I can tell. Strange when ya think about it, ya know? Famous people like that gent always get some sort of notice or a biography, but for this gent...nuthin! Maybe the bastard did purchase all our souls, but at least we all had souls to purchase, I'm thinkin'. Just lookin' into that feller's eyes you could see he was an evil bastard. The few photographs that are still floatin' around of him...hell it's easy to see. That feller wasn't remembered by nobody and to my way of thinkin', leastways, it's no wonder why..."

"A, a, about the girls... Sir?" Jessie coughed out.

"Yeah, them girls. I know that the Baroness lady was flat broke when she died from an overdose when she got back to Europe. The fake Sultana married over there but was killed in the war.

Some of the other folks I talked about lived and died here, buried over in the cemetery over near the library. Their kids are all growed now, old as me, most of 'em. And as for that Holly gal, I heard she moved west and started a real nice family. I also heard that she visited up here once when she was in her forties and came east to bury her mother. I'll say this for her, she was true to her word about little Robare inheriting the bastard's estate, though no one really knows if he actually, uh, inherited *all of it!*"

About the Author

Greg and Joy May split their lives between their home in the Philippines, where WWII shipwreck hunting occupies their every waking hour, and plying the byways of the USA in their semi-truck where Greg is a long haul trucking Instructor and Professional Driver.